# THE WREXHAM KILLINGS

## DI Ruth Hunter Crime Thriller #16

### SIMON MCCLEAVE

STAMFORD
PUBLISHING

# THE WREXHAM KILLINGS

## By Simon McCleave

A DI Ruth Hunter Crime Thriller
Book 16

First published by Stamford Publishing Ltd in 2023

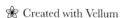 Created with Vellum

Your FREE book is waiting for you now!

Get your FREE copy of the prequel to
the DI Ruth Hunter Series NOW
http://www.simonmccleave.com/vip-email-club
and join my VIP Email Club

Also by Simon McCleave

**THE DI RUTH HUNTER SERIES**

**THE DC RUTH HUNTER MURDER CASE SERIES**

**THE ANGLESEY SERIES - DI LAURA HART**

**(Harper Collins / AVON Publishing)**

# About the Author

## SIMON McCLEAVE

Simon is a two million bestselling crime novelist. His first book, 'The Snowdonia Killings', was released in January 2020 and soon became an Amazon Bestseller, reaching No 1 in the Amazon UK Chart and selling over 400,000 copies. His fourteen subsequent novels in the DI Ruth Hunter Crime Thriller Series have all been Amazon Best Sellers and many have hit the top of the UK Digital Chart. He has sold over 2 million books since 2020.

The Ruth Hunter Snowdonia books are currently in development as a television series to be filmed on location in North Wales in 2023.

Simon also has a very successful crime series set on Anglesey with Harper Collins (Avon). 'The Dark Tide', the first of the series, was the highest ever selling Waterstones' Welsh Book of the Month.

Simon McCleave was originally born in South London. When leaving University, he worked in television and film development. He was a Script Editor at the BBC, a producer at Channel 4 before working as a Story Analyst in Los Angeles. He worked on films such as 'The Full Monty' and television series such as the BBC Crime Drama 'Between The Lines'.

Simon then became a script writer for television and film. He wrote on series such as Silent Witness, Murder In Suburbia, Teachers, Attachments, The Bill, Eastenders and many more. His film, 'Out of the Game' for Channel 4 was critically acclaimed - 'An unflinching portrayal of male friendship.' (Time Out)

Simon lives in North Wales with his wife and two children.

*To Neil, Sam, Mia, Macy and Tracey x*

# April 2021

IT WAS A MILD SPRING NIGHT AS THE YOUNG WOMAN staggered through the field and then glanced up at the expanse of clear, vivid stars that flecked the night sky. In her early 20s, she had dark blonde hair pulled back into a ponytail. Her face was pale and attractive.

But something felt wrong. Very wrong. Her stomach was twisted with anxiety and fear.

For a moment, she squinted up at the night sky. There was something slightly different about the sky tonight. With no clouds to obscure them, the stars seemed unusually clear. A curved line ran from the brightest star in the east, through a row of smaller stars, to another in the west which seemed to have an amber glow. The shape seemed to mirror the slight crescent of the moon itself.

There was a cool breeze on the young woman's face. *Where the hell am I?* she wondered as she now focussed on where she was walking. She tried to piece together what had happened. The dark events that had led up to her walking through this field. It was an incoherent, alarming jumbled mess.

As she sucked in a lungful of fresh air she felt woozy, but could tell that she wasn't drunk. Her disorientation wasn't down to alcohol or drugs. She had an overwhelming sense that she had been attacked. There was a pounding throbbing pain at the back of her head. Clasping her hand to the back of her skull, she felt that her hair was sticky and matted. *Is that blood?*

Stumbling on unsteadily, her feet swished through the thick grass. She tried to make sense of what had happened earlier that night. She remembered raised voices. And a struggle and then a fight. Someone had hit her across the back of her head. *What the hell happened and how did I get here?*

The moon had dropped slightly in the sky over to her right. With a tinge of apricot, it illuminated the darkness like some alien beacon. The night air was quiet, but not silent. There was the distant sounds of cars. A dog barked somewhere far away and the noise of its deep bark echoed around her.

The young woman stopped to get her bearings. She couldn't just keep walking aimlessly. Then she felt something enormous looming over her. Her eyes travelled slowly up the brickwork, eventually resting on the top of the giant menacing structure.

Then she recognised it.

It was the Pontcysyllte Aqueduct – or *Traphont Ddwr Pontcysyllte*. A vast Georgian 18-arched iron and stone structure, just south of Wrexham, that carried a canal across a huge valley with the River Dee below.

'Jesus', she muttered under her breath, feeling a little startled that she hadn't noticed it before now. Even though she knew the structure, for a few seconds she couldn't remember how or why. And then it came to her. She had been canoeing across it on a school trip. That was it. She recalled her teacher telling them that not only was the aqueduct the longest in the UK, it was the highest in the whole world. She recalled feeling a little scared about the prospect of her first time canoeing being across something that was 130ft high. In fact, she remembered being angry at the teacher for telling them that and frightening her.

*What the hell am I doing here?* she wondered. She knew that this place was several miles from Wrexham.

In the distance, there was the sound of the River Dee, rushing over rocks as it snaked its way 70 miles from its source at the heart of Snowdonia, then east past Chester and then over to the sea between Wales and the Wirral Peninsula in England.

Closing her eyes, the dizziness in her head seemed to be getting more and more intense.

Now she knew exactly where she was, but had no memory of how she'd arrived there. And then, as she searched her memory, she couldn't seem to recall where she lived – or even her name.

*Oh my God!*

Her pulse quickened and her stomach tightened with an overwhelming sense of terror.

*What's going on? This is really scaring me.*

As she moved closer to the thick masonry piers and iron clad arches, the spotlights that illuminated the structure cast a strange vanilla glow over where she stood.

Glancing down at her jeans, she saw that they were stained by splashes of a dark liquid which seemed to have now dried. Her first instinct was that it must be red wine.

Then, as she turned over her hands, she saw that her palms were also streaked with dark red. She sniffed at her skin. It didn't smell of wine. It smelled almost metallic. And then the dark realisation.

It was blood.

Pulling at her hoodie, she saw that it too was covered.

*Oh God! Is that my blood? What the hell happened to me?*

Trying to get her breath, she could feel her head spinning.

It was all too much.

Her legs suddenly felt like lead and gave way beneath her.

And then as she fell, everything went black.

# Chapter 1

Detective Constable Georgina Wild – or Georgie as she was known to her family, friends, and colleagues – stirred and blinked open her eyes. Her instant reaction was that she wasn't sleeping in her own bed. The material against her face felt textured like a cushion rather than a soft pillow. If she had to guess, she had slept the night on a sofa with a flimsy blanket draped over her. Taking a breath, she manoeuvred herself onto her elbows and then sat up.

Then she became aware of someone else's presence in the room.

Sitting in the large armchair opposite was Detective Inspector Ben Stewart. He was still holding the large kitchen knife that he'd threatened her with the night before.

And then everything came back to her in a horrible, stomach-churning flash.

Ben was in his late 30s, piercing blue eyes, dark blond hair and very handsome - like a young Robert Redford. He worked for the Modern Slavery and Human Trafficking Unit, as part of the National Crime Agency out of

Manchester. It was the UK's primary law enforcement unit against organised crime and human, weapon, and drug trafficking.

Georgie and Ben had been working for the previous ten days on a double murder case that involved a human trafficking and slavery ring working out of Denbigh in North Wales. Vulnerable teenagers and young people were being trafficked over from the Indian subcontinent to work in terrible conditions for virtually no pay. And while working the case, Georgie and Ben had become romantically involved.

However, the previous evening, Georgie had discovered that Ben was the mysterious man known as *The Boss* who was behind the ring. And that he was responsible for murdering two young Indian men who had posed a threat to it. It had shaken her to her very core. And when she confronted Ben with what she suspected, he had told Georgie that he wasn't going to let her leave his flat.

Pushing her hair back from her face, Georgie looked over at Ben. He had clearly slept the whole night in the armchair.

*How the hell am I going to get out of here and away from him?*

'So … now what?' she asked with a cold sneer. Her fear had been replaced by an overwhelming anger.

Ben sat forward and scratched his jaw with a pensive expression. 'Well, I need coffee before we do anything.'

She narrowed her eyes as she looked at him. 'How could you have murdered two innocent people in cold blood?' Even as she said it, she felt a chill shudder through her whole being. She had kissed and embraced this man. She had even imagined a future where they were together. How had she got this so incredibly wrong?

Ben shrugged with an icy expression. 'They were just in the way. That's all. It was business.'

'Don't be so bloody ridiculous, Ben!' she snapped. 'You're talking about human life here. They had families. What, and you just killed them because they posed a threat to your business?'

'I don't have to justify myself to you,' Ben replied indifferently.

'Don't you?' Georgie said with a look of bewilderment. 'What about everything we talked about? Are you telling me that none of that was really you?'

She could feel the emotional pain and anger welling inside.

Ben didn't reply as he got up, yawned, and stretched. It was almost as if he was trying to demonstrate his callousness and lack of remorse.

Georgie took a breath as the fury rose in her chest. 'Who the fuck are you, Ben?'

He gave her a withering look. 'I think you need to be quiet now,' he said quietly.

'You do know that as soon as I don't turn up to work this morning, they're going to start to wonder where I am,' Georgie growled.

Ben shook his head as he got up and stretched again with a groan. He was still holding the knife. 'No. No, they won't.'

Georgie frowned. 'Well they will.'

Ben pulled Georgie's phone from his trouser pocket. He'd taken it from her last night. He held it up. 'You're going to send DI Ruth Hunter a message to say that you're not feeling well and you won't be in today.'

Georgie snorted. 'And why the hell would I do that?'

Ben gestured to the knife and then fixed her with an icy stare. 'Because I'm telling you to.'

'Oh, right,' she said in a sarcastic tone. 'And you're going to stab a defenceless pregnant police officer are you?'

In a flash, Ben was standing over her. His teeth were gritted and his face was screwed up in rage. He took the length of the blade and pushed it hard against the skin of her throat. 'Let's get one thing clear from now on, shall we?' he shouted.

Georgie's heart was now hammering against her chest. His sudden eruption had startled her. The man standing over her bore no resemblance to the person she had been working with and grown attracted to in the past ten days. His mouth was twisted as he glared at her.

'As you've so eloquently pointed out, I've already killed two people in cold blood to protect myself,' he thundered as he moved his face a few inches from hers. She could smell his stale breath. 'So, I won't hesitate to end your life if you fuck with me. Do you understand?'

As the adrenaline surged through her veins, Georgie could feel that she was shaking all over. The knife felt like it was cutting into her skin.

She nodded and replied, 'Yes, I understand.'

Ben took a breath as he tried to calm himself. His eyes roamed around the room for a few seconds. Then he moved the knife away from her neck, looked at her, smiled, and put his hand gently to her face. She flinched.

'I'm sorry,' he said. His voice was quiet, even gentle. 'I didn't mean to scare you. But you need to do what I tell you. Okay?'

*Woah. He is seriously unhinged,* she thought to herself.

Georgie nodded. Ben's sudden switch from utter fury to cool composure was unsettling.

He ran his fingers softly down her cheek. It made her wince with revulsion.

'You do understand that, don't you?' he said, as though he was making perfect sense.

'Yeah, I understand,' she said now with a deliberately empathetic tone.

It was clear that challenging Ben with her own anger was going to put her in danger. Maybe a softer, gentler approach would eventually get him to lower his guard and allow her to escape.

Ben handed her the phone. 'Send a text to say that you won't be in,' he said.

Aware that the knife was still in his hand and close to her face, Georgie took the phone and began to type.

He moved so that he could look over her shoulder. 'I don't need to remind you not to do anything stupid, do I?' he said with an air of menace.

'No,' Georgie replied under her breath as she typed. 'I'm not going to.'

*HI BOSS*

> *I'm not feeling great this morning. I think it's more than just morning sickness if I'm honest. I'm going to stay here and get some rest today.*
> *Sorry.*
> *Georgie xx*

SHOWING BEN THE SCREEN, HE READ IT AND THEN NODDED to indicate that she could send it.

DI Ruth Hunter, her boss, had been incredibly supportive of Georgie ever since she fell pregnant after a fling with an old flame and decided to keep the baby. Ruth had become increasingly like a mother figure to her recently and she would have no problem with Georgie taking a day's rest. Georgie now had to work out how to let

Ruth know that the message was fake and that she had been abducted.

She pressed send and Ben snatched the phone from her and put it back in his pocket.

'Right, we can go upstairs to freshen up,' he said, gesturing to the hallway and stairs with his knife. 'Then coffee, toast and we'll get on the road.'

He said it in a strangely matter of fact way as though he and Georgie were a married couple going out for the day.

'Where are we going?' she asked in a nonchalant tone.

Ben gave her a half smile. 'We're going on a magical mystery tour.'

# Chapter 2

Detective Sergeant Nick Evans took the boiling kettle and poured the water onto the tea bag in his favourite Welsh Rugby mug. On one side was the Welsh Rugby badge. On the other it read, *I support two teams – Wales and whoever England are playing.* His eyes moved easily around his kitchen. It was such a relief to be home.

The past few weeks had been an emotional roller-coaster. He had been wrongly accused of murder which had led to a living nightmare. Imprisonment, going on the run and retribution. However, his name had been cleared and he had been exonerated by the Crown Prosecution Service of all charges. And that meant he could return to work as a detective at Llancastell CID. He had his life back with his wife Amanda and their daughter Megan. He would never take them or his life for granted again.

As he waited for the tea to brew for a few seconds, Nick grabbed his copy of 'The Promise of a New Day – A book of Daily Reflections'. As a recovering alcoholic, with over four years of sobriety under his belt, he started the day in the same way as the majority of other people in recovery did. He would spend ten to fifteen minutes setting up his day in the right way. Often he would read something that had a positive message or thought. Sometimes he would meditate, often using an app on his phone. And, most importantly, he would remind himself how grateful he should be to be alive, with a healthy happy family, a roof over his head, a job that he loved, and that he was sober. When he was drinking, Nick was never grateful for anything. He was full of self-pity, self-loathing, and resentment. He had come such a long way in the past four years. It felt like a miracle. And if he had carried on the way he was drinking, he could well be dead by now.

Going over to the fridge, Nick took out the milk. For a moment, he was taken back to his horrendous life in active alcoholism. Five years ago, he would have woken up alone with an overpowering sense of anxiety and panic. There would be the terrible fear as he tried to piece together the previous evening. Where was the car, what happened, did I speak to or text anyone? And then the next overwhelming thought.

I need a drink.

His brow would be sweaty and his hands shaky. Coming downstairs, he'd open the fridge with a sickening dread that there was no more alcohol in the house. And then a surge of comfort and relief as he reached for the bottle of vodka, wine, or a can of beer inside. Sometimes it was all he could do to even keep it down and not throw up. Dry retching was another delightful side effect of active alcoholism. But once he had a decent amount of alcohol in his bloodstream, all the anxiety and fear dissipated in a lovely, warm blanket of booze. And so it went on in an endless cycle of pain and despair.

*Thank God I don't have to do that today,* he thought to

himself as he picked up his tea with a steady hand, and headed through to the living room.

His eye was drawn to a framed green poster up on the wall for the *Green Man Festival 2018*. It was the first live music event that he and a heavily pregnant Amanda had attended while in sobriety. Held in the Brecon Beacons, and featuring mainly indie and alternative bands, they had had an amazing time. He recalled them singing along to *War On Drugs* at the top of their voices.

Hearing a noise, Nick saw a figure coming down the stairs.

It was Amanda.

Even with bleary eyes and bed hair, he thought she was absolutely beautiful.

'Hey,' she said in a croaky voice as she came into the living room. She moved towards him and wrapped her arms around his waist. 'First day back at work. How does it feel?'

'I can't wait,' Nick admitted. 'I feel like an excited schoolboy.'

She squeezed him. 'Aw. Good to get some normality back.'

Nick smirked. 'Well …'

'Well what?' she asked with a quizzical look.

'I had a lot of time on my hands when I was sitting in that prison cell,' Nick explained with a twinkle in his eyes. 'I just thought if I ever get my life back, I'd like there to be some changes.'

Amanda raised an eyebrow suspiciously as she put her phone down on the sofa. 'If you say more 'blow jobs', I will actually punch you.'

'Oh,' Nick sighed, pulling a crestfallen face. 'Right. I take that as a no then?'

Amanda laughed and gave him a playful punch. 'You're such a twat sometimes, Nick Evans.'

He moved forward, put his hands on her shoulders and looked into her chestnut eyes. 'Being serious, I realised how lucky I am to have you. And I probably take you for granted.'

'That is true,' Amanda said with a wry smile. 'You are very lucky to have me.'

Nick laughed. 'Yeah, don't push it.'

'Anything else occur to you while you were swanning around in prison?'

Nick looked indignant. 'I wasn't bloody *swanning*!'

'Come on,' she teased him. 'Nice room, television, all your meals cooked for you. It's virtually a Premier Inn.'

'I'd like to see Lenny Bloody Henry share a cell with a violent, recovering smackhead,' Nick joked, and then looked at her. 'Anyway, I've got some money tucked away in an ISA,' he said. 'You know, for a rainy day.'

'Okay,' she said. 'That's very grown up of you.'

'Yeah, well I'm doing my best to act my age these days.'

'Except when you're very tired and you act like a petulant toddler.'

'And we never went on a honeymoon when we got married,' Nick said, ignoring her. 'So, I thought if we can get someone to look after Megan, maybe me and you could go away somewhere incredibly romantic.'

'Rhyl?' she suggested with a grin.

'Mmm, I was thinking more like Rome,' he said with a smile.

'Yes. Rome does sound better than Rhyl,' she said as she leaned in to kiss him. The kiss lingered and became passionate. 'That's a lovely idea.' They kissed again and he pulled her closer to him.

Nick then gave her a knowing look.

'Easy tiger. We haven't got time for that this morning,' she said as she moved towards the hallway.

'Shame.'

'I've got to get ready and you've got to get to work,' she called as she went up the stairs.

Sipping at his tea, Nick went to perch on the edge of the sofa.

At that moment, Amanda's phone buzzed with a text message.

He couldn't help but reach over and look at the screen.

ARE WE STILL MEETING UP LATER? X

BEFORE HE COULD CHECK THE NUMBER, THE MESSAGE HAD disappeared and he didn't have Amanda's passcode to unlock her phone.

He told himself there was probably a good explanation for the message. A friend or his stepdaughter Fran. But there was part of him that was concerned.

## Chapter 3

Stretching out her back and shoulders, Detective Inspector Ruth Hunter gave a yawn and a groan as she sat in the DI's office on the far side of Llancastell CID. Her phone buzzed. It was a text from Georgie saying that she wasn't feeling well and was taking the day to rest. After the frantic nature of the past week - two murders linked to a trafficking and modern slavery gang in Denbigh – Ruth was more than happy for Georgie to spend some time at home. She replied with a text to tell her to take a couple of days if she needed.

Checking her watch, Ruth got a little buzz of excitement. Her right-hand man and partner, Detective Sergeant Nick Evans was returning to work today after a very traumatic few weeks. Ruth had told Nick to take some compassionate leave but he was insistent that the best thing for him was to return to work as soon as possible. His wife, Amanda, would be at work. And his daughter Megan – Ruth's goddaughter – in reception at the local primary school. Nick said that rattling around the house on his own was the last thing he needed.

Detective Sergeant Dan French knocked on her open door. In his early 30s, French was a no-nonsense, no-frills copper with an impressive dedication to the job. Ruth knew that if she asked him to do something, it got done thoroughly with no fuss.

'Boss, I've spoken to our police liaison in India,' he said. 'They're still trying to track down Kabir Malik. They think he might have flown down to Mumbai.'

CID officers at Llancastell believed that Malik was running the trafficking and slavery ring from his offices in Denbigh. However, he had disappeared to India before they could confront him with what they knew. And it was going to be a very long and challenging process to try and extradite him from India without concrete evidence.

'Okay, thanks Dan,' Ruth replied with a sigh.

'You heard from Georgie?' French asked.

'She's not well. I've told her to take a couple of days off,' Ruth explained.

'Sounds sensible,' he agreed.

'I've seen that there are some NPPF two-step Inspector's exams coming up at the end of the year,' Ruth said knowingly. 'Are you thinking of entering them?'

She knew that French had all the qualities needed to move quickly up the ranks of CID but she suspected he just needed a gentle shove.

'Bit premature isn't it, boss?' he asked hesitantly.

'Don't undersell yourself Dan. It's going to take eighteen months to two years to get everything in place to consider promotion. I don't see why you shouldn't be thinking about that now.'

Even though he tried to hide it, French's face lit up with pride. 'I just didn't think you saw me like that.'

'Well, I do,' Ruth stated. 'If you put together that application for the exams, I can sign asap.'

'Thanks, boss,' French said gratefully. 'I'll get on it.'

They were interrupted by a ripple of applause that grew into cheers.

Ruth looked out and saw that Nick had come through the doors into CID. He had a beaming smile on his face as several detectives approached to shake his hand and pat his back. He had always been an incredibly popular member of the CID team and everyone had been very concerned about him.

'Here he is,' French said with a wry smile. 'The prodigal son.'

Nick approached and came into Ruth's office. It might not have been very professional but she gave him an enormous hug.

French turned and left them to it.

'Christ, you're a sight for sore eyes,' Ruth said quietly as she moved back to look at him.

Nick looked a little overwhelmed. 'I've only been away a few weeks but everything looks different.'

'Come and sit down,' Ruth said.

She and Nick had been through so much since Ruth first arrived from the Met. After a tricky start, they were now close personal friends.

'Thanks,' Nick said, taking a seat.

'And you're sure you should be in?' Ruth asked.

'Where else would I want to be?' he asked with a grin.

'Well true,' Ruth agreed. 'We certainly don't do this job for the pay or the work/life balance do we? The girls must love having you back home?'

Nick nodded. 'I think we all just want to get back to the way it was before everything happened. We had a lovely little life.'

'Yeah,' Ruth nodded thoughtfully. 'Sometimes I forget what I've got to be grateful for.'

'Well I won't be doing that for a while,' Nick said. 'Amanda suggested you come over for Sunday lunch next week. I know Megan would love to see you.'

'I haven't seen them for a while, so yes,' Ruth said, feeling a warm glow.

Detective Constable Jim Garrow knocked at the door and looked at them. 'Good to see you back, sarge.'

'Thanks, Jim,' Nick replied.

Garrow turned to look at Ruth. 'Boss, uniform have called in an unconscious woman that's been found at the foot of Pontcysyllte Aqueduct.'

Ruth nodded. She knew where that was. About seven or eight miles south of Wrexham.

Nick raised an eyebrow. 'Christ, did she jump off it and survive?' The aqueduct was a well-known location for suicides.

'Apparently not,' Garrow said. 'She does have a head injury, but it's not consistent with a fall.'

'Why have they called us?' Ruth asked. A lot of the time, the people found unconscious overnight were alcoholics or drug addicts. And that wasn't part of CID's remit.

Garrow gave her a dark look. 'Her hands and clothing were covered in someone else's blood.'

## Chapter 4

Georgie was sitting in the passenger seat as Ben drove them north west from Llancastell. There was a sinister atmosphere in the car. Ben had the knife nestled on the driver's seat between his legs. Even if Georgie did manage to get out of the car, she knew that Ben was stronger and faster than her. If she was going to escape, it would need to be something far more effective and cunning than her merely fleeing from the car.

Glancing out of the window, Georgie spotted the last lingering clouds that had been scattered and evaporated by the morning sunshine. She stared at the rising green hills and meadows that were dotted untidily by sheep. What she would give right now to be walking carefree across the countryside of North Wales.

Buzzing down the window, she let the fresh air blow against her face. She took a deep lungful. Even though she hadn't been physically sick that morning, the nausea of her pregnancy still lingered in her stomach and her throat.

She put the window back up and glanced over at Ben. She wondered how he had managed to hide so convincingly behind his easy-going, charming façade. He'd managed to hoodwink everyone at Llancastell CID and, presumably, the Modern Slavery and Human Trafficking Unit.

'So, magical mystery tour, eh?' Georgie asked in a bright tone. She wanted to get some idea of where they were going and why. 'What does that involve?'

'Just visiting a few old acquaintances,' Ben said mysteriously. 'But we need to pick someone up on the way.'

'Are you going to tell me who?' Georgie asked.

There were a few seconds of silence.

'My son, Arlo,' Ben replied.

*What?*

Georgie narrowed her eyes. 'You have a son?' In all the conversations that she and Ben had had, he never revealed that he had a son.

'Yes,' Ben frowned. 'So what?'

'You never mentioned to me that you had a son.'

'It's none of your business, is it?' he snapped.

'No, I suppose it's not,' she admitted, remembering that her relationship with Ben up until now had been a total lie. 'Where is he?'

'In school,' Ben explained.

Georgie looked confused. 'Does he know that you're picking him up?'

'No. It'll be a lovely surprise.'

'Does the school know that you're taking him out for the day?'

Ben glared at her. 'It's got nothing to do with them.'

'I'm pretty sure it has,' Georgie stated. 'Who does he live with?'

'His mother.'

'And she knows, does she?'

Ben didn't answer.

'You can't just show up and take your son out of school,' Georgie said, shaking her head.

'Why not?'

'Because if he lives with his mother and you don't have permission,' Georgie said, 'it's tantamount to abduction and they'll call the police.'

'Yeah, well I don't care about any of that,' Ben said, and then gave a disturbing grin. 'After all, I am the police.'

## Chapter 5

F rench and Garrow came out of the lift on the first floor of the Llancastell University Hospital and turned left. The air smelled of hospital food and disinfectant. As they got to the double doors, Garrow saw an elderly man dressed in a robe tottering towards them with a drip on wheels attached to his arm, so Garrow stopped to hold the door for him.

'Thank you, young man,' the elderly man said with a smile. His eyes were bloodshot and his skin flecked with liver spots.

French looked back at Garrow.

'Young man, eh?' Garrow said with a slightly smug grin. 'I wonder at what age I'll stop being *young man*?'

French rolled his eyes. 'Probably when you stop asking silly questions like that.'

'Got out on the wrong side of bed this morning, sarge?' Garrow asked with an amused raise of his eyebrows. He wasn't going to let French's grouchy manner affect his mood.

'Something like that,' French mumbled. 'Actually, I was

up 'til the early hours watching the American football play-offs.'

'Right,' Garrow said with a bemused nod.

'Yeah, I know sport isn't really your thing,' French laughed.

'Who's your team then?'

'New York Giants.'

'Any good?'

'No, they're bloody terrible. But I've got a few mates and we all got to pick our teams about ten years ago. The Giants had just beaten the New England Patriots in the Superbowl. So, like a right glory hunter, I picked The Giants and they've been dreadful ever since,' French groaned.

'Oh well,' Garrow shrugged as they arrived at the Intensive Care Unit. 'My taid supports the Wrexham football team and that seems to make him very depressed too.'

French raised an eyebrow. 'Not anymore.'

Garrow gave him a quizzical look. 'How do you mean?'

'Did you not see the news? They were bought a couple of months ago by that Ryan Reynolds and another actor Rob McElhenney. They've invested loads of money. Looks like Wrexham are going places. I haven't been for a couple of seasons but it would be great if they do well. Get out of the bloody National League.'

'Well that would cheer my taid up,' Garrow said. He wasn't quite sure who the two actors were but he knew their names.

As they entered the ICU, they took out their warrant cards and approached the central nurses' station.

'DS French and DC Garrow, Llancastell CID,' French said quietly. 'You had a young woman brought in unconscious this morning?'

A middle-aged nurse with coal black hair nodded and then pointed to a small room down the corridor to their left. 'Actually the doctor is in with her now.'

'Thanks,' French said as they turned and headed away.

As they arrived at the room, Garrow saw that the door was open by about a foot, and inside a young female Asian doctor was looking at an ECG readout and writing notes. She had a name badge that said Dr Gupta.

French pushed open the door slowly and flashed his warrant card.

'Oh hi,' the doctor said quietly with a kind smile.

'How's she doing?' Garrow asked under his breath as they went in.

'She's still unconscious,' the doctor explained. 'There is a nasty wound to the back of her skull but she's breathing on her own. She's due to have a CAT scan and an MRI this morning so we can see the extent of her injuries.'

French nodded. 'Have you managed to find out who she is yet?'

'No, I'm afraid not,' the doctor admitted. 'There were some officers here earlier but she didn't have a purse or a phone. When we removed her clothing, we did find a couple of things in her pocket.' The doctor went over to a small clear plastic wallet and held it up. 'I've put them in here for you.'

'Thanks,' French said.

Garrow looked over at the young woman. She was in her mid-20s with long blonde hair, fair skin, and high cheekbones.

'Did you run a toxicology test?' Garrow enquired.

The doctor nodded. 'Yes. There were no signs of alcohol or drugs in her system.'

Garrow looked at her. She certainly didn't look like she was a drug addict or homeless. Then he spotted the smears of blood on the palms of her hands and looked at French. 'Sarge, we're going to need a forensic officer to come in and take a swab of that blood.'

Garrow also noticed some intricate and delicate tattoos of flowers around both of her wrists.

French nodded and looked at the doctor.

'Of course,' the doctor replied.

The young woman's eyes started to move behind her eyelids. She stirred with a groan.

The doctor moved swiftly to her side and said very gently, 'Hello. Can you open your eyes for me?'

After a few seconds, the woman managed to open her eyes. She looked completely baffled as she took in her surroundings.

'It's okay,' the doctor reassured her in a soothing tone. 'You're in hospital. You've had a nasty bang to your head but you're going to be okay.'

The woman looked terrified.

'Can you tell us your name?' the doctor asked.

The woman frowned as her eyes roamed around the room anxiously.

The doctor gave her a kind smile. 'If you can tell us your name …'

'I don't know,' the woman murmured.

The doctor frowned and looked up at French and Garrow.

'You don't remember your name?' the doctor asked her calmly.

'No,' the woman replied, looking upset.

## Chapter 6

**B**en Stewart and Georgie drove through Penyffordd, a quiet village that was in Flintshire, close to Buckley and Mold. Its name derived from the Welsh *Pen-y-ffordd* which meant the highest or furthest point of the road. Heading north, they passed *The Millstone Pub* before taking a right onto Chester Road.

Georgie had spent the past twenty minutes running through every scenario of how she could escape. Unless she could find some kind of weapon, there was no hope of overpowering Ben. She concluded that if she could find a way of alerting someone, preferably police officers, that she had been kidnapped, without drawing Ben's attention, that would be her best chance of being rescued.

Looking up, she noticed that Ben had pulled the car over outside St Joseph's Primary School.

She glanced over at him. 'This is where your son goes to school?'

Ben ignored her as he took out police issue handcuffs. 'Give me your hands.'

'What?' Georgie asked with a frown.

'Give me your hands!' he snapped loudly.

'You can't handcuff me,' Georgie protested.

Ben grabbed the knife. 'Don't make me cut off one of your fingers.'

Georgie held out her hands. He pulled them roughly towards him and then cuffed them to the steering wheel so there was no possibility of her getting out of the car.

Then Ben got out of the car, opened the rear door and pulled out something that had been hidden under the driver's seat. It was something heavy wrapped in a piece of material.

Georgie got the instant smell of gun oil and knew exactly what was inside.

As he unwrapped the material, Georgie saw that there was a Glock 17 handgun inside. Ben took it, checked the magazine and then slipped it into the waistband of his trousers under his jacket.

'Jesus, what the hell are you doing with that?' Georgie asked.

'I'll be back in a minute,' Ben said.

'Why are you taking a gun into a primary school?' she asked, trying to remain calm.

'In case anyone gets in my way or tries to stop me,' he replied as he looked around furtively. Then he fixed her with a stare. 'If you try anything, I will shoot you.'

Georgie just looked at him but said nothing as Ben slammed the back door of the car shut. She then watched as he jogged along the pavement, across the playground, and into the school building.

For a moment, she felt sick with nerves at the thought of him walking into a school with a handgun and taking his son.

Then she realised she needed to do something – and fast.

Glancing around, she looked urgently for anything that might alert someone to her presence in the car. She looked at the car horn that was at the centre of the steering wheel.

Twisting her hands and wrists, she stretched up her fingers towards the rectangular button.

'Jesus!' she muttered in frustration as she shifted her arms.

She managed to get her little finger onto the horn and she pressed against it.

Nothing.

*Fuck!*

She didn't have enough power in her little finger to depress the horn enough for it to sound.

With every ounce of energy, she stretched again.

Nothing.

Her eyes roamed frantically around the car, looking for something else.

At the centre of the dashboard was the car's Tetra police radio with a handset.

There was no way that she could get her hands to it though.

Twisting her body, she began to move her face towards the red emergency button on the handset. When it was pressed, it would send out an emergency alert across the whole police network that the specific officer identified by that handset was in need of help immediately. Clearly, the radio would be recognised as belonging to Ben and his vehicle. And within minutes, using GPS tracking of the vehicle and the radio, there would be marked police cars in attendance.

Stretching out her neck, she edged her nose towards the red emergency button. The skin on the tip of her nose brushed against it.

*Come on, for God's sake.*

Glancing up, she saw Ben with a small boy walking out of the school and across the playground.

*Shit, shit, hurry up,* she told herself.

Straining her neck and shoulders, she tried to give herself just half an inch to depress the button.

Ben and the boy were now at the gate that led out to the pavement.

'Come on!' Georgie growled out loud as she screwed up her nose.

Then she felt her nose move the button by a fraction – but not enough to send out the emergency call.

Ben appeared at a rear door and opened it.

Georgie shot back and glanced around, trying to look unflustered.

A young boy with white-blond hair, milky skin and blue eyes got into the car. He looked like he was about nine or ten years old. He had a quizzical look on his face.

'Here you go, mate,' Ben said as he leaned in, pulled the seatbelt across the boy and then fastened it.

Georgie looked at the boy from the passenger seat – her hands were still handcuffed to the steering wheel.

'Hi there,' she said. 'I'm Georgie.'

The boy noticed the handcuffs and looked even more perturbed.

Ben opened the driver's door, got in and immediately unlocked the cuffs.

'This is Arlo,' Ben said, and then gestured to the cuffs. 'This is my friend, Georgie. Don't worry, we play this stupid game with handcuffs sometimes to see if we can get them off.'

Arlo frowned but nodded as if he believed Ben.

'Hi Arlo,' Georgie said with a kind smile, and then looked at Ben.

'What's a family emergency?' Arlo asked.

Ben turned to look at him. 'You don't need to worry about that mate. That's just something I told Mrs Tate so you could come out of school.'

Arlo furrowed his brow. 'I don't understand.'

'Well, me and Georgie were planning on a trip to the seaside today. Abergele,' Ben said brightly. 'We thought we could all go on the beach, get fish and chips, go in the arcade. That sort of thing. How does that sound?'

Arlo nodded enthusiastically. 'Yeah, that sounds cool.'

Ben started the car and they pulled away.

Georgie looked over at him – what the hell was going on?

## Chapter 7

G arrow and French were now sitting in a doctor's office in the Intensive Care Unit of Llancastell University Hospital. Thick files, bulging manila folders and dog-eared medical books filled the shelves. Detailed posters of the human anatomy and its skeletal structure lined the walls.

The young woman had become incredibly distressed at her apparent loss of memory and had been administered a mild sedative so she could sleep.

The young Asian doctor walked in, stethoscope hanging around her neck, holding a folder and some images. 'So, I've got the CAT scans back.'

'Anything on them?' French asked.

The doctor sat down on the other side of the desk and shook her head. She showed them the images from the scan. Garrow peered at them but he clearly didn't know what he was looking for or why the doctor was actually showing the scans to them.

'The good news is that there is no serious neurological damage to her brain,' she explained, running her index finger over the image. 'She has severe concussion so we'll need to keep her under observation.'

'What about the memory loss?' French asked.

The doctor considered this for a second and then explained, 'It could be post traumatic amnesia.'

'Okay,' French said, clearly none the wiser.

'It's not uncommon when someone has received a blow to the head that results in unconsciousness,' the doctor stated. 'She'll be confused. She might not be able to remember recent events. She might even struggle to recognise family and friends.'

'And how long does that last?' Garrow asked. The young woman was covered in someone else's blood. As far as they knew, there had been no serious incidents in the past 24 hours in the area, so where had the blood come from? They needed her to remember what had happened to her as soon as possible.

The doctor pulled a face. 'I'm sorry but there's no definitive answer for that.'

French sat forward on his seat and looked at her. 'But if you had a guess, in a typical case of this kind?'

'There is normally a correlation between the amount of time the patient was unconscious and the time it takes for the memory to return,' she explained. 'It could be a few hours, even a few days or weeks. There is no way of knowing.'

'That's fine. And thanks for your help,' French said as they got up. 'Please contact us if there is any change.'

'Of course,' the doctor replied.

Garrow gave her a kind smile as they left the office, noticing how tired she looked. He guessed that a twelve-hour shift in the ICU could be pretty draining. When he was a teenager, Garrow had excelled at both maths and sciences. Much to the delight of his parents, he had toyed with the idea of studying medicine at university. When he eventually told them of his plans to join the police force they couldn't help but hide their disappointment, despite telling him that he needed to follow whatever career path he felt would fulfil him and make him happy.

Lost in these thoughts for a few seconds, Garrow went past the nurses' station and headed out of ICU. Then he looked down at the clear plastic envelope. He could see a couple of train tickets but there was also some kind of till receipt.

They got to the lift and French pressed the button.

'Anything interesting?' French asked.

Fishing around, Garrow pulled out the till receipt and looked at it.

'A meal at the Cross Foxes pub in Erbistock,' Garrow replied. 'Dated three days ago.'

# Chapter 8

Georgie, Ben and Arlo were making their way north towards Abergele. Pulling down the visor, Georgie could see Arlo looking contentedly out of the window. Ben gave her a suspicious look as she moved the visor up again.

Ignoring him, she looked out at the beautiful Welsh countryside. In the distance, a small village with a squat stone church stood at the foot of a series of overlapping hills. A church steeple rose from the centre like an exclamation point. In the fields that bordered the road, sheep grazed obliviously. Some had bulging bellies as they were pregnant. Georgie watched half a dozen or so lambs scamper along a rocky outcrop. It made her think of her own pregnancy. She knew that the stress of being kidnapped wasn't good for her or her baby.

'Dad, I need a wee,' Arlo said from the back of the car.

'You'll have to hold on, mate,' Ben said sternly.

Georgie turned and gave Arlo a kind smile. 'I think it's only half an hour until we get there.'

Arlo grimaced and then shook his head. 'I really need to wee.'

Georgie looked over at Ben and shrugged.

'Okay,' Ben huffed angrily as he slowed the car and then pulled into the opening to a field. He turned and gave Arlo a half smile. 'Go and have a wazz by those bushes over there, mate.'

Arlo nodded in a way that showed he was keen to please his dad. He opened the back door and trotted away to some bushes.

'Where's Arlo's mum?' Georgie asked as she watched him from the car.

'Arlo's mum? That bitch?' Ben snorted. 'Arlo's mum shagged a CPS lawyer called Simon behind my back. Now they're married and Arlo lives with them. And she's trying to stop me having any access to him.'

Georgie looked over at Ben. 'She wouldn't be able to do that.'

'I punched her prick of a husband a few months ago when I dropped Arlo off,' Ben explained. 'He said he wanted Arlo to call him 'Dad'. So, I took matters into my own hands and ...' He took a visible deep breath. 'None of that matters any more, does it?' he said very quietly.

It was as if he'd let his guard down for a few seconds and now regretted it.

Georgie frowned as she looked at him. 'What happened to the person I was with last week?'

Ben shrugged. 'That was all bullshit.'

'No,' Georgie said calmly as she shook her head. 'Not all of it. No one is that good a liar.'

'Wanna bet?' Ben sneered. His armour was up again.

'What's in Abergele?' Georgie asked.

'None of your business,' he snapped.

'But it's not just a trip to the seaside, is it?' she asked. Her instinct thought there might be more to the journey.

'Just dropping in on an old friend,' Ben said, narrowing his eyes. 'I've got a score to settle.'

At that moment, the back door opened and Arlo got in.

'Better, mate?' Ben asked.

'Yeah,' Arlo said with an innocent nod.

'Right,' Ben said, starting the engine again. 'Abergele here we come, eh?'

## Chapter 9

G arrow and French pulled into the car park of the Cross Foxes pub which sat up on a bank of the River Dee.

Getting out of the car, Garrow glanced down at the swirling river that was banked either side by high trees and tall reeds. With the spring sunshine dappling and sparkling off the river's eddying surface, it was a beautiful view. In the distance, a man in a khaki bucket hat and thigh high waders stood in the river and then cast his fishing line out into the water.

'Good place to catch salmon,' French said, gesturing to the man. 'Or trout, if I remember correctly.'

'Lovely spot,' Garrow remarked as they headed into the pub.

'My taid used to have a fishing licence for the Dee,' French remembered. 'He taught me to fish when I was about ten. That's why I know exactly where this pub is. We'd come here after. He'd have a bitter shandy and I'd have a Coke and a packet of crisps.'

'Sounds idyllic,' Garrow said.

'Yeah, it really was,' French said, lost in thought for a moment. 'Right, we'd better go in, eh?'

Garrow watched French for a few seconds. He was very guarded about his family and rarely mentioned his parents or relatives. Garrow didn't know if this was just French maintaining a professional distance at work, or if there was more to it than that. However, it wasn't something that Garrow was going to pry into.

The bar area had low beams and a dark red tiled floor which gave it a traditional old-fashioned feel. The enormous blackboard featured an array of world wines, the duck egg blue shutters and the carefully arranged photos and old adverts marked it out as more than just a local.

Spotting a man in his 30s behind the wooden bar, French and Garrow approached as they took out their warrant cards.

'DS French and DC Garrow, Llancastell CID,' French explained.

'Oh right,' the man said, looking a little concerned. He had a neatly trimmed dark beard and a red checked shirt tucked into his jeans that strained a little at his ample stomach. 'How can I help?'

French took the receipt and handed it to him. 'Can you confirm that this is a receipt from this pub?'

The man took the receipt and immediately nodded. 'Yes. It's from here.'

French pointed to the bottom of the paper. 'We're trying to track down the person who had this meal. There's a time and date at the bottom.'

'Okay,' the man nodded and went over to the computerised till. 'It's Table 5 which is outside, so I can check if they booked it for that time.' He tapped away for a few seconds and then gave them an apologetic look. 'Sorry.

They must have been a walk-in. I can have a look at how they paid and see if I can get a name from that?'

'Please,' French nodded.

Garrow glanced at the row of speciality beers – EPA Pale Ale, Brakespear Bitter and Aspall Draught Cider. Garrow didn't really drink in any meaningful way. He didn't know why. Being drunk had never really appealed to him. But he was partial to a decent pint of local bitter once in a while. He remembered enjoying a couple of pints of Welsh Highland Bitter – but at 5.2%, it was strong and knocked him for six.

'Sorry,' the barman said with the same apologetic face. 'The person must have paid cash as there's no record here.'

Garrow thought for a moment and then said, 'I know this is a long shot but the person we're looking for is a young woman, mid-20s, blonde hair. And she had a couple of tattoos on her wrist.'

The barman's expression exchanged. 'Actually, I do remember her. She came in with another woman about the same age.'

French looked over at him. 'I don't suppose you remember a name? Or anything that might help track her down?'

The barman looked over at a young man with dark curly hair who was just finishing taking a food order at a nearby table. 'Andrew?' he called over.

Andrew approached with a quizzical expression.

'These gentleman are police officers,' he explained. 'You served Table 5 on Friday afternoon. Two women in their 20s? Do you remember?'

Andrew nodded a little gormlessly. 'Yeah.'

French looked at him. 'Do you happen to remember either of their names? We're particularly interested in the blonde woman that was sitting at that table. Is there anything you can think of that might help us track her down?'

Andrew looked decidedly awkward.

Garrow sensed he might be hiding something. 'It's really important, Andrew,' he said quietly. 'However trivial you might think it is.'

Andrew looked concerned. 'Why? Is she all right?'

French fixed him with a look that was intended to let him know this was serious. 'Whatever you know, you need to tell us right now.'

'I've got her number,' Andrew explained nervously as he pulled out his phone. 'I had some spare tickets for a gig. And we got talking, so she gave me her number. Her name's Lucy. Here,' he said, showing them the screen.

'Thank you,' Garrow said as he jotted the number down in his notebook.

## Chapter 10

Having taken the A541, Georgie, Ben and Arlo were cutting across country on their way towards Abergele. As Georgie looked out, she noticed that the weather had changed quite suddenly. The bright sunshine had been replaced by dark granite-coloured clouds. Her window was down and the air had become heavy and portentous.

Arlo was engrossed in the back of the car, playing a game on his phone with AirPods in his ears. Since Ben's sinister statement that he was going to Abergele to settle a score with 'an old friend', Georgie had wondered what that meant exactly. It didn't sound good, whatever it was. She didn't know if it had anything to do with the trafficking and slavery gang that she now knew Ben was running.

Then her thoughts turned to what Ben's plans were for her. She was a police officer and she knew that he had committed two murders, as well as running a modern slavery ring out of Denbigh. Part of her wondered why she was still alive. Had Ben drawn the line at murdering a pregnant woman? Or was he just considering what to do with her? All she knew was that she had to alert someone to their abduction without his knowledge.

Looking right out of the open window, Georgie took a deep breath. Her stomach was a ball of tight anxiety. She thought she recognised where they were. *Afonwen?*

'I know this place,' she said under her breath, almost as if she was talking to herself.

Ben didn't respond.

'Herons Lake is just over there,' Georgie said. Part of her was exhausted from sitting in strained silence. It felt a relief just to break the monotony. 'My mum and dad took me there when I was a kid and we camped by the lake.'

Ben looked at her, his face full of thunder. 'That's nice for you,' he said bitterly.

She didn't know quite what he meant by that. His comment sounded almost childlike.

'Were you close to your parents?' she asked him.

Ben snorted but didn't say anything.

There were a few more minutes of silence. Given his whole demeanour, she guessed that there had been some kind of issue between Ben and his parents.

'Don't you like talking about your mum and dad?' Georgie asked tentatively. Maybe if she could get a more personal conversation going with Ben that might convince him not to harm her. 'Are you close to them?'

'For fuck's sake!' Ben snapped loudly. 'If you think I'm going to talk to you about my family, then …'

There was another awkward silence.

However, Georgie could see that there was an inner rage growing inside him. His whole body was tensing and his hands seemed to be gripping the steering wheel tightly.

'Sorry …' she said under her breath as she turned to look out of the window again. 'I didn't …'

'You want to know about my family?' he growled angrily.

'No, it's fine. I shouldn't have asked,' Georgie conceded. 'It's none of my business is it?'

'But you're making it your business though aren't you?' he said with an underlying indignation.

'Let's leave it shall we?' she said, trying to pacify him.

'Oh no. You want us to trade our little fucking stories about parents and grandparents in a 'getting to know you'? Is that what you want, is it?' He virtually spat the words from his mouth.

Georgie looked over at him and gave a little shrug. 'I'm sorry. I didn't mean to pry. If I've upset you then …'

'No, no. If you want to know,' Ben shook his head full of rage. 'I didn't know any of my grandparents. They lived in South Wales. We had nothing to do with them. And my dad was a nasty, violent alcoholic who beat my mum, me and my sister black and blue on a regular basis. I didn't go on camping trips or do anything. All I can remember is my dad coming back from the pub every night, smashing things up and thumping the shit out of us. And if I said anything or tried to stand up to him, he locked me in the coal cellar. Once he left me in there for two days. No light. Pitch black. No food. I had to piss, shit and then try to sleep in there.'

Georgie didn't say anything for a few seconds. 'I'm so sorry,' she whispered.

'No, you're not!' he barked at her. He seemed utterly overwhelmed by rage. 'And I don't want your fucking pity either.'

Georgie nodded. She regretted having broached the subject. However, part of her felt a perverse sense of relief that Ben had exploded. It had revealed a dark, emotional pain that might go a little way to explaining his damaged, twisted character.

Even though it was a risk, Georgie wanted to know more. 'What about your mum? Are you still in contact with her?'

Ben shook his head. 'No,' he said under his breath as he stared at the road ahead.

Georgie nodded. 'Right,' she said in an empathetic tone.

'My dad came back on the night of my thirteenth birthday,' Ben said quietly. 'She'd been distracted by baking me a cake, and the stew had dried out. So, he beat her to death on the kitchen floor in front of us.'

There was a beat and then Ben looked over. 'Is there anything else you want to know?' he asked with a dark expression.

'No,' Georgie replied with an apologetic shake of her head.

## Chapter 11

'How are we getting along with your mystery woman with amnesia?' Ruth asked as she came out of her office and wandered through CID. The fact that the young woman had blood all over her hands that clearly wasn't her own was a major concern.

Ruth looked over at Garrow and for a second she remembered just how far he'd come since joining CID. Garrow was known by some of the detectives as *Prof* or *The Prof*. He was university educated for starters. However, unlike when Ruth had joined the force in 1992, it was now quite common to have a degree. In fact, nearly 40% of officers joining these days had a degree or an equivalent qualification. That was a far cry from Ruth's first posting at Lavender Hill nick in Battersea. As far as she knew, only Superintendent Rupert Holloway had been to university – and he stuck out like a sore thumb and seemed to rub most of the rank and file up the wrong way. Along with his degree in social sciences, Jim had a methodical, cerebral, even intellectual way of investigating crimes that was a little different to other detectives. What he lacked in instinct, he more than made up for with his sharp mind. Plus, he didn't have any airs or graces about him which made him popular with the CID team.

'I've run her prints through the database but didn't get a hit,' Garrow explained.

'Forensics?' Ruth asked.

'A scene of crime officer has taken a swab from her and from the blood we found on her clothing,' Garrow said.

Ruth frowned. 'How long is it going to take to pull DNA from that?'

Garrow pulled a face. 'Tomorrow at the earliest, boss.'

'Anything else?' she asked.

French came over. It was getting hot in the CID office and he'd rolled up his shirt sleeves. 'We found a receipt from the Cross Foxes pub in Erbistock. She met a young woman in there early evening on Friday. She didn't book and didn't pay with a card. *But* she gave her number to a member of staff so we think her name is Lucy.'

Garrow nodded. 'I'm running a check on the number now. We should be able to get a full name and address by the end of the day.'

'Good work,' Ruth said. In the past year, Garrow and French had become a tight team, and their contrasting ways of approaching a case complemented each other. 'I haven't seen her clothing but what did SOCOs make of the amount of blood we found on her?'

'Doesn't sound good.' French ran his hand over his jaw. 'Forensics believe that there was enough blood on her clothing and hands to suggest a major injury. Possibly fatal.'

Ruth narrowed her eyes. 'But we've got no reports of anything in the Wrexham area in the past 48 hours that would match that?'

French shook his head. 'No, boss.'

Ruth gave them a dark look. 'Which means there's someone out there severely injured or dead that we haven't found yet.'

## Chapter 12

Garrow and French had been called back to the ICU unit at the hospital as the woman they thought was called Lucy was now fully conscious and out of danger. She had been moved to a small single room in a nearby ward.

As they went in, Lucy was sitting up in bed, looking lost in thought and confused.

'Hi,' Garrow said gently as she glanced over at them. 'We're police officers from Llancastell. We were here earlier when you came round?'

Lucy shook her head and looked baffled. 'Were you?'

Garrow and French went over to two grey plastic chairs and sat down.

'We believe that your name is Lucy,' French explained. 'Does that make any sense or ring any bells for you?'

Lucy shook her head and then looked upset. 'I'm really sorry,' she whispered as her eyes filled with tears.

Garrow leaned forward in his seat. 'I know this is very difficult for you, so take as much time as you need.'

Lucy wiped her face with a tissue, sniffed, and then

adjusted the pillows as she sat up. Then she looked at Garrow with a furrowed brow. 'I had blood all over my hands. And someone came and took a sample.'

French nodded. 'That's right.'

'What happened?' she asked.

'I'm afraid we don't know yet,' Garrow said quietly. 'Can you remember anything at all?'

Lucy closed her eyes and shook her head. 'I'm really sorry. I wish I could.'

'You don't need to apologise,' Garrow reassured her.

'I think I can remember some kind of fight. People were shouting,' she explained. 'But it's all so vague.'

'Any idea who those people were?' French asked.

'No,' she replied sadly.

'You have an injury to the back of your head,' Garrow said. 'Do you have any idea how you got it?'

Lucy shook her head again. 'This is so embarrassing …'

'Really, there's no need to feel embarrassed whatsoever,' Garrow said with a kind expression.

'And you were found unconscious at the bottom of the Pontcysyllte Aqueduct, near Llangollen,' French explained. 'Does that mean anything to you?'

Lucy furrowed her brow. 'The Aqueduct?' She took a few seconds. 'I know it but I just don't remember being there recently.'

'We do also know that you were at the Cross Foxes pub in Erbistock on Friday afternoon,' Garrow informed her. 'You were with another woman about the same age as you?'

Lucy's eyes suddenly roamed the room as if she had thought of something. 'Sian.'

Garrow raised an eyebrow. 'Sian?'

'I was with Sian,' Lucy said. 'Sorry, I know that doesn't help much.'

Garrow's phone buzzed. He looked at the caller ID, saw that it was a Wrexham number and guessed that it was someone from the security team at the mobile phone company.

Getting up, Garrow looked at Lucy and gestured to the door. 'I'm just going to take this call.'

He walked into the corridor outside.

'DC Garrow?' he said, answering the call.

'Hi, this is Jamie from the security team at O2,' said a friendly male voice with a Geordie accent. 'You were looking for an address for one of our customers, is that correct?'

'Yes, that's right,' Garrow said, feeling positive that they might be getting closer to discovering who Lucy was and where she lived. He pulled out his notebook and pen.

'The customer connected with that number is a Lucy Morgan,' Jamie explained. 'The address we have on the account is 19 Bryn Close, Acton Park, Wrexham.'

Garrow scribbled down the address. 'That's great, thank you.'

Ending the call, Garrow went back into the room and looked over at Lucy. 'I have some good news. I'm pretty sure your name is Lucy Morgan. And you live in Acton Park in Wrexham.'

Lucy shrugged. 'Okay ... It doesn't register.'

'We'll go and have a look at the house,' French said, getting up.

Garrow gave her a kind smile. 'And if we find anything significant, we'll come back. There might be something there that will jog your memory.'

Lucy smiled back at him. 'Thank you. That's very kind of you.'

## Chapter 13

Georgie, Ben and Arlo were now speeding along the
A525 as they travelled through the village of Tref-
nant which was in Denbighshire, about halfway between St
Asaph to the north and Denbigh to the south.

As they slowed and then stopped at some temporary
lights, Georgie glanced to the right and saw a beautiful 19th
century church set back from the road. A sign read – *Holy
Trinity Church, Trefnant*. Between the road and the church's
entrance was a large churchyard with a colourful array of
spring flowers, gravel paths, and several wooden benches.
It looked incredibly peaceful.

However, Georgie was lost in thought. She was still
trying to process Ben's outburst and the dark abuse he had
witnessed as a child. As a police officer, she had seen some
pretty upsetting and harrowing abuse within families on
many occasions. Ben's description of his father's abusive
behaviour, and seeing his mother beaten to death in front
of his eyes, was one of the worst she'd ever heard. She also
knew the devastating impact that kind of childhood
trauma could have on the rest of a person's life – addic-

tion, violence, and often the repetitive cycle of abusive behaviour.

As the lights changed, they pulled away and turned left onto a main road.

'We need petrol,' Ben said under his breath, almost as if talking to himself.

Ben almost immediately turned and pulled into the forecourt of a small rural petrol station and stopped the car. The white brickwork of the main office was discoloured. An old rusty satellite dish had been bolted to the flat roof. The concrete where they had parked was stained, dirty, and strewn with weeds.

However, Georgie wasn't focussed on her surroundings. Instead, her eyes immediately flicked over to the Tetra radio at the centre of the car's dashboard and the red emergency button. If Ben was distracted enough when putting petrol into the car and going into the shop to pay, maybe she would have a chance to hit the button to signal to other officers that something was wrong.

'Right,' Ben said as he opened the driver's door. He then looked at her and muttered. 'Don't do anything stupid.'

Georgie didn't reply.

Taking out his AirPods, Arlo looked over. 'Can I have a drink, Dad?'

'Not yet, mate,' Ben said calmly. 'As soon as we get to the seaside we'll get drinks, fish and chips, ice cream. Anything you want, mate.'

Arlo looked a little disappointed but nodded, replaced his AirPods and went back to whatever he was doing on his phone.

Ben slammed the door, and Georgie watched him go over to the petrol pump. To her dismay, she saw that it was a pump that allowed card payments.

*Shit!* she thought. There was now no need for Ben to go inside.

Watching through the back rear window, she saw Ben put the nozzle into the car and heard the deep vibrating hum as the pump started.

She just needed him to look away for a few seconds so she could reach for the radio handset.

With her fingers primed, she watched him like a hawk but he was gazing into the car and keeping a watchful eye on her.

*Come on, come on. Just look away.*

However, Ben moved back to the driver's door and opened it. He leaned in, reached for the Tetra radio handset and unclipped it from the main body of the dashboard.

He gave her a derisive look as he gestured to the radio that was now in his hand. 'Just in case you do something silly like radio for help.'

He slammed the door loudly and went back to the pump.

*Bollocks! Now what?*

Moving around slowly, she kept a watchful eye outside.

She had an idea.

Ben seemed less interested in looking in at her now he'd taken the radio. Instead, he was looking up at the pump's display. She also knew that while he put in his bank card and paid for the petrol, Ben would have to turn his back on them for about 30 seconds to a minute.

And that would be her chance.

*Right, let's do this.*

Her pulse was now racing. She tapped Arlo's knee furtively.

He frowned as he looked at her.

She gave him a look as if to signal that she wanted to talk to him.

He took one AirPod out.

With her eyes half on Ben outside, Georgie gave Arlo a smile. 'You playing a game on your phone?'

Arlo smiled cheerily and nodded. 'Yes. It's called Hanging Donuts.'

'Oh right,' Georgie said, taking a nervous gulp.

Ben took the nozzle out of the car and went over to replace it and then pay.

*Right, now!*

'Mind if I take a quick look?' she asked him, holding out her hand. 'My nephew might like it.'

Her heart was hammering in her chest.

Arlo smiled. 'Yeah, okay,' he said as he handed the phone to her.

With another glance outside, she saw that Ben was using the machine to pay and had his back turned.

Taking the phone, Georgie said 'Thanks.'

Frantically looking at the screen, she minimised the game.

Then she looked for the green text button to compose a text message.

Looking up, she saw that Ben was taking his card out of the machine.

She was running out of time.

*Shit! Shit!*

With frenetic tapping, Georgie composed a message:

*HELP, POLICE OFFICER DC WILD AND CHILD KIDNAPPED, CAR reg TG19 YGY*

. . .

Ben was putting the card into his wallet and turning.

Tapping in 999, Georgie sent the text, opened up the game and handed the phone back to Arlo.

Her heart was pounding.

'Looks good,' she said, feeling sick with worry.

Arlo smiled and popped his AirPods back in.

Turning round, she saw Ben appear at the door.

*Shit! Did he see me with Arlo's phone?*

Georgie held her breath, bracing herself for Ben's reaction.

He opened the car door, got in, and then looked directly at her.

Silence.

'Everything all right?' he asked as he then glanced back at Arlo.

Arlo was back playing his game with his AirPods in.

'Yeah, fine,' she replied slowly, letting out her breath in relief.

'Good.' Ben started the engine and they pulled away.

## Chapter 14

Glancing out of the window, Georgie could feel the tension mounting inside the car. She had no idea if her emergency text had been received. She did know that it would have been taken seriously. However, when the registration was run past the DVLA, the police would soon realise that it belonged to Detective Inspector Ben Stewart of the Modern Slavery and Human Trafficking Unit. With this information, they might contact Ben directly to see if everything was okay and if the message was a hoax. Yet since the Sarah Everard case last month in which the young woman was abducted and murdered by police officer Wayne Couzens, the climate in the UK police force had changed. It was clear that there were predatory sex offenders, and potential murderers, within the force.

As they negotiated a long bend, a road sign signalled that it was ten miles to Abergele. The sun broke through the clouds, casting shadows across the interior of the car.

Georgie glanced over at Ben. She knew there was a chance that if they were stopped by the police, she would never see or speak to him again. She knew that he was a corrupt police officer and a cold-blooded murderer. And she certainly wasn't making any excuses for his actions. But what he'd told her about his upbringing did make her see him in a slightly different light.

'For what it's worth,' she said gently, 'what you told me about your childhood. I'm really sorry that happened to you.'

'I don't want to talk about it,' Ben snarled.

'Okay,' Georgie said.

'I should never have told you any of that,' he said, shaking his head. 'Just forget it, okay?'

'It's not something you just forget.'

There was a long awkward silence.

Ben was glancing at his rear-view mirror intently.

Moving her head, Georgie looked over at the wing mirror.

There was a marked police car behind them.

Her stomach tightened.

Ben looked increasingly agitated.

Suddenly, the police car's lights burst into life with a flash of blue light.

'What the fuck do they want?' Ben asked suspiciously, and then looked over at Georgie.

She shrugged as her pulse began to race. 'How would I know?'

'Bloody hell,' Ben growled as he pulled the car over to the side of the country road. Then he glared over at her. 'Now is not the time to try and be a hero,' he warned her.

'What's going on?' Arlo asked from the back of the car as he took one of his AirPods out.

'Don't worry, mate,' Ben reassured him. 'I just need to speak to these police officers for a minute. Nothing to worry about.'

'Do you work with them?' Arlo asked.

'Something like that,' Ben said. 'Just carry on playing your game, mate, okay?'

Arlo nodded and followed his father's suggestion.

Glancing in the wing mirror again, Georgie saw a young uniformed police officer get out of the passenger side of the car and start to wander down towards them.

Taking his warrant card from his jacket pocket, Ben buzzed down the window and a few seconds later the constable arrived, leaned down and looked in.

'Everything all right, constable?' Ben asked calmly.

'Yes, sir,' the constable said as he peered at the warrant card. 'Everything okay, miss?' he then asked.

'Yes, we're absolutely fine,' Georgie reassured him as her pulse raced.

'Okay, if you could just stay there for a second please, sir,' the constable said. He then moved away for a second and said something into his Tetra radio. There was a crackle on his radio. Even though it wasn't entirely audible, the dispatch operator clearly said *Detective Constable Georgina Wild.*

She saw Ben flinch as his eyes roamed nervously.

Coming back to the car, the constable peered back at them. 'I'm sorry, sir, but I am going to have to ask everyone to get out of the vehicle for a moment while I ask you a few more questions.'

Ben narrowed his eyes. 'Are you kidding me, constable?' he snapped. 'You've just seen my ID. What the hell is the problem?'

'If everyone could just step out of the car, sir. I'm sure this won't take more than a couple of minutes and then you can be on your way,' the constable explained calmly.

'For fuck's sake,' Ben huffed.

Georgie could see that he was about to explode as he tensed his hands around the steering wheel.

Suddenly, Ben put the car into gear and quickly slammed his foot on the accelerator.

The car lurched forward with a roar.

'Jesus!' Georgie gasped as she grabbed the sides of her seat and closed her eyes for a moment.

'How did you do it?' Ben yelled at her.

'What?' Georgie asked.

'How the fuck did they know you were in this car with me?' Ben said through gritted teeth.

'I don't know, do I?' Georgie replied angrily. 'You've got my phone. I haven't been anywhere or done anything.'

Ben glared at her. 'Yeah, well I'd better not find out this has anything to do with you or …'

'What's happening, Dad?' Arlo asked, sensing that they were suddenly driving fast – or maybe he'd heard the raised voices.

'It's okay, mate,' Ben said calmly. 'It's just some police training thing I've got to do. The police car behind is pretending to chase us.'

Arlo looked very confused.

Georgie could hear the sirens getting closer as Ben pushed the car faster and faster.

Overtaking a transit van, they swerved around a corner with a squeal of rubber from the tyres.

'Cool,' Arlo said excitedly. He had clearly bought into his dad's story.

Georgie was feeling sicker with anxiety with every second.

'You're not going to outrun them, Ben,' she pleaded with him as they careered around a corner and she clutched at her seat for dear life.

'Wanna bet?' Ben snorted, gripping the steering wheel, his knuckles white. He stared at the road ahead intently.

Glancing back, she looked at Arlo to check that he was definitely wearing his seatbelt.

He was glancing around with a mixture of excitement and confusion.

'You okay, Arlo?' she asked.

'Yeah,' he said with an emphatic nod as he looked back at the patrol car that was about two hundred yards behind them. 'This is fun.'

As Georgie looked ahead, she saw that they were hammering towards a car pulling a caravan.

'Shit!' Ben murmured.

The back of the caravan seemed to be getting bigger and bigger.

To avoid hitting it, Ben needed to slow down or they were going to plough straight into the back of it.

But he wasn't slowing at all.

Georgie gave him a terrified look. 'Ben,' she said fretfully.

'Shut up,' he hissed under his breath.

Looking ahead, she put her hands up. It looked as if they were going to hurtle into the back of the caravan.

'Oh my God,' Georgie said, closing her eyes in terror.

Suddenly, Ben pulled the car onto the other side of the road.

There was a piercing squeal of brakes.

Opening her eyes, Georgie could see a line of traffic coming the other way. It was lined up behind an enormous articulated lorry which was no more than fifty yards from them.

*Shit! We're not going to make it!*

Holding her breath and squinting, Georgie watched as Ben threw the steering wheel left.

The back of the car went out of control with the force of the turn.

Georgie winced. If Ben lost control, the car could roll and could end up anywhere.

Wrestling with the steering wheel, Ben got the car back under control.

'That was close, Dad,' Arlo said triumphantly.

'Hey,' Ben said puffing out his cheeks. 'I wasn't worried for a second.'

'Weren't you?' Arlo asked with a tone of pride.

'Not one bit, mate,' Ben said, looking over at Georgie with a dark smirk. She wanted to punch him in the face for playing Russian Roulette with her and Arlo's lives.

Georgie looked at the line of vehicles that were going past on the other side of the road. There had to be at least thirty. She knew that meant the pursuing police car was stuck behind the dawdling caravan – and would be for several minutes.

'Arlo?' Ben said.

'Yeah?'

'Have a look behind us, mate,' Ben said. 'Any sign of that police car?'

'No,' Arlo said, looking out of the back. 'I think you've lost them. Does that mean you've won the game?'

Ben looked over at Georgie. 'Yeah. That's exactly what it means, mate.'

As he pressed down on the accelerator, Georgie felt herself being pushed back in her seat as they sped away.

Five minutes later, Ben pulled the car off the road and into the middle of a field.

As they stopped, Arlo leaned forward. 'What are we doing here, Dad?'

Ben pointed to a car park and large hotel that was

about five hundred yards away. It had *Mardon Country Hotel* written up on the main wall.

'Think we might need to hold up in there for a bit, mate,' Ben explained.

'Are we staying the night?' Arlo asked excitedly.

'Why not,' Ben replied.

## Chapter 15

S itting at his desk, Nick looked around the CID office. Some of the detectives were at their desks typing at computers or talking on phones. Other desks were empty where officers were out and about. In that moment, Nick was struck by enormous gratitude for what he had both at work and at home. However, he couldn't seem to get the text message on Amanda's phone out of his head. He knew it would be nothing, and the sensible thing would be to ask her about it later.

Getting up, he could see that Ruth was hard at work in her office at the computer. She had told him to take the morning just to settle back in. If he was honest, all he wanted to do was get working on the current investigation.

'How we doing, Jim?' Nick asked.

'Think we've got something, sarge,' Garrow replied.

'Go on,' Nick said as he approached.

'O2 have given us a name and billing address for the woman with amnesia,' Garrow explained. 'Lucy Morgan. It's the mobile number that the guy at the Cross Foxes gave us.'

'Sounds like it's her then,' Nick said. 'Where does she live?'

'Wrexham,' Garrow said, looking at the email on the screen. 'Acton Park. I've spoken to the letting agent for the house and he's going to meet us there.'

'Good work,' Nick said, realising that Garrow and French were more than capable of handling the investigation.

'Thanks,' Garrow nodded, as he got up and went over to talk to French at his desk. French got up, and they both walked across the CID office and left.

As Nick turned, he saw Ruth coming out of her office. She looked troubled.

'You okay?' he asked as he approached.

'No,' she said quietly as she gestured for him to follow her into her office.

Nick sat down and looked at her. 'What is it?'

'A text was sent to the 999 emergency line from a mobile phone about 30 minutes ago,' Ruth said, looking at some notes she had scribbled down. 'It read - *Help, police officer DC Wild and a child kidnapped, car reg TG19 YGY.*'

Nick frowned. 'What?'

'That car belongs to a Detective Inspector Ben Stewart. He works for the Modern Slavery and Human Trafficking Unit. And he's been working for the past ten days on a double murder investigation revolving around a trafficking ring based in Denbigh bringing kids and young people over from India.'

'And he was working with Georgie?' Nick asked.

'Yes,' Ruth said, and then pulled a face.

'What?'

'Ben and Georgie became … romantically involved,' Ruth explained.

'Right,' Nick said, feeling a little lost.

Ruth pointed down to her notes. 'Problem is, a patrol car just outside Abergele pulled Ben's car over because of the message. One of the officers went to the car. Ben showed him his warrant card, but a woman fitting Georgie's description, and a young boy, were inside the car. The officer got suspicious but when he asked Ben and the others to step out of the vehicle, he drove off. They chased them for about five miles but then lost them.'

Nick raised an eyebrow. 'Georgie sent that text.'

'Sounds like it,' Ruth said, and then gave Nick a dark look. 'And that means for some reason, Ben has kidnapped her and a young boy and they're now on the run.'

## Chapter 16

G arrow and French stood outside a neat looking
bungalow on Bryn Close, a cul-de-sac close to
Acton Park, a suburb to the north-east of Wrexham.
Dating back to the Bronze Age, Wrexham was the prin-
cipal town in North Wales. It had a history of coal-mining
and industry going back to the 18<sup>th</sup> century and was a
proud, working class town with a strong community spirit.
The acquisition of its football club by Hollywood actors
Rob McElhenney and Ryan Reynolds two months ago had
been a major news story, bringing excitement and a touch
of glamour back to the town.

Garrow looked up and saw that the dark clouds of the
morning had cleared and now it was a beautiful spring
afternoon. The sky was an azure blue with wispy clouds
that looked like pulled candyfloss. A small private plane
flew overhead, banked to the right, and then headed east
towards England. The border with Cheshire was only five
miles away, situated along the River Clywedog.

The letting agent, a slightly overconfident, balding man
in his 40s who kept whizzing his large bunch of keys

around his index finger, had met them at the property. Lucy Morgan had been renting the property for just over a year and there had been no problems with her as a tenant.

The letting agent opened the white front door and looked at them. 'Any idea how long you're going to be?'

'Depends on what we find in there, I'm afraid,' French replied as he took out his blue forensic gloves.

Garrow did the same. Lucy had been covered in someone else's blood so they had no idea if they were about to walk into a major crime scene. They couldn't take any chances.

The letting agent's face fell as he watched them put on their forensic gloves. 'Oh right ... Erm, if you guys can let me know when you've finished and close the door on the way out, I can come and lock up later.'

Garrow nodded. 'Just so you know, there is a possibility that we'll need to get a forensic team in here.'

'Right, okay.' The letting agent pulled a face. 'I'll leave you to it then.'

As he walked away, spinning his keys, French gave Garrow a look. 'Well he was bloody irritating.'

'Yeah, definitely over-compensating for something,' Garrow agreed as they went into the bungalow.

The house was neat and tidy with a subtle colour scheme of soft browns, greys, and olive greens which gave it a tasteful air. The furnishings were simple and sophisticated, indicating a well-educated mind – not to mention several bookshelves filled with tomes of both classic and contemporary literature.

On the walls hung posters and photographs; some were of London art exhibitions, others of plays at the theatre, plus a few pictures of family and friends. In the living room, a small upright antique piano stood in one corner, and a tapestry hung above the fireplace. On the mantelpiece, a few knick-knacks and candles had been arranged with careful thought.

Spreading out, French and Garrow quickly checked the two bedrooms, living room, tiny dining room, kitchen and bathroom.

'Nothing here that might explain the blood on Lucy's hands and clothes, sarge,' Garrow said as they reconvened in the hallway.

French pointed to a framed graduation photograph of Lucy – wearing a cloak and cap, and with a scroll in her hand. 'Bright girl by the looks of it,' he said.

'2.1 Hons degree in English Literature from Bath University,' Garrow said. 'That's impressive.'

'I'll take your word for it,' French said, as he looked around and gestured to the living room. 'I'll have a look in here and see if there's anything that might indicate where she was last night.'

'I thought I might take a few things from here to her in hospital to see if it jogs her memory at all,' Garrow said as he took the photo down from the wall. He couldn't help but look at the photo and think how attractive Lucy was. It must be so incredibly frightening to have no memory of who you are and where you live.

Moving into the kitchen, Garrow's eyes roamed around, looking for anything that might help them.

There were various photographs behind magnets on the fridge. A few were of Lucy on nights out with friends, and there were several with a woman in her late 40s, whom Garrow assumed was Lucy's mother. Taking the photos down, he placed them in the evidence bag.

Then he spotted a small calendar hanging from the wall on the other side of the fridge.

Going closer, he scoured it for yesterday's date.

*Mum? Pub? Home?*

'Think I've got something, sarge,' he called.

French marched into the kitchen and came over. 'What is it?'

'According to this calendar,' Garrow explained, 'Lucy might have been meeting her mother at a pub or at home yesterday evening.' He pointed to the photos that he'd taken. 'I think that's her in these photos.'

French looked at him. 'We're going to need an address for her then.'

## Chapter 17

Ruth was feeling sick with worry since learning of Georgie's text message and the chase involving the car she was travelling in with Ben and a young boy, whose identity she didn't know yet. The last time she had spoken to Georgie she had intimated that her and Ben were possibly going to enter into a romantic relationship. How the hell had that gone so horribly wrong? Georgie was pregnant, so she was vulnerable.

Sitting forward at her desk, she saw a silly, romantic text from Sarah. It made Ruth smile for a moment, as she thought about how lucky she was to have Sarah in her life.

Looking outside, Ruth could hear that the CID office was full of concerned chatter. The news of Georgie's kidnapping was only just filtering through.

Getting up from her desk, Ruth prepared herself to *address the troops*.

'Okay everyone,' she said loudly as she walked to the centre of the room. 'If we can settle down. We do have a major incident developing that most of you are now aware of. We believe that Georgie has been abducted by DI Ben

Stewart, who was working with us here last week. At the moment, we have no idea what his motive is. Georgie sent me a text early this morning to say that she was feeling unwell and wouldn't be coming to work today. It's my belief that the text was actually sent by Ben Stewart. Georgie is not responding to phone calls or texts to her mobile phone. Twenty minutes ago, I authorised uniformed officers to force their way into Georgie's house. However, there was no sign of her there or anywhere in the area.'

Nick looked over and signalled to his phone. 'Boss, we've got a St Joseph's Primary School in Penyffordd on the line. Ben Stewart took his 9-year-old son, Arlo, out of school, claiming that there was a family emergency. One of the teachers was suspicious and rang Ben's ex-wife, Annabelle. She had no idea why Arlo needed to be taken out of school and wasn't aware of any family emergency.'

'Do we have any background on this?' Ruth asked.

'The teacher told me off the record that there had been an acrimonious divorce between Ben and Annabelle after she had an affair,' Nick explained. 'She seemed to think there was an ongoing dispute about Ben's access to Arlo.'

Ruth gave Nick a knowing look. 'Which might well explain why he's chosen to take him.'

Nick thought for a few seconds. 'Do we have any idea why Ben would have abducted Georgie in the first place?'

'None,' Ruth admitted, sounding frustrated. 'To all intents and purposes, Ben is a smart, young DI. He and Georgie were clearly attracted to each other. Obviously Georgie is pregnant so she didn't think it could go anywhere. But the last I knew, they were going to see if they could make a go of it.'

Nick looked confused. 'I wonder what the hell happened to change all that?'

'I'm completely stumped,' Ruth admitted.

'We must be able to get a GPS track on the car,' Nick said, thinking out loud.

'Unless he ditches it.'

'Yeah, he'll know that we can track down his car,' Nick agreed.

'Do we have any idea where they might be heading or why?' Ruth asked.

Nick looked down at his notes. 'They were stopped about eight miles outside Abergele.'

'Okay, let's dig into Ben's background and see if we can find anything that links him to Abergele. If you ring the Modern Slavery and Human Trafficking Unit in Manchester, we can get his personnel file sent over. But let's see if we can find out where his family is. Parents, siblings.'

'Yes, boss,' Nick nodded.

'And I think we need to hold a press conference asap,' Ruth said. 'Get the media to circulate photos of all three of them plus descriptions.'

'I've already spoken to the media office at St Asaph and they're on it,' Nick reassured her.

Ruth looked at Nick as they wandered over towards her office. 'Thank God you're back,' she said under her breath.

## Chapter 18

Daylight was fading by the time French and Garrow got to the address that they'd been given for Lynne Morgan, Lucy's mother. She lived in the middle of Wrexham – *Wrecsam* - in a small house directly opposite The Racecourse Ground – *Y Cae Ras* in Welsh - which was where Wrexham AFC played their home games in the National League. Built in 1864, it was the world's oldest international football stadium.

French stepped forward and rang the doorbell.

'Must be a pain when Wrexham are playing at home,' Garrow said, gesturing to the main road and the football stadium. When he had been a uniformed officer, he'd policed a few football games in Shrewsbury and they'd been fairly unpleasant.

'Unless she's got a season ticket and then she's laughing,' French said as he went to the doorbell and rang it again.

Nothing.

Garrow moved over to a downstairs window, cupped his hands and tried to look inside. There were shutters and net curtains so it was virtually impossible to see anything inside.

They had no idea whether Lucy had even made it to her mother's home on Friday evening as planned according to her calendar. The incident that had caused Lucy to become covered in blood might well have happened before she'd even arrived.

'You looking for Lynne?' a voice asked in a North Wales accent.

They glanced over and saw a thick-set, middle-aged man, grade one ginger hair, putting out his bins. He was wearing a red Wrexham AFC shirt.

Garrow went over and took out his warrant card. 'DC Garrow, Llancastell CID. We're looking for Lynne Morgan.'

The man frowned. 'I'm not sure she's in.'

'But she does live here?' Garrow asked to clarify as French came over.

'That's right,' the man said with a nod. 'Has done for donkey's years.'

'Have you seen her today?' French asked.

The man thought for a few seconds. 'I'm not sure. I thought I saw her going to work this morning but that might have been yesterday.'

'Okay,' Garrow said, reaching for his notebook and pen. 'Where does she work?'

'She's a barmaid at the Horse and Jockey in town, like,' the man explained.

'Have you seen her since Friday evening?' French enquired.

'I'm really sorry.' The man pulled a face. 'I think I have but I couldn't swear to it.'

French gestured to the house. 'Anyone else live with you who might have seen her?'

The man looked back and then shouted, 'Trace?'

A woman in her 40s, petite, blonde with delicate features, came out onto the doorstep.

'What's the matter?' she asked loudly as she clocked Garrow and French and gave them the once over.

'These blokes are coppers,' the man explained. 'Sorry, police officers. And they're trying to find Lynne.'

'Oh, been up to no good has she?' Trace laughed.

Garrow gave her a polite smile. 'We're just trying to establish when was the last time either you or your husband saw her.'

'Christ, now you're asking,' Trace said, putting her hands on her hips. 'I can't remember, can you Gav?'

'No,' Gav agreed.

French fished out a card and gave it to them. 'If you do see her, can you tell her to give me a call as soon as possible.'

'Yeah, no problem,' Gav said.

Trace looked over. 'Her son lives there at the moment. Steve. He's just got out of the army, hasn't he Gav?'

'Yeah,' Gavin replied, and then gave them a dark look. 'Being in the army has, you know …' Gavin pointed to his temple. 'Fucked him up a bit, like. Between you and me, we think he's a bit of a druggie.'

'Okay, thanks,' Garrow said, wondering if the information about Steve Morgan had anything to do with his sister.

## Chapter 19

Glancing out at the packed media room at Llancastell Police Station, Ruth was aware that the search for Ben, Georgie and Arlo was just starting to filter into the national news – even though the details were sketchy. She was fuming that the story had been leaked already, although she was confident that it hadn't come from anyone in her CID team. They were all too invested in Georgie's safety to do anything as reckless as talk to a journalist. She knew the same couldn't always be said for some of the younger uniformed officers in Llancastell.

Ruth's phone buzzed and she looked at her most recent update.

*BBC Wales @ BBC Breaking News*

*Sources claim that a woman and a 9-year-old boy have been abducted by a serving North Wales police officer. It is believed that they are now on the run.*

Ruth had to admit that a social media explosion could only help them to track down Ben, Georgie and Arlo. After her press conference, there would be thousands on the lookout for a man, woman and boy in the North Wales area fitting the descriptions and photos that were being distributed and released as they spoke. Even though it was early evening, Ruth knew that it was important that the story hit the evening news on the major television channels.

Checking her watch, Ruth stared out at the assembled journalists. A figure marched up the side of the room towards her. It was Kerry, the Chief Corporate Communications Officer for North Wales Police, who had come across from the main press office in St Asaph. Ruth had met her on various occasions over the last few years and found her arrogant and irritating.

Kerry sat down next to her. 'Evening, Ruth.'

Ruth gritted her teeth. 'Evening, Kerry. Sorry to drag you all the way over here at this time.' Ruth wasn't sorry at all, but she needed to keep Kerry onside as much as possible in the next few days until Georgie and Arlo had been found safely.

'No problem,' Kerry said with a slightly smug smile. Then she looked at Ruth quizzically. 'I understand that this DI Ben Stewart has been working with you here for the past week?'

'That's right,' Ruth said, wondering where Kerry was going with this. Everything Kerry said was calculated, with some kind of agenda.

Kerry pulled a face. 'Gosh, you must feel pretty embarrassed about that?'

Ruth raised an eyebrow. 'How do you mean?'

'I'm not being critical or anything,' Kerry said.

*Which means that's exactly what you're about to be,* Ruth thought guardedly.

'But he's made you look pretty stupid,' Kerry explained, unable to hide her condescension. 'You're all supposedly experienced detectives. And yet you had no idea that this man you were working with was clearly about to go off the rails and kidnap your colleague and an innocent boy. I mean, it's hard to imagine that you didn't pick up on any of that, isn't it?

Ruth took a breath. *God, you're such a self-righteous bitch.*

'I guess it is,' Ruth said, smiling through gritted teeth.

Ruth and Kerry had never seen eye to eye on how to handle the press. Kerry seemed to believe they needed to be manipulated with careful control of when and how information about a case was released. In contrast, Ruth believed that they should keep them fully informed and up-to-date. They stood a better chance of catching criminals if they used the media to appeal for witnesses and kept local communities fully in the loop.

Glancing down at the microphones and tape recorders, Ruth realised it was time to start. *Let's get on with this before I slap this woman,* she thought.

'Good evening, I'm Detective Inspector Ruth Hunter. This press conference is to update you on the case and to appeal to the public for any information. We believe that a serving police officer, DI Ben Stewart, has abducted DC Georgie Wild, an officer from this police station, along with his 9-year-old son, Arlo Stewart. If you have any information about their whereabouts, please contact us on the North Wales Police helpline. We are looking for anyone who has spotted someone fitting our descriptions of these three people to come forward. We do believe that Ben Stewart was heading towards the Abergele area ... Now, I do have some time to take questions, if there are any.'

A reporter peered up at her from the front row. 'Lee Hunt, Mirror Group. Given the recent case of Sarah Everard who was murdered by a serving police officer,

Wayne Couzens, do you believe that the lives of both hostages are in serious danger?'

*Bloody great! I don't want to have to talk about this now.*

'At this stage, I'm not willing to speculate on anything like that,' Ruth said firmly. 'Our sole purpose is to locate Georgie and Arlo safely and bring them home unharmed.'

A television journalist made a gesture from the back of the room and Ruth nodded. 'Keira Bowie, BBC News. Detective Inspector, do you know if Detective Inspector Ben Stewart was showing signs of being under great stress, or was there any indication that he was going to commit these crimes in recent weeks?'

'I don't think it's helpful for me to discuss Ben Stewart's mental health in the lead up to this incident,' Ruth explained. After Kerry's barbed comment, she was starting to wonder how they had missed Ben's true nature.

'A source has told me that you were in fact working on a murder case with DI Ben Stewart last week. Is that correct?' Keira Bowie continued.

*For fuck's sake!*

'I'm not sure that question is relevant to the current situation. Right, thank you everyone. No more questions,' Ruth said, trying desperately not to show that she was feeling rattled.

Ruth stood and gathered up her files. She noticed Kerry giving her an all-too-familiar supercilious look.

Kerry got up and blew out her cheeks. 'Don't worry, Ruth. I'm sure that we can do some sort of damage control on all this.'

*Please fuck off.*

'I'm not worried Kerry.' Ruth shrugged. 'This is nothing that I haven't handled before.'

'Good for you.' Kerry moved closer and lowered her voice to a virtual whisper. 'The trick is not to show them that they've got to you, Ruth. It's your press conference and you're in control.'

Ruth wanted to punch her in the face, but instead gave her a forced smile. 'Thanks, Kerry. I'll bear that in mind.'

Spinning on her heels, she walked out of the conference room.

## Chapter 20

It was nearly 8pm by the time Garrow arrived at the University Hospital in Llancastell. Even though he had technically finished his shift, he had some of the personal effects from Lucy's home. He hoped they might jog her memory as to what had happened to her. He also had the information about her mother – where she worked, lived etc …

As he walked along the hospital corridor, Garrow couldn't help feel a little jolt of excitement at seeing Lucy again – which he knew was completely inappropriate and unprofessional. Having seen the art and theatre posters on her walls, her eclectic book collection and her degree photo, he knew that they had a lot in common. At least they had before Lucy developed amnesia. She was smart, cultured, attractive and close to Garrow's age.

Resolving to put that out of his mind, Garrow entered the ward and saw Dr Gupta coming the other way. She looked up and gave him a half smile of recognition.

'Hi,' Garrow said.

'Any developments about what happened to Lucy?' Dr

Gupta asked.

'I'm afraid not.' Garrow then gestured to the bag of photos he'd taken from Lucy's home. 'We went to her house today. I've brought these with me in the hope that it might help jog her memory.'

Dr Gupta nodded but looked a little concerned. 'It might help but please tread carefully. Her emotions will be all over the place at the moment.'

'Of course,' Garrow said with a considerate nod. 'Any more test results?'

'As I said before, nothing on the CAT scan or MRI,' Dr Gupta explained. 'As far as we can see there is no lasting physical damage. But obviously the psychological trauma needs to be managed.'

'Will she be discharged then?' Garrow asked, wondering quite how Lucy would cope going to a home that she might not even recognise.

Dr Gupta nodded. 'We'll observe her tonight and tomorrow and take it from there.'

'We're trying to track down her mother,' Garrow explained. 'I'll try again and let her know that Lucy needs her help.'

'That would be very helpful. Thank you,' Dr Gupta said with a kind smile, and then continued down the corridor.

Garrow went over to the door to Lucy's room. It was open by about a foot. He knocked on it and looked in.

Lucy, who was propped up on pillows and watching the television, looked over and gave him an uncertain half smile of recognition.

'Hi Lucy,' Garrow said quietly. 'Is it okay if I come in?'

'Yes, of course,' Lucy replied as she adjusted herself in the bed. Then she gave him a quizzical look. 'Sorry, I don't even know your name.'

'Jim,' Garrow said as he went over and sat down next to the bed. 'How are you feeling?'

She thought for a few seconds. 'I'm not really sure. Confused,' she confessed with a slightly befuddled laugh.

'Of course,' Garrow said, and then pulled a face. 'I should have brought you something. Grapes.'

'Oh, I don't like grapes,' Lucy admitted. 'But thank you.' Then she frowned. 'How is it that I know I don't like grapes but I can't remember my name?'

'I guess the memory is an incredibly complex organ,' Garrow suggested.

'With over 100 billion nerve cells, I guess it is,' Lucy added, and then gave a little laugh. 'And I didn't know I knew that either.'

Garrow gave her a wry smile. *She really is cute.* He then looked at her. Her eyes were clear, blue and entrancing. 'I went to your home today,' he explained very gently.

'Ooh, is it nice?' she asked in a jokey voice.

'Yes, it is.'

But then her condition seemed to dawn on her and her expression changed.

Garrow leaned forward on his seat. 'I've brought some things from your house. Some photos. I thought they might help. But if you don't feel up to looking at them, that's fine. We've also tried to contact your mother, Lynne.'

'Lynne?' she whispered, as though saying the name might remind her. 'Lynne,' she said taking a deep breath. 'No,' she whispered as she shook her head sadly. It didn't register with her. Then she blinked as though she was on the verge of tears.

'I do have a photograph of you and your mum together,' Garrow said quietly. 'Would you like to see it?' he asked hesitantly.

Lucy nodded but looked unsettled. 'I think so.'

Delving into the bag, Garrow pulled out the photograph of Lucy and Lynne sitting together at a table in a pub. It looked like it was a selfie taken by Lucy fairly recently.

'Here you go,' he said.

She took the photo but her hands were a little shaky. Peering at it, she searched the image with her eyes. Then she shook her head sadly. A tear rolled down her face and she wiped it away. 'I can't remember her,' she whispered.

'I'm sorry,' Garrow said. 'Maybe this wasn't such a good idea.'

'No. I need to remember, so I have to do this,' Lucy said as she sniffed. She looked at him and then gestured to the bag. 'Please. Can I look at another one?'

'Of course,' he replied. 'This is one of you with your mum. And we think this is your brother, Steve.'

'Steve?' she asked with a frown.

'Apparently, he lives with your mum but he was in the army,' Garrow explained.

Lucy looked at the photo. 'Steve?' she whispered. Then her hand shook visibly and her eyes widened.

'What is it?' Garrow asked. He was concerned that something about the photograph had disturbed her.

Lucy continued to shake as her eyes roamed frantically around the room. 'I do recognise him. And there was a terrible fight.' Then she looked directly at Garrow with a distressed expression. 'Someone had a knife.'

'Do you know who?' Garrow asked.

With tears welling in her eyes, Lucy shook her head. 'No. I'm sorry.'

Garrow couldn't help but reach out and put a comforting hand on her arm. She looked so upset.

## Chapter 21

Georgie glanced out of the hotel window down into the car park. Ben had clearly calculated that it wouldn't be long before the whole of North Wales Police were looking for them. Luckily, he hadn't discovered that she had used Arlo's phone to text 999.

Having been to the hotel shop, Ben had bought a variety of things that would change their appearance slightly. He had now disappeared into the bathroom and Georgie could see that Ben was attempting to dye his distinctive blond hair a dark brown or black. She couldn't tell. He had also bought a couple of baseball caps, sunglasses, some low strength reading glasses, plus a whole new outfit for Arlo so that he could change out of his school uniform.

Georgie felt frustrated that Ben seemed to have thought of everything. She didn't know why she was surprised. He was an experienced police officer who would know exactly how a manhunt of this kind would be conducted. And that gave him a huge advantage. Looking over at Arlo, she saw that he was on the bed watching the television with the sound turned down while playing on his phone at the same time.

What were Ben's plans? Why were they going to Abergele? What did he intend to do with Arlo, or hadn't he thought that through? And what did he have in mind for her in the long run? She didn't want to think about that too much.

Coming out of the bathroom, Ben now had wet, dark black hair that was swept back with gel. He wore a thick pair of reading glasses, a baggy, dark green plaid shirt and beige slacks.

*Jesus, he looks completely unrecognisable*, she thought. In fact, his transformation was chilling.

He glanced at her and then looked over at Arlo. 'What do you think, mate?'

Ben had told Arlo that wearing disguises and changing their appearance was just part of another game.

Arlo sat up and grinned. 'Wow! You look completely different.'

'That's the idea,' Ben said as he went over to one of the shopping bags and pulled out a navy baseball cap with the word *Vox* written on it in big white letters. 'Here you go. Put this on,' he said as he tossed it over to Georgie.

'Not really me, is it?' she said sarcastically.

'Yeah, just put it on,' Ben said as he glared at her.

'Dad! Dad!' Arlo shouted as he pointed up at the flatscreen television mounted on the wall. 'There's a photo of you on the TV.'

As Georgie looked up, she saw that the local BBC news was on the screen. There was a photo of Ben, followed by a photo of her and then Arlo.

'That's me!' Arlo yelled in excitement.

As Ben scrambled around to find the remote control, Georgie saw Ruth giving a press conference.

'Why is there a photo of us on there?' Arlo asked, now completely confused.

'Don't worry about that, mate,' Ben said, trying to reassure him as he turned the television off and looked over at Georgie.

'Maybe we've won a competition,' Georgie suggested with more than a hint of irony.

'Have we, Dad?' Arlo asked gleefully.

Ben shot Georgie an angry look. 'No, we haven't.' Ben then looked at his watch. 'Right, it's bedtime for all of us now. I'll sleep in this bed with you, mate. And Georgie is on that sofa.'

Arlo frowned. 'Won't she be uncomfortable?'

Georgie smiled over at him. 'I'll be fine, Arlo. Don't worry.'

'You see?' Ben said as he went over to the lights and began to turn them all off. 'Let's get some sleep, eh mate?'

## Chapter 22

It was midnight by the time Ruth arrived home. She was exhausted. The search for Georgie and Arlo had proved frustrating. So far, they hadn't been able to trace the location of Ben's car and, despite the press conference, there hadn't been any confirmed sightings of them yet.

Taking off her shoes, Ruth felt the ease of letting her feet sink into the carpet.

*God that feels better.*

Ruth's partner, Sarah, came out of the living room and looked concerned.

'I thought I told you not to wait up for me,' Ruth said, but secretly she was glad she had.

'Any news?' Sarah asked as she gave Ruth a hug.

'Nothing,' Ruth replied. 'They pulled the car over this afternoon, and now it seems to have vanished.'

'How long have you got?' Sarah asked. She knew that as Head of Llancastell CID, Ruth wouldn't be home for that long.

'Shower, change of clothes and then I'll try and get

three or four hours' sleep before heading back in,' Ruth explained.

'Come and sit down,' Sarah said, taking her hand. 'Have you eaten anything?'

'I grabbed a sandwich.'

'Glass of wine?' Sarah suggested.

'Although that would be perfect,' Ruth admitted, '… it'll just make me even more tired tomorrow.'

As they made their way down towards the living room, Ruth heard the sound of footsteps.

She turned to see Daniel, dressed in pyjamas, padding along the hallway behind them.

'Hey, what are you doing up, buster?' Ruth asked with a smile.

Ruth and Sarah had a temporary foster licence to look after Daniel after his father was killed. He had been living with them for quite a while now.

'I wanted to see you,' Daniel explained as he yawned.

Ruth crouched down and gave him a big hug. 'It's good to see you.'

'Why are you so late?' he asked with a frown.

She put her hand reassuringly on his shoulders. 'Just work stuff.'

'Catching bad guys?' he asked.

'Something like that,' Ruth replied with a smile.

'Can I have some milk?'

'Of course you can,' Ruth said. 'Come on.'

'Daniel ate pink fish for the first time tonight,' Sarah said proudly as they all made their way to the kitchen.

'Did you?' Ruth asked, as she went in and pulled open the fridge.

Daniel shook his head. 'It's called salmon, Sarah. I'm not a baby.'

Ruth laughed and raised an eyebrow as she looked at Sarah. 'He's not a baby, Sarah.'

'And then I saw you on the news,' Daniel said.

'Did you?' Ruth asked. She tried to make sure that she never discussed her work with him.

'We were watching the football,' Sarah explained, pulling an apologetic face. 'But Daniel turned it over when I was putting the bins out.'

'Oh dear,' Ruth said.

'Are you looking for a boy who's a bit younger than me?' Daniel asked.

'That's right. His name is Arlo.'

'Have you found him yet?'

'No, not yet,' Ruth replied. 'But I'm sure he's going to be okay, so you don't need to worry.'

Daniel nodded thoughtfully.

Ruth poured him a glass of milk and handed it to him. 'Probably time to go back to sleep.'

At that moment, Ruth's phone buzzed. It was Llancastell Police Station.

'I'd better take this,' Ruth said to Sarah.

'I'll take him up,' Sarah said as she manoeuvred Daniel out of the kitchen. 'Come on, buster.'

'Why do you call me buster?' Daniel asked.

'Because it's better than twerp, isn't it?' joked Sarah.

'What's a twerp?' Daniel asked as they disappeared down the hallway.

'DI Hunter?' Ruth said, answering her phone. It was late so she assumed it was important.

'Evening ma'am,' said a male voice. 'Uniformed patrol has found the target vehicle you've been looking for belonging to DI Ben Stewart.'

'Any sign of our suspect or DC Wild or the boy?' Ruth asked, knowing already that it would have been mentioned.

'I'm afraid not, ma'am,' the officer replied. 'The car had been abandoned in a field close to a village called Llansannan.'

'How far is that from Abergele?' she asked.

'Seven or eight miles,' he replied.

'Okay, thank you for letting me know,' Ruth said. 'Goodnight, constable.'

'Night, ma'am.'

Ruth ended the call.

It sounded as if Ben had dumped the car almost immediately after they had been chased.

Slumping down on the sofa, Ruth gave an audible sigh of frustration. Even though she knew Georgie was tough and resourceful, Ruth felt overwhelmed for a moment by the fact she had been abducted. And she didn't even know why.

## Chapter 23

'Read me another chapter,' Megan demanded.

Nick had been lying on her bed for about half an hour and they had already read three chapters of '*Olive and the Unicorn.*'

'I would love to,' Nick said with a smile as he moved a strand of hair from her beautiful face. Luckily she took after Amanda with her hair and big chestnut eyes. 'But I'm scared that Mummy will tell me off for not spending time with her too.'

Megan frowned and looked at him. 'You're scared of Mummy?'

'Yeah,' Nick laughed. 'Very scared. Aren't you?'

'No,' Megan giggled indignantly. 'Mummy's not scary.'

Nick smiled and raised his eyebrow. 'Erm, I think you'll find that Mummy can be terrifying.'

'Now you're just being silly,' Megan said, shaking her head. 'Daddy?'

Nick sat up on the bed as he prepared to give her a kiss goodnight and head downstairs. 'Yes, poppet?'

'You know when you went away a few weeks ago on work?' she asked.

She was referring to when Nick was being held on remand at HMP Rhoswen before he escaped and went on the run.

'Yes, when I was away on work,' Nick said quietly, wondering quite where Megan was going with this.

'Did you stay in a hotel?' she asked.

For a second, Nick thought about the smelly cell he'd shared on the Vulnerable Prisoners Wing. 'Yes, I stayed in a hotel.'

'Was it a nice hotel?' she asked.

'It was all right,' Nick replied. 'But I definitely prefer being at home with you and Mummy.'

'Good,' Megan said as she turned and put her head on her pink pillow. 'I don't want you to go away on work again.'

'Don't worry. I won't,' Nick said. 'I promise.' He leaned over and kissed her on the forehead. 'Night, angel.'

'Night, night,' Megan said as he pulled the duvet up around her shoulders.

Filled with the overwhelming joy of being home, Nick padded down the landing and downstairs.

As he came into the living room, Amanda was wearing her glasses and reading a book curled up in the armchair. She had only just started to wear reading glasses and was a little self-conscious about them.

'Those glasses really suit you,' Nick said with a wry smile. 'You remind me of that woman from the 60s.'

Amanda pushed the glasses down the bridge of her nose and tried to look sexy. 'Sophia Loren?'

'No. You know, what's her name,' Nick said. 'Myra Hindley.'

Amanda scowled and gave him the finger. 'Make a sentence out of 'off' and 'fuck.'

'But seriously,' Nick continued, 'I think they're sexy.'

'Do you?'

'Yeah, in a Rose West kind of way,' he laughed.

Getting up from the armchair, Amanda stormed towards him and gave him a playful punch in the chest. 'You're such a twat! You know I'm self-conscious wearing glasses.'

'Sorry,' Nick said as he pulled a face.

'Nobhead,' she said as she then put her arms around his waist.

'Your nobhead though,' he pointed out.

'Unfortunately, yes,' she said, rolling her eyes. 'Actually, I have a confession to make.'

Nick wondered if it had anything to do with the text from this morning. Up until that point, he'd forgotten all about it.

'That sounds ominous,' he said with a knowing look.

'I forgot that I'd agreed months ago to do the main share at an AA meeting up in Mold,' Amanda explained. 'Anyway, they asked if I was still okay to do it and I lied and said I wasn't well.'

'I think that's fine given the last few weeks,' Nick said and then frowned. 'Oh, so that was what the text was about this morning.'

Amanda narrowed her eyes. 'How do you know I got a text about that this morning?'

'You left your phone on the sofa,' Nick said. 'It buzzed, so I looked at it.'

'You checking my phone, Detective Sergeant Evans?' Amanda asked with a wry smile.

'Guilty as charged,' Nick laughed.

'Don't you trust me then?' Amanda teased him.

'Of course I do,' Nick said, pulling her closer to him. 'We've been through so much. I love you and Megan more than anything in the world.'

He leaned in, kissed her passionately and pulled her in close.

Amanda responded for a few seconds.

'Hey, easy Tiger,' she said, putting her hand to his face. 'There's pasta boiling over in the kitchen.'

'Is that a metaphor?' he asked with a knowing grin.

'No.'

'Oh,' Nick laughed again. 'And they say romance is dead, eh?'

## Chapter 24

It was dawn and the first chinks of light had started to come through the hotel window. Georgie shifted uncomfortably on the sofa, moved the blanket, and lay on her back. She could hear that both Ben and Arlo were sleeping in the bed on the other side of the room.

The problem now was that Georgie couldn't make her escape without taking Arlo with her. She was a police officer and she wasn't about to leave a 9-year-old boy in the hands of a murderer – even if he was his father too. Ben was clearly mentally unstable and dangerous, so she needed to make sure Arlo was safe.

Was there a way of alerting police to their presence in the hotel? She glanced over to the phone beside the bed. There was no way of using it without waking Ben.

There was the sound of voices chattering quietly outside and the clink of a trolley. If Georgie was going to guess, there were members of staff outside in the corridor. Then she looked over to the door. What if she could slip out of the door for a moment and speak to a member of staff before creeping back inside?

Her pulse started to race as she sat up on the sofa and moved the blanket, making sure that she didn't make a noise. Standing up slowly, she heard her knee click.

*Shit!*

In the tense silence of the room, it sounded like a gunshot.

Peering over at the bed, she checked that Ben hadn't stirred.

Taking slow, small steps, she crept cautiously towards the door. Her heart was pounding against her chest.

What if opening the door woke Ben? He might attack her. However, she had noticed that Ben had gone to great lengths so far to protect Arlo from what was going on.

She took another step. The carpet was thankfully thick and her socked feet seemed to make virtually no noise as she went.

Holding her breath, she reached the door.

*Here we go, take it nice and steady,* she reassured herself.

Stretching out her hand, she took the metallic door handle in her fingers.

Then she moved it about an inch.

'Going somewhere?' asked a voice.

She flinched.

*Jesus!*

Ben was glaring over at her.

'I'm going to the bathroom,' Georgie said, feigning indignance at his question. 'If that's okay with you?'

'Bathroom door is over there,' Ben said, pointing. He looked incredibly suspicious. His dyed hair made him look more intimidating.

'Right,' Georgie said with a nod as she moved away, went to the bathroom door and closed it behind her.

Blowing out her cheeks, she could feel her hands

shaking as she turned on the tap and splashed her face with cold water.

She looked at her reflection in the mirror. *How is this all going to end?* she asked herself.

Opening the bathroom door, she saw that Ben had now pulled the curtains and Arlo was getting himself together.

'Come on, we're going,' Ben said gruffly.

'Going where?' Georgie asked.

She saw Arlo looking over at them. He had clearly picked up on the friction and tension in the room.

'Oh, we're going to the seaside this morning, aren't we?' Georgie said in a sing song voice in an attempt to allay Arlo's anxiety.

'That's right,' Ben said, grabbing a plastic bag that contained Arlo's uniform, food wrappers, price tags and the box of hair dye. Georgie knew that he wasn't stupid enough to leave anything in the room that might indicate they had changed their appearance in any way. The police and public were looking for a blond man with a woman and a boy in school uniform.

Ben went to the door and ushered them into the hotel corridor.

Georgie gave Arlo a reassuring smile. 'Did you sleep all right, Arlo?'

He nodded as they walked along the corridor. 'I've never stayed in a hotel before.'

'Haven't you?' Georgie said.

Pointing to the fire escape staircase, Ben opened the door. 'Let's go down this way.'

Georgie assumed that Ben was trying to avoid CCTV as much as he could, especially any cameras that had been placed in the hotel lift.

Arriving on the ground floor, they came out through a

door and saw the hotel lobby up ahead. It was still early and so the hotel was deserted.

Marching over to the wall, Ben headed for a fire alarm. He elbowed it sharply so that the glass broke.

A piercing electronic noise shattered the silence.

A few members of staff scuttled from behind the reception, talking in loud voices and then disappeared.

Georgie moved protectively towards Arlo – she had no idea what Ben was doing.

Ben darted towards the reception desk and checked that no one was around. With a swift movement, he pushed himself over the counter and disappeared through a door into an office.

Hotel guests, still bleary eyed, confused, dressed in robes, pyjamas or trackies, started to appear in the lobby trying to find out if there was a fire or if the alarm had been set off accidentally.

'What's he doing?' Arlo asked, looking over at Ben who had reappeared again. He hopped back over the counter.

'I'm not sure,' Georgie admitted.

'Come on,' Ben said with a sense of urgency as he gestured them towards the main entrance.

'What were you doing, Dad?' Arlo asked as Ben ushered them through the automatic glass doors.

'A friend of mine said we could borrow his car, mate,' Ben said as they started to walk through the car park.

Ben held up a set of car keys that he had clearly taken from the hotel office.

There a was a bleep, and the indicators of a black BMW X4 flashed on and off further up.

'Here we go,' Ben said brightly as he looked over at Georgie with a supercilious grin. 'Decent car, eh?'

'Yeah, your friend's got good taste,' Georgie replied sarcastically.

Ben opened the back door and helped Arlo to get in. 'Here we go, mate.'

Georgie got into the passenger seat as Ben got in the other side and took a quick glance at the dashboard.

'Automatic, shame,' Ben muttered to himself as he pushed the ignition button and then reached for the seat-belt. 'Right everyone, we're back on track. Abergele, here we come.'

They pulled away and sped out of the car park.

## Chapter 25

I t was 8am and French and Garrow were outside Lynne
Morgan's home again on the Mold Road. The traffic
was heavy and the air was thick with exhaust fumes.

French gave an authoritative knock on the door and
took a step back.

As Lucy's next of kin, it was important that they made
contact with her mother Lynne as soon as possible. If Lucy
was going to be released from hospital, then she was going
to need support from her family until, hopefully, her
memory gradually returned.

Glancing over at the enormous Mold Road Stand of
the Racecourse Football Ground, Garrow saw a van was
parked up on the pavement with a large, red ride-on
mower. He presumed it was to cut the grass of the pitch
inside.

'They're going for promotion this year,' French said,
gesturing to the stadium.

'Are they?' Garrow said. He had no real interest in
sport whatsoever.

'Been out of the Football League for nearly fourteen

years now, so I hope they do go up,' French said. 'It would be great for this city.'

Garrow frowned. 'I thought Wrexham was a town?'

French shrugged. 'It is. But it should be a city. St Asaph is a bloody city, for God's sake.' French then nodded towards the ground. 'My dad took me to the greatest night in Wrexham's history. They beat the mighty Arsenal in the cup in January 1992. Everyone remembers the Mickey Thomas free kick, but it was Steve Watkin who scored the actual winner. Christ, I was only six.'

Garrow nodded. 'I'm pretty sure my taid told me about it.'

French took a step forward and knocked on the front door again but it looked like no one was in.

Garrow looked at his watch. 'Seems a bit early for her to go to work at the Horse and Jockey?'

'Maybe she just popped out to the shops,' French suggested.

Tracey, the woman who lived next door, came out of her front door. She was dressed in a smart navy trouser suit and had a laptop bag slung over her shoulder.

'Still no answer?' she asked as she came down the path.

'No,' Garrow replied. 'And you haven't seen her or her son?'

Tracey shook her head and looked confused. 'No. I've been worrying about her ever since me and Gav spoke to you yesterday. I hope nothing bad's happened to her, you know.'

Garrow nodded. 'We'll let you know.'

Tracey gestured to the pavement. 'Anyway, I'd better get to work.'

French opened the letterbox and looked inside.

'I can't see anything,' he said.

To the right hand side of the front door was a gate

made from dark wood and black steel. Garrow went to it and guessed that it was at least eight foot high. Giving the handle a pull, he could feel that it was locked.

Then he looked over at French. 'I'm going to hop over this sarge and have a look around the back.'

French nodded. 'Okay. I'll wait here in case someone answers the door. Besides, I'm older than you so I don't fancy hopping over that this morning.'

'Right you are,' Garrow said with a wry smile as he went over and gripped the cold steel of the gate.

Putting his foot up, he pulled himself up onto the main frame of the gate.

'Oi, what he's doing?' shouted a man loudly as he sat in a white transit van in the traffic outside.

French took out his warrant card and held it up.

'Oh right you are,' the man said with a cocky grin. 'Fucking coppers.'

Garrow threw his leg over the top of the gate and then looked down.

*Bloody hell, that looks a long way down from here,* he thought to himself as he gripped the top of the gate, turned himself around, and then lowered himself to the path below.

Moving along the side of the house, he cupped his hands at a ground floor window and looked inside. A vase of dried flowers and some framed photographs were obscuring most of his view, but he could see an empty sofa with a floral pattern.

He walked down the rest of the side passageway and into a small, well-tended garden. Flowerbeds were neat and there was a table, chairs, and a rattan sofa on a patio.

*Nothing particularly suspicious so far,* he concluded.

On the far side of the patio, there was a large ground

floor window and door which he assumed led into the kitchen.

Trying the handle of the door, he could feel that it was also locked.

He went to the window and peered in.

The first thing he saw was a dark red smear across the white fridge door.

*Shit! Looks like blood.*

Cupping his hands to block out the sunlight, he squinted.

As his eyes roamed the kitchen, he spotted something that made his heart sink.

There was a body slumped on the floor on the other side of the kitchen table.

'Jesus!' he gasped under his breath.

Sprinting back to the gate, he saw French at the other end of the path.

'Sarge!' he shouted loudly. 'There's someone lying in the kitchen. I'm going to break in.'

French nodded with a sombre face. 'I'll call for the paramedics.'

Charging back into the garden, Garrow grabbed one of the garden chairs and hurled it through the glass of the back door.

The glass exploded with a crash.

He leant inside and reached down to the handle – there was no key.

His heart was hammering inside his chest.

Stepping back, he took a run up and then hit the door-frame with everything he had.

The door flew open, hitting an interior wall in the kitchen. The remaining glass fell out and broke noisily on the floor.

Taking a few steps forward, Garrow sped across the kitchen and round the table.

His stomach tightened as he saw Lynne Morgan's blue-grey face looking up at him from the floor.

Her eyes were still wide open.

*Bloody hell.*

Trying to keep it together, Garrow reached for his forensic gloves and snapped them on.

It was clear that Lynne had been dead for some time.

Crouching down, he saw a deep gash in her throat.

Her clothes, hands, and the floor were covered in dark blood, most of which had now congealed into black stickiness.

He clicked his radio. 'Control from eight zero, over.'

After a few seconds, his radio crackled. 'Eight zero, this is Control, go ahead, over.'

'I have a possible homicide at 23 Mold Road, Wrexham,' he explained. 'Request scene of crime and CID officers here asap, over.'

'Received eight zero, stand by.'

Standing up, he went carefully down the hallway towards the front door. This was now a crime scene so forensics were going to be vital.

Opening the front door, he looked at French.

'Who is it?' French asked.

'Lynne Morgan,' Garrow replied. 'She's been dead for a while.'

'Any idea how she died?'

Garrow gave him a dark look. 'Someone slit her throat by the looks of it.'

French looked shocked. 'Jesus.'

As French put his gloves on, he followed Garrow down the hallway and back into the kitchen.

For a few seconds, they both looked at the grisly scene.

Then French turned to look at him. 'I guess this explains where the blood on Lucy Morgan's hands and clothing came from.'

Garrow nodded but his instinct was that Lucy couldn't have done this to her own mother. Could she?

## Chapter 26

'Right everyone, listen up,' Ruth said as she strode into the middle of Incident Room 1 at Llancastell nick. 'We've had to move everything over here as we have two major incidents to investigate at the same time. Between the confines of these four walls I'm going to say that getting Georgie and Arlo Stewart back safely is our number one priority. So, I'm going to let Dan and Jim take the lead on our investigation into Lucy Morgan until further notice.' Ruth went over to a scene board which had been prepared overnight for Georgie's abduction. 'Right, what have we got on Ben Stewart? Nick?'

Nick grabbed a file, got up and headed to the centre of the room. Ruth felt pleased to have Nick back as her deputy SIO.

'Okay, so this is Detective Inspector Ben Stewart,' Nick said, looking out at the CID team and then pointing to a photo of Ben on the scene board.

'Any idea why Ben has chosen to go to this area?' Ruth enquired.

'I spoke to Ben's ex-wife, Arlo's mother,' Nick

explained. 'She has no idea why Ben has headed towards Abergele. As far as she knows, he has no friends, family or connection to the area.'

Ruth frowned. 'Have we found out anything else about his background that might help us?'

'I've got his personnel file sent over from the Modern Slavery and Human Trafficking Unit in Manchester,' Nick replied. 'Apparently there have been several concerns raised about Ben's mental health since his divorce. He's been in counselling for over a year.'

Ruth gave a frustrated sigh. 'But he was still allowed on active duty until he snapped and now we're picking up the pieces?'

'Looks that way,' Nick said.

'Family?' Ruth asked.

Looking down at the file, Nick pointed to a document inside. 'I've got here that both parents died when he was still young. He was then taken into care. I'm waiting to see if social services have anything on their records. However, there are some handwritten notes down here. Ben appeared in Mold Crown Court in 1998 to give evidence in the trial of a man called Marvin Peters. I've run Peters through the PNC. He was the house manager of a children's home in North Wales. He served five years of a ten-year sentence for systematic sexual abuse. He's on the sex offenders register.'

A uniformed police officer came into IR1 and headed towards Nick.

'You think he abused Ben?' Ruth asked, thinking out loud.

'Possibly. If Ben was asked to give evidence, then I think it's likely,' Nick said.

'And where is Marvin Peters now?' Ruth asked.

The uniformed officer looked at Nick. 'I've got that address from the database you requested, sarge.'

'Thank you, constable,' Nick said, taking the printout as the constable turned and left.

Ruth raised an eyebrow. 'What's that?'

'Marvin Peters is now living in a nursing home,' Nick stated.

'Where?'

Nick gave her a dark look. 'Abergele.'

# Chapter 27

The area outside Lynne Morgan's home was now a hive of activity. The road had been cordoned off with blue and white evidence tape and was being managed by several uniformed police officers dressed in luminous green jackets. Two marked patrol cars were also parked across either end of the Mold Road with a big blue sign that read *Road closed due to police incident.*

A group of neighbours stood in a huddle behind the cordon discussing what might have happened. A couple of journalists and photographers had also arrived on the scene to see if there was a major story developing.

Garrow and French were beside the SOCO van as they changed into the white forensic suits, rubber boots, masks and hats they had been handed.

Garrow was thinking of Lucy laying in her hospital bed, completely unaware that her mother had been brutally murdered. Was she responsible for her mother's death? It was highly likely that her hands and clothes had been covered in her blood. Or had she arrived at her mother's home as planned, only to find her mother being attacked? Maybe the killer had hit Lucy on the back of her head, causing her to black out and lose her memory.

'Penny for them,' French said, looking over and clearly seeing Garrow deep in thought.

'I'm just trying to match the woman I've been talking to in hospital with the carnage in there,' Garrow admitted.

'We have to stick to the evidence at the moment,' French told him. 'We know Lucy was present at the time, or just after her mother's death. That's all we know.'

'We need to find Steve Morgan asap too,' Garrow stated.

French frowned. 'If he was living here, where the hell is he now?'

'Seems suspicious that he's disappeared,' Garrow said, thinking out loud.

'Come on.' French gestured that they needed to go inside to see what the SOCOs had found so far.

There were now aluminium stepping plates placed along the hallway down to the kitchen. It prevented officers damaging any forensic evidence that might have been left on the carpet.

As they went into the kitchen, Garrow saw that a SOCO was leaning close to take photos of Lynne Morgan's body. Another SOCO was holding a small ruler to give the photographs something for measurement and scale.

'Detective Sergeant French?' a voice said.

A figure nearby had pulled down their mask. It was Professor Tony Amis, the Chief Pathologist for this part of North Wales.

'Hi Tony,' French said. 'What can you tell us?'

As Amis stepped forward, the two SOCOs crouched over the body moved away.

'Your victim had her throat cut,' Amis said as he

crouched down and pointed. 'We have a vertical distribution of blood on her clothes so she was standing up when she was attacked and for several seconds afterwards. The right end of the injury starts below the ear at the upper third of her neck and deepens gradually with the severance of the right carotid artery. The left sided end of the injury was at the mid third of the neck with a tail abrasion.' Amis then looked up at them. 'You know what that means?'

'No idea,' French admitted.

'Your killer slashed the victim from right to left,' Amis said with a knowing expression.

'They were left handed?' Garrow asked.

'Very good, Detective Constable Garrow,' Amis said with a smile as he looked at French. 'He's good. You should keep him.'

Garrow gave French a wry smile, most of which was hidden by his mask.

'I know that all sounds a bit Miss Marple or Columbo,' Amis chortled, 'but it's incredibly difficult for a right-handed person to inflict a wound like that. It would be completely unnatural.'

'But it would be possible?' Garrow asked.

'Of course,' Amis admitted, 'but in the high emotion of a murder, most people are under a huge amount of stress and so they revert to whatever comes naturally. I can tell you more when I've carried out my preliminary post-mortem.'

'Anything else that might help us, Tony?'

Amis leant over, took Lynne's hand and turned it to show them. 'There is a substantial amount of skin and some blood under her nails, especially on this hand. She definitely put up quite a struggle.' Amis then looked up at them. 'And your killer would have significant scratch marks somewhere on their face or body.'

## Chapter 28

Ben, Georgie and Arlo turned into a quiet residential street on the outskirts of Abergele. Ben slowed the car and then turned into a parking space outside a huge three-storey Georgian house. A large white sign read – *Abbeygate House – Residential and Nursing Care and Support.*

'Right, here we go,' Ben said, as though this was a planned stop they all knew about.

'Why are we stopping here?' Arlo asked, looking out.

'I've just got to pop in and say hello to an old friend,' Ben explained cheerily.

Georgie looked over at him. Was this connected to Ben's earlier comment that he had a score to settle with *an old friend*?

'You sure you don't want me and Arlo to wait in the car for you?' Georgie suggested, fearing that whatever Ben had planned, it would be better for Arlo not to be around.

'No, no,' Ben said, opening the driver's door. She could see that the Glock 17 handgun was now in his trouser waistband, under his jacket. 'I want Arlo to meet him,' Ben said.

'Okay,' Arlo said, as he got out and then looked at Georgie. 'I don't mind.'

Georgie gave him a reassuring smile.

The street was still and quiet except for the distant unsettling cries of gulls. Above them, the sky grew darker by the second, and a large grey mass began to sweep across the sun like a thick blanket.

They followed Ben up the steps and into a neat reception area. A young woman, with cropped hair that had been dyed dark red, sat behind a desk peering at a computer screen.

'Hi there,' Ben said with a friendly smile. 'We've come to see Marvin Peters.'

'Oh right,' the woman said as she nodded and peered at the screen. 'Can I take a name?'

Georgie watched him intently, wondering quite why they were there and what Ben was planning to do. It was making her feel very uneasy, especially as Arlo was standing there oblivious that anything sinister was about to take place.

'Ben Stewart,' he replied casually.

The woman frowned. 'Sorry. I don't have you down here as one of Mr Peters' registered visitors.'

'Really?' Ben said, looking confused. 'He's my great uncle. I've brought my son to meet him for the first time.'

The woman pulled an apologetic face. 'Sorry. We can only let registered visitors see our residents. It's a security thing.'

'Oh well, maybe another time,' Georgie said, putting her hand on Arlo's shoulder to signal that they should go. Maybe this was a lucky escape for them all.

'We've come all the way from Llancastell,' Ben said, and then he pulled out his warrant card. 'If you're worried about security, I am a serving police officer.'

The woman glanced at the warrant card but at that distance didn't register that the photo didn't completely match Ben's current appearance.

'Let me go and have a word with the house manager,' the woman said, getting up and heading over towards a closed door. She opened it and stuck her head inside.

'Whatever you're planning,' Georgie said under her breath, 'I don't think Arlo needs to be involved. Let me take him back to the car.'

Ben ignored her as the woman returned.

'Okay, we will allow you to see Mr Peters this time,' she said with a smile, 'but if you want to visit him again, you will need him to add you to his visitors list.'

'Thanks, that's great,' Ben said brightly. 'I'll make sure I remind him.'

The woman pointed. 'He's in room 17. I can take you down there if you want?'

Ben shook his head. 'That's all right,' he reassured her. 'We'll find it.'

They turned, made their way through the double doors and into a long corridor.

'Is he really your great uncle?' Arlo asked.

'Well, I guess he was a bit like an uncle,' Ben said. 'He was in charge of looking after me when I was about your age.'

Arlo nodded but clearly didn't understand.

A few seconds later, they arrived at a white door that had a gold number 17 on it.

Ben knocked and opened it. 'Marvin?'

A man in his early 80s was sitting in a large armchair watching a nature documentary on the television. He gave them a quizzical smile.

'Hello, Marvin,' Ben said in a friendly tone. 'How are you? It's good to see you.'

Georgie's stomach tightened. She had no idea who Marvin Peters was, or what he'd done to Ben, but she could sense that something horrible was about to happen.

'Yes?' Marvin said, looking bemused.

'This is my son, Arlo,' Ben said, going over to where Marvin was sitting. 'Say hello to Marvin, Arlo.'

'Hello,' Arlo said, looking shy.

Marvin pushed himself up out of his armchair. 'I ... I don't understand,' he stammered, looking baffled. 'Who are you?'

Ben snorted and shook his head. 'Who am I?'

'Yes,' Marvin said with a furrowed brow.

Ben put his hand on Marvin's shoulder. 'Why don't you sit back down in your chair, Marvin, and I'll tell you all about it.'

'Erm, I ...'

Ben pushed Marvin back gently so he was forced to sit down. 'There you go.'

'Ben?' Georgie whispered. 'You don't need to do this.'

Arlo gave her a puzzled look – he didn't know what she meant.

'Arlo,' Ben said, pointing to Marvin. 'Marvin used to look after me when I was about your age. I was in a children's home. He took really good care of me, didn't you, Marvin?'

The blood had drained from Marvin's face as his eyes widened.

Georgie knew exactly what Ben was implying.

'I ... I think you should leave,' Marvin muttered, looking terrified.

Ben crouched down and moved so that his face was close to Marvin's. 'Do you remember me, Marvin? Ben Stewart. I had blond hair. Does that ring any bells?'

Marvin gave an almost imperceptible nod – he was now shaking.

Ben looked up at Georgie and Arlo. 'Say goodbye to Marvin, Arlo.'

'Bye,' Arlo said, giving a little wave.

Georgie looked at Ben. 'I can't let you do this.'

Ben stood up, opened his jacket to show her the gun. 'You and Arlo can join Marvin, if you like. Or you two can wait outside while I say my fond farewells to my old friend.'

'No,' Marvin said, trying to get up out of the chair. 'You can't do this …'

Feeling sick to her stomach, Georgie took Arlo by the hand and went to the door. 'Come on, Arlo. We'll wait outside for your dad.'

'Are we going to the beach soon?' Arlo asked as Georgie closed the door behind them.

'I'm sure we are,' she reassured him as they stood in the corridor. Her whole body tensed. She was a police officer and she had been forced to allow a cold blooded murder to take place.

The door opened and Ben came out with a smile. 'Right, who's up for getting some breakfast and going to the beach?' he asked brightly.

'I am!' Arlo cried.

Ben took him by the hand. 'Come on then, mate.'

## Chapter 29

Garrow and French walked along the hospital corridor. Garrow could feel the tension in his stomach. He knew they had to break it to Lucy that her mother had been murdered. Even though there was significant evidence that Lucy had been involved somehow in her mother's death, Garrow's instinct was that she wasn't the one who had slit Lynne Morgan's throat.

Entering the ward, the sister approached them. She had sharp features, bright blue eyes, and immediately gave off a no-nonsense attitude. She must have recognised them from their previous visits.

'Are you the police officers who have been talking to Lucy Morgan?' she asked, sounding a little like a teacher.

'That's right,' French replied.

Garrow frowned. 'Is everything all right?'

'Yes,' the sister said briskly. 'Actually, in the past few hours Lucy has started to get some fragments of her memory back. And once she's seen the hospital's trauma psychiatrist, she can be discharged and go home.'

'Right,' Garrow said, but he couldn't hide his solemn expression.

The sister gave them both a curious look. She had clearly picked up on the fact that they were about to deliver some distressing news.

'I'll leave you to it then,' the ward sister said and left.

Garrow and French walked along the corridor until they came to the door to Lucy's room.

'You mind if I go in there alone?' Garrow asked.

'Why?' French asked, looking a little surprised.

'I've built up a bit of a rapport with her, so it might be less harrowing if I go in on my own,' Garrow explained, even though he knew it wasn't strictly protocol.

French raised an eyebrow. 'She's a murder suspect, Jim. She's not the victim.'

'We don't know any of that yet, sarge,' Garrow pointed out.

'I think you're getting a bit too close to all this, don't you Jim?' French said, giving him a suspicious look.

Garrow shrugged but didn't reply. He knew that French was probably right and that he was being unprofessional.

'Go on,' French said, gesturing to the door. 'I'll give you ten minutes.'

'Thanks,' Garrow said quietly under his breath, and then opened the door and went in.

Stirring from her sleep, Lucy blinked open her eyes, looked at him and then gave a half smile.

'I don't remember your name,' she said in a croaky voice as she propped herself up in bed.

'Jim. Short for James,' he said as he came over and sat down on the chair.

'Jim,' Lucy said as her face brightened a little. 'I've had

a few memories come back today. It's very strange. Stuff from when I was a child. Even a couple of things from uni.'

'That's good,' Garrow said. 'Anything from the evening before we found you?'

Lucy blinked and shook her head. 'Sorry, no.'

Taking a breath, Garrow looked at her and sat forward on the seat. He was about to turn her life upside down with what he told her. 'Lucy, I'm afraid I've got some very bad news for you. And there's no easy way to tell you this … We went to your mother's house earlier today and found her dead. I'm so sorry.'

Lucy looked stunned as she shook her head. 'I don't understand,' she whispered. Her breathing was quick and shallow as if she couldn't catch her breath. 'What happened to her?'

'She was killed,' Garrow said very gently.

Then Lucy looked directly at him. 'The blood on my hands?'

Garrow nodded. 'I really am so sorry.'

'Oh my God.' Lucy looked completely overwhelmed. 'I was there when she was killed. Why can't I remember?' Then her eyes filled with tears. 'You don't think …'

Garrow swallowed nervously.

'You think I killed her?'

'No … We just don't know what happened yet,' Garrow said, trying to reassure her.

'I can't believe this is happening,' Lucy said with a sniff as she wiped tears from her face. Then she met his eyes. 'It's like I'm in some terrible nightmare and I'm going to wake up any minute.'

Garrow put out his hand and put it comfortingly on her arm as he looked at her.

'Look, I don't think you had anything to do with what happened to your mother,' he said gently. 'But you were there. So, I'm going to find out what happened. I promise you.'

## Chapter 30

As Ruth and Nick sped across North Wales towards Abergele, Ruth had her mobile phone clamped to her ear. She was trying to contact the Abbeygate Residential Home to tell them to be on the lookout for Ben. However, no one was picking up the phone.

'No answer again,' Ruth said frustratedly. 'Why don't these people pick up the bloody phone?'

Nick pointed to a sign that read – *ABERGELE - Tref Farchnad Hanesyddol* – *Historic Market Town.*

'We're going to be there in a minute,' Ruth said. 'Don't think I've been here before.'

The Abbeygate Residential Home loomed into view.

'Here we go,' Nick said as they pulled into a parking space outside.

Getting out of the car, Ruth felt the bluster of the fresh sea breeze about her face. She glanced around to see if there was any sign of Ben, Georgie or Arlo.

Nothing.

She prayed that they weren't too late.

They trotted up the stone steps and into the reception

area of the home itself. A young woman with short dyed red hair looked up and smiled. 'Hi there. How can I help?'

Ruth pulled out her warrant card. 'DI Hunter and DS Evans, Llancastell CID. I need to check on a resident that you have here. Marvin Peters?'

The young woman gave them a bemused frown. 'He's popular today.'

'How do you mean?' Ruth asked, but she was already one step ahead and fearing what the young woman was going to say.

'Marvin has already had some visitors today,' she explained. 'His nephew and his family.'

*Shit!*

Ruth shot an uneasy look at Nick.

'Are they still here?' Nick asked.

'No,' she replied innocently. 'They left about twenty minutes ago.'

'Can you remember his nephew's name?' Ruth asked.

'No, sorry.'

'Blond, mid 30s?' Nick asked.

The young woman shook her head. 'No. He had dark hair and glasses.'

Ruth frowned. That description didn't match Ben.

'Can you tell us what room Marvin is in?' Ruth asked with a sense of urgency.

'Yes, room 17,' she replied, looking confused. 'Is everything all right? His nephew was a police officer too.'

Ruth and Nick looked at each other and broke into a jog across reception, through the double doors, and down the corridor.

'This is not good,' Ruth muttered under her breath as they ran.

'I've got a horrible feeling we're too late.'

Getting to the door, Ruth opened it slowly and peered

inside. The television was on but there was no sign of Marvin.

'Mr Peters. We're police officers,' Ruth said as she and Nick went inside.

There was a body lying on the far side of the room between a large armchair and the wall.

*Jesus Christ!*

Rushing over, she saw an old man.

His face was drained of colour and his eyes were wide open.

There were contusions around his neck where he had been strangled.

'He's dead,' Ruth said with a dark expression.

## Chapter 31

Georgie, Ben and Arlo had driven west down the coast to Colwyn Bay. Georgie presumed that having murdered Marvin Peters, Ben was keen to get out of Abergele as quickly as possible. Colwyn Bay – or *Bae Colwyn* - was a large seaside resort on the North Wales coast overlooking the Irish Sea.

Georgie, Ben and Arlo were now wandering through the town centre in search of some food. Georgie had no idea what Ben's plan was now that he had murdered Marvin Peters. Maybe he didn't have one. However, she was pretty sure that Ben wasn't about to turn himself in.

Arlo stopped in front of a toy shop and peered in through the window.

'So, what's the plan now?' Georgie asked under her breath.

'I've got a few more people I'd like to visit on our trip,' Ben said casually.

'What are you talking about, Ben?' Georgie snapped angrily.

'My father for starters,' Ben said with a shrug. 'I think Arlo should meet his taid, don't you?'

Arlo continued to be distracted by the window display.

'But you told me your father murdered your mother?' Georgie said under her breath.

Ben looked at her. 'He did. That's why we're going to see him. He's in a care home up the coast in Llandudno.'

Georgie narrowed her eyes and hissed, 'You can't drag us around while you go on a killing spree of people from your past.'

'Why not?' Ben asked. 'The planet will be a better place without them.'

'Who made you God, Ben?' Georgie said in utter disbelief.

Ben ignored her.

Arlo turned and looked at them. 'Can we get some food now, Dad?'

Ben ruffled his hair with a smile. 'Of course we can, mate.'

Georgie watched Ben stroll away and realised that she'd been kidnapped by a psychopath.

# Chapter 32

The whole of the Llancastell CID team were now in an impromptu briefing in IR1. Ruth was keen to get everyone up to speed on both investigations, especially as two major crimes meant that manpower was being stretched.

'Okay, so we know that Ben has abducted Georgie and Arlo,' Ruth said, pointing to the scene board. 'We still have no idea why he abducted Georgie in the first place, although my suspicions are that it is connected to the slavery and human trafficking case that they were working on together. I can't see any other reason. Nick, what have you got?'

Nick got up. 'Right. We know that Ben suffered sexual abuse at the hands of Marvin Peters. He took both Georgie and Arlo to the care home in Abergele where Peters was living, and killed him. We have no idea if Georgie or Arlo witnessed the murder. We do know that Ben has completely changed his appearance. He now has dark hair and glasses. And Arlo is no longer wearing his school uniform. What we don't know is how they are travelling as he abandoned his stolen car.'

'Can we check the system for any reported car thefts in the Abergele area?' Ruth suggested.

'Yes, boss,' Nick replied. 'We have no idea where they are heading next or what Ben intends to do with Georgie or Arlo. But given the fact that he killed Marvin Peters, I would suggest that he is incredibly dangerous.'

'If he was abused by multiple men, maybe he's going after someone else?' Garrow suggested.

'Good point, Jim,' Nick agreed. 'I'll check the case and trial files from Mold in 1998. Otherwise, we're relying on them being spotted by a member of the public.'

As Nick went and sat down, French looked over at Ruth. 'I did a quick online check on the PNC, boss. The Mardon Country Hotel just outside Abergele reported a car theft from their car park early this morning.'

'Thanks Dan,' Ruth said. 'Have we got a registration?'

French nodded. 'Yankee, Foxtrot, one nine, Yankee Lima Oscar. It's a black BMW X4.'

'Right, let's get that circulated to traffic and ANPR,' Ruth said, feeling encouraged that this might be a significant lead. 'And let's see if we can trace the car's GPS as a matter of urgency please.'

## Chapter 33

Georgie walked through the BayView Shopping Centre with Ben and Arlo. It was the same as every other shopping centre that she had ever been to – Boots, Costa, Argos, Shoe Zone etc … Maybe it was the time of day or just the demographic of Colwyn Bay, but most people seemed to be elderly.

Georgie's mind was a whirring mess. However, she did know that she needed to get herself and Arlo to safety. She couldn't allow Ben to drag them around the coast of North Wales while he carried out a series of revenge killings. She also knew that being inside a busy shopping centre might provide her and Arlo's only chance of escape. Once they were back in the car and on the road, it was going to be a lot harder to get away, especially as Ben was armed.

Her eyes darted right and left, frantically searching for anything that might provide both a distraction and a chance to escape. She could feel the tension building. In a matter of minutes they would be outside again and heading towards the seafront where Ben had parked their stolen BMW.

Up ahead were the escalators that led up to the ground floor where the exit to the main road was situated.

Georgie looked at the long escalator for a moment.

Slowing her walk, she manoeuvred herself so that she and Arlo were walking directly behind Ben as they approached the bottom of the escalator leading up.

Georgie could feel her pulse quicken.

*Come on, Georgie, it has to be now.*

Glancing anxiously back, she saw that there were two young couples with very young children in pushchairs behind them.

Georgie put her hand on Arlo's shoulder. 'Let's let these people go first, shall we?' she suggested under her breath.

Ben stepped onto the escalator and looked back to check that Georgie and Arlo were following.

Georgie moved herself and Arlo out of the way in an innocent gesture to allow the couples to go on before them.

'Do you need a hand with any of that?' she asked with a polite smile.

Out of the corner of her eye, she could see that Ben was travelling up the escalator.

The young couples, children and pushchairs got onto the escalator.

Glancing up, Georgie's eyes met Ben's. For a moment, he didn't seem particularly concerned.

But then he realised that he was going up and Georgie and Arlo were yet to step onto the escalator.

Grabbing Arlo's hand, Georgie made a dash back the way they had come. 'Come on, Arlo. Let's race your dad back to the car but go a different way shall we?'

Breaking into a sprint, Arlo smiled. 'Okay!'

They hammered through the shopping centre, weaving in and out of the elderly shoppers coming the other way.

Up on the left was a sign and turning to the multi-storey car park. Georgie thought that heading into that would make it incredibly difficult for Ben to follow them.

'Let's go this way,' Georgie said, reaching and taking Ben's hand and trying not to yank his arm out of its socket.

With her feet clattering on the flooring, they crashed through the double doors into the cold, gloomy basement of the car park. The air smelled of damp and engine oil.

Slowing down a little, Georgie knew they now needed to get somewhere safe and try to contact Llancastell CID so that they could be rescued.

They jogged along the row of parked cars, their footsteps echoing off the low concrete ceiling above them.

Over to the right was an exit door and a pay and display machine. Beside that was an office attached to a car hand-wash. A man in his 20s was vacuuming a large 4x4 Toyota. Behind him was a sign advertising the prices for various types of washing and valeting.

'I'm just going to talk to this man,' Georgie panted as they approached. 'Tell you what, why don't you go and sit in that office for a minute while I talk to him.'

Georgie ushered Arlo into the office where there were a couple of chairs for waiting customers, along with a water cooler and a television mounted to the wall.

'Can I help, madam?' the man said as he turned off the hoover. 'Is your car down here?'

'Listen, I'm a police officer,' Georgie said with great urgency. 'And I need your help. Me and that little boy have been kidnapped. We've managed to escape. I need to borrow your phone so I can phone for help.'

The man took a moment to absorb what she'd said.

'Please,' she said, glancing around anxiously.

Then he nodded, 'Yes, of course.'

'Thank you, thank you,' Georgie gasped as she frantically took the iPhone that he had fished from his pocket. Her hands were shaking as she dialled 999.

'Where are they now?' the man asked, glancing around anxiously.

'I think we lost him,' Georgie said as she waited.

'Hello. Emergency. Which service please?' the operator asked.

'Police, please,' Georgie said, her voice shaking.

'PUT THE PHONE DOWN NOW!' boomed a voice that reverberated around the whole car park.

It was Ben.

He was striding across the car park towards them aggressively.

'Is this him?' the man asked nervously.

'Yes,' Georgie said, feeling sick with nerves.

The man grabbed a screwdriver from a nearby cleaning trolley and then brandished it as Ben approached.

'Stay back there!' the man shouted at Ben.

'Hello, you're connected to the police service – go ahead now,' the operator said.

Georgie pressed the 5 button twice to signal that she could no longer talk on the phone.

'Stay back! I mean it,' the man shouted, but Ben wasn't slowing down.

'Ben!' Georgie yelled. 'This has to stop right now!'

With a swift movement, Ben pulled the Glock 17 from the back of his jeans waistband. As he continued to stride forward, he aimed at the man's thigh.

CRACK!

A thunderous explosion of noise filled the car park.

'Argh!' the man screamed, clutching his thigh and falling to the concrete.

Ben then pointed the gun at Georgie's head.

'Drop the fucking phone right now or I'll blow your head off,' he growled.

'How is this going to end, Ben?' Georgie pleaded with him as she put the phone down on the ground, knowing that the police operator would be aware that she was in danger but couldn't speak.

Ben took another step forward and pushed the hard metal barrel of the handgun into Georgie's forehead.

For a moment, Georgie held her breath.

Ben had gritted teeth and a wild look in his eyes. She had no idea if he was going to shoot her in that moment.

'You ever try to take my son from me again and I promise you, I will kill you without hesitation,' Ben hissed. 'Do you understand me?'

Georgie nodded – the pressure of the gun against her skull was painful.

'Dad?' whispered a voice.

It was Arlo.

He was standing outside the office now, looking horrified.

'It's okay, mate,' Ben said, looking completely thrown. 'It's fine. Just a misunderstanding.'

'What now?' Georgie asked. 'We just drive over to Llandudno to see your dad, do we?' Georgie hoped that this information would now be relayed to whoever was running the investigation.

The man was still writhing on the floor, groaning.

'You shot that man?' Arlo said, looking utterly terrified.

'Yeah, he's a drug dealer.' Ben tried to reassure him as he reached out and put his hand on Arlo's shoulder. 'Come on, we need to get out of here.'

Ben glared at Georgie and signalled that they were

leaving. She clearly didn't have a choice but hoped that the intel that they were now heading for Llandudno had got through.

'I'm so sorry,' she said to the man as Ben pulled her away.

## Chapter 34

Ruth perched herself on a table – she was still in the middle of the CID briefing.

'Dan, can you get us up to speed on our investigation into Lynne Morgan's murder?' Ruth asked.

French got up and headed to the centre of IR1. 'Lynne Morgan was brutally murdered at her home in Wrexham on Friday night. Her daughter, Lucy, who lives in Acton Park, was found by the Pontcysyllte Aqueduct the same night. She had a head injury and was covered in her mother's blood. Lucy is suffering from acute traumatic amnesia, although some of her memory is starting to return. Professor Amis found significant traces of skin under Lynne's fingernails. Forensics are going to see if they're a match to Lucy's DNA.'

'A match would be pretty compelling evidence against Lucy,' Ruth said.

'Except we don't have a motive,' Garrow pointed out.

'Have a look at Lucy and Lynne's financial affairs,' Ruth said. 'See if there's anything there. And pull all calls from Lynne's phone.'

'Lynne has a son, Steve, who lives with her,' Garrow explained. 'We can't seem to locate him at the moment.'

Ruth thought that sounded suspicious. 'Can we track him down through his work?'

French shook his head. 'It looks like Steve has found it difficult to hold down employment ever since he was discharged from the army.'

Nick frowned. 'Why was he discharged?'

'Steve is suffering from complex PTSD,' Garrow explained. 'His company was blown up by an IED in Helman Province in 2012. I've run him through the PNC.'

'Anything interesting?' Ruth asked.

'Long history of alcohol-related crime. Drunk and disorderly, assault and resisting arrest. He got a six month suspended sentence in 2017 for attacking a bouncer.'

A phone rang on a nearby desk and Nick answered it.

'Okay. He sounds troubled. Let's try and track him down asap,' Ruth said. 'Lynne Morgan's house is opposite The Racecourse Ground, isn't it?'

'Yes, boss,' French replied.

'Have we looked at the CCTV on that stretch of the road yet?' Ruth asked.

'Still waiting for the council to send it over,' French explained.

'Okay, everyone,' Ruth said, to signal that the briefing was over. 'Let's get to work.'

As detectives filed away to their desks, Nick put the phone down and looked urgently at Ruth.

'What was that?' she asked.

'There's been a shooting at a multi-storey car park in Colwyn Bay,' he explained. 'The shooter's description matches our latest description of Ben. The injured man told officers that a woman had told him she and a young boy had been kidnapped. Sounds like he tried to defend them but Ben shot him in the leg and took off with Georgie and Arlo.'

'Shit,' Ruth sighed in frustration. 'Any idea where they went?'

Nick went over to his computer. 'There was an emergency call from a mobile phone in Colwyn Bay. The caller signalled they couldn't talk but the operator recorded the call. They think it was Georgie using the injured man's phone but they haven't managed to check the number.'

'Have we got the recording?' Ruth asked.

Nick pointed to his computer. 'The emergency operator is sending it over now.' Nick peered at the screen and then clicked on the MPEG audio file.

There was the sound from a mobile phone:

A man's voice shouted *'Stay back!'*

Then a voice that Ruth instantly recognised as Georgie. *'Ben! This has to stop right now.'*

*CRACK!*

The sound of a gunshot and the scream of a man who had clearly been shot.

Ben's voice then shouted, *'Drop the fucking phone right now or I'll blow your head off!'*

There were a few seconds where the voices were mumbled and inaudible.

Then Georgie's voice said, *'We just drive over to Llandudno to see your dad, do we?'*

Ruth looked over at Nick. 'Llandudno.'

## Chapter 35

It had been 15 minutes since Garrow and French had received a call from the duty sergeant to say that Steve Morgan had arrived at the station and wanted to speak to them. As they walked into Interview Room 3, Steve virtually leapt up from the table in an anxious rage.

'I've been in here for ages and no one will tell me what's going on!' he thundered. With coal-black short hair, he was in his early 30s, stocky, with a puffy face and bloodshot eyes. Garrow deduced that he had been drinking heavily in the past few days.

'Steve Morgan?' French asked, gesturing for him to sit down.

'Yes,' he huffed. 'I need to know where my mum is. Her house is a crime scene but I was told to come here for more information.'

Garrow looked at him with a serious expression. 'If you could sit down for a minute please Steve, then we can go through everything with you?'

'Is she all right?' Steve asked frantically as he sat down reluctantly.

French leaned forward. 'I'm afraid I have some very bad news to tell you.'

The blood visibly drained from Steve's face.

'Your mother was found dead at her home earlier today,' French said very gently. 'I'm very sorry for your loss.'

'What?' Steve said, pulling an incredulous face. 'No. What are you talking about?'

'I'm really sorry,' Garrow added.

'What do you mean?' Steve said, his eyes shifting as he tried to comprehend what they had told him. Then he looked at them. 'Why is it a crime scene?'

'I'm really sorry to tell you this, but we believe that your mother was murdered,' French said quietly.

'What?' Steve's eyes widened in horror. 'Why are you saying that? What do you mean she was murdered?'

'Detective Sergeant French and I entered your mother's house early this morning,' Garrow explained. 'We found your mother in the kitchen.'

'Oh God,' Steve said as he started to tremble. 'No …'

French looked at him. 'Just so you know, we are going to record the rest of this interview, just in case we need to use anything that you tell us in court. Do you understand that, Steve?'

Steve frowned. He was lost in thought and emotion. 'Erm … yeah,' he muttered.

French leaned forward, pressed the red button of the recording equipment and there was a long electronic beep.

'Can you tell us where you were on Friday night, Steve?' French asked.

Steve still looked lost. 'I was at a mate's house … I've been there all weekend.' Then he sat forward, blew out his cheeks and wiped a tear from his face. 'I need to see her.'

'Of course.' Garrow gave him an understanding nod. 'We can arrange that for you.'

'Oh God, I just can't believe this is happening,' Steve said, his voice trembling. 'What about Lucy?'

'Your sister is safe,' French explained. 'But she did receive a blow to the head and she is currently suffering from amnesia.'

'What?' Steve furrowed his brow. 'You mean Lucy was there when it happened?'

'Yes,' Garrow replied. 'We believe that Lucy was in your mother's house when she was killed. But she has amnesia, so she has no recollection of what happened.'

'Where is she now?' Steve demanded.

'I believe that she has been discharged from hospital and taken home,' Garrow replied.

There were a few seconds of silence as Steve ran his hands through his hair. His eyes filled with tears. 'I can't believe any of this has happened.'

'Steve,' French said. 'Can you think of anyone who would want to harm your mother?'

'No, of course not.' He looked at them. 'Mum never hurt a fly. Everyone loved her.'

'How would you describe her relationship with your sister, Lucy?' French asked.

'Fine.' Steve shrugged. 'They had their moments, like all mums and daughters. But ...' He shook his head. 'Do you think someone broke into her house or something. A burglar?'

'We're not sure at the moment,' French stated. 'However, there are no signs of a break-in so we're going on the assumption that your mother was killed by someone she knew.'

Steve looked shocked. 'That doesn't make any sense.'

'Can I just check that you were out of the house on

Friday night and didn't return until today?' French enquired.

'Yeah, that's right.' Steve then frowned. 'Why do you keep asking me where I was? I didn't have anything to do with this. She's my mum!' he growled.

## Chapter 36

Ruth and Nick were hammering across country from Llancastell up to Llandudno. Ruth had already put the local police on alert that Ben was heading to the town but they didn't have the address of where he was heading yet. She had also contacted an Armed Response Unit and made them aware that Ben was on his way to Llandudno and that he was armed and dangerous. They needed to be on standby as soon as she had the location.

She buzzed down the window and took a deep breath of fresh country air. The cumulus clouds lay like a crocheted cloth across the blue sky. The hedgerows on either side of the road were dotted with colour. The snowdrops, which had flowered as early as January, were being replaced by the lemon-yellow of primrose. Verges were also now beginning to bloom in the yellows of buttercups and dandelions.

Reaching into her pocket, Ruth pulled out a stick of nicotine gum and popped it into her mouth.

'It's weird,' Nick said as he glanced over. 'When you

buzz down the window, I instantly expect to get a waft of cigarette smoke.'

'Not any more,' Ruth said, pointing to the gum she was now chewing in her mouth. 'I promised Daniel I'd quit. And Sarah.'

'Good for you,' Nick said.

'Oh, I'm not happy about it,' Ruth laughed. 'Smoking was one of my favourite things to do in the whole world. And giving it up has been a nightmare.'

'Right,' Nick said with a knowing nod. 'Yeah, well I know a bit about quitting an addiction … What does it taste like?'

'This is meant to be mint,' Ruth explained, and then pulled a face. 'But it tastes like someone's thrown pepper into my mouth,' she admitted.

'Lovely,' Nick said with a smile. 'And of course, it does mean that you can't say 'You drive, I'll smoke.'

'Yeah, I think 'You drive, I'll chew' doesn't quite have the same ring to it.'

Nick chortled. 'Not really.'

There was music playing very quietly on the radio. She recognised it as *Who Are You?* by *The Who*.

'I love this,' Nick said, turning it up a bit.

'I saw them play this at Glastonbury,' Ruth admitted.

Nick frowned. 'You saw The Who play at Glastonbury?'

'Hey, I used to be pretty cool when I was younger,' Ruth protested with an amused smile.

'Come on,' Nick said. 'You think Spandau Ballet are edgy.'

Ruth gave him the finger. 'Me and Sarah went to Glastonbury in 2007. It was raining and the place was muddy and under water. But no one seemed to care that much.

And we saw Amy Winehouse, The Killers. And Shirley Bassey did that Sunday afternoon slot which was amazing.'

'And you saw The Who,' Nick said.

'Yeah, that was my least favourite bit,' Ruth admitted.

Nick shook his head. 'The Who are rock royalty.'

'It was lost on me,' Ruth grinned. 'It sounded like a mess.'

At that moment, Ruth's phone buzzed. It was a message from CID.

'I've got the address for Gethin Stewart,' she said, referring to Ben's father. 'He's in a care home on Trinity Square.'

Ruth tapped a number into her phone.

'Hello?' said a male voice with a thick Welsh accent.

'Sergeant Williams?' Ruth asked. He was her contact at Llandudno Police Station.

'Speaking?'

'It's DI Ruth Hunter,' she explained. 'Gethin Stewart is a resident at the Carden Residential Care Home on Trinity Square.'

'Okay, I know where that is,' Williams replied.

'That's where we believe Ben Stewart is heading,' Ruth said. 'And we think it's his intention to kill his father. He is armed and very dangerous, so I suggest that we evacuate as many of the residents as we can. I have an Armed Response Vehicle on standby. They should be at the home within ten minutes. I'll be there in fifteen.'

'Understood, ma'am,' Williams said, but he sounded uneasy.

Ruth ended the call and grabbed her radio. She glanced over at the sat nav. They would be arriving in Llandudno in 12 minutes.

'Alpha three zero, this is three six, over,' she said.

'Three six, this is Alpha three zero receiving, go ahead, over,' replied an officer from the Armed Response Unit.

'We now have our target location,' Ruth explained. 'Proceed to Carden Residential Care Home, Trinity Square, Llandudno, Lima three zero, three gamma whiskey, over.'

'Target location received and understood, out.'

Ruth blew out her cheeks as she weighed up how the next half hour was going to play out.

'You okay?' Nick asked, sensing that she was lost in thought.

'I'm just worrying that we've got an unstable gunman, a pregnant police officer, and a 9-year-old boy heading into a town where we also have armed officers,' Ruth admitted.

Something else buzzed on Ruth's phone and she looked down.

'If Ben thinks that he doesn't have anything to lose now he's murdered Marvin Peters, that makes him incredibly dangerous,' Nick said darkly.

Ruth glanced down at the document she had been sent. It was a series of case notes from 2001. It made for shocking reading.

'What's that?' Nick asked, gesturing to the phone.

'I've pulled some notes from our national database,' Ruth explained. 'Ben accidentally killed his mother in 2001 when he was thirteen.'

Nick raised an eyebrow. 'What?'

'Apparently, he took his father's shotgun to stop him attacking his mother who was semi-conscious. The gun went off accidentally and killed his mother. He was never charged but he and his sister were taken into care. Gethin Stewart was charged with GBH and negligence.'

'And Ben was then abused by Marvin Peters while in the children's home,' Nick said.

'I'm not condoning anything he's done,' Ruth said. 'But I can see why Ben has gone off the rails and wanted to kill Peters and his father.

## Chapter 37

French and Garrow were in the lift in the Llancastell University hospital heading down to the basement where the mortuary was located. Garrow was getting frustrated – he couldn't seem to get Lucy out of his head.

Half an hour earlier they had received a call from Professor Amis to say that he had found something 'interesting' in Lynne Morgan's post-mortem that he needed to talk to them about.

'You haven't said much since we interviewed Steve Morgan, sarge?' Garrow said as the lift moved slowly down with a metallic clunk.

'Not much to say, is there?' French said with a shrug. 'He's got an alibi for Friday night. And he doesn't have any motive to harm his mother. I thought he seemed genuinely upset, didn't you?'

'Possibly,' Garrow said unconvincingly.

French frowned. 'You're not convinced?'

'Ex-soldier, complex PTSD, alcohol abuse, with a history of violence,' Garrow replied. 'If he was in a black out, anything could have happened. We've seen enough drunks who've done terrible things only to wake up and not remember a thing.'

French narrowed his eyes. 'You think he slit his own mother's throat? That seems very deliberate and personal.'

The doors to the lift opened with a noisy shudder and they stepped out into the windowless basement corridor.

'We don't know what their relationship was like,' Garrow said. 'Maybe she was suffocating or trying to control him and he just snapped.'

'Maybe,' French said, sounding unconvinced as they got to the double doors to the mortuary and pushed them open.

The temperature instantly dropped. Garrow got the odour of disinfectants and preserving chemicals. He remembered the first time he'd attended a post-mortem. Nick had taken him along when he was still on probation in CID. He recalled the shock of seeing the dead body of a young man who had been stabbed to death in a brawl outside a pub. It had felt so horribly surreal seeing his white corpse just laid out on the steel gurney like a ghostly mannequin. It had taken him several days to get that image out of his head.

However, as Nick explained that day, he had now grown fairly accustomed to seeing dead bodies. He wasn't sure that was a good thing but it was part of the job.

Amis turned on an electric saw, which then squealed as it hit the body's breastbone. Not only did it grate on Garrow's teeth, but it made his stomach churn. There were still parts of a post-mortem that were very unpleasant.

Turning off the saw, Amis noticed Garrow and French. He pulled down his sky blue surgical mask and gave them a half smile.

'Ah, Llancastell's answer to Bodie and Doyle,' Amis quipped, laughing at his own little joke.

Garrow gave French a quizzical look.

'The Professionals,' French said dryly by way of an explanation.

Garrow presumed he was talking about the 80s television series but he'd never seen an episode.

'Bit before your time DC Garrow?' Amis asked with a smile. 'You probably weren't born were you?'

'I was born in 1993,' Garrow explained.

'Dear God,' Amis laughed as he reached over and took a mug of steaming tea. The mug featured two large green animated bugs with the amusing slogan – *What doesn't kill you … mutates and then tries again.*

'What can you tell us, Tony?' French asked.

Garrow's eyes rested on Lynne's body. Her chest was open exposing her lungs and other vital organs inside.

'Cause of death is what I suspected,' Amis said as he pointed to the deep cut across the throat. 'The right end of this injury starts below the ear at the upper third of her neck and deepens gradually with the severance of the right carotid artery. The left sided end of the injury was at the mid third of the neck with a tail abrasion. She would have haemorrhaged and bled to death in less than a minute.'

French looked a little irritated. Garrow knew that Amis seemed to have had this effect on most of the CID team at one time or another. He seemed to go around the houses before getting to the actual reason why he'd called them in.

'You said there was something 'interesting' that you'd found?' French said, trying to hurry Amis along.

'Oh yes,' Amis said with a guffaw. 'Of course. Your victim had sexual intercourse less than half an hour before she was killed.'

'Was it consensual?' Garrow asked.

Amis nodded. 'Looks that way. I couldn't find any

evidence of any bruising or anything that might suggest sexual assault or rape.'

'How can you be so certain of the timescale?' Garrow asked.

'The semen was still inside the vagina and hadn't progressed to the cervical canal,' Amis explained. 'That process normally takes around thirty minutes. However, once your victim was dead, the process stopped. And I have managed to retrieve some semen so your forensic guys can get a DNA profile from that.' Amis then pointed to her fingernails. 'I've also managed to get a decent amount of skin from under her nails, which will also give you a DNA profile.'

'And if we match the DNA of the semen and skin to the same person,' Garrow said, thinking out loud, 'it's likely she was murdered by the person she had just had sex with.'

'That would be my presumption,' Amis said.

'Right, thanks Tony,' French said, indicating that it was time for them to go.

'There is something else,' Amis said. 'I've looked at the semen sample and there is no sperm present.'

Garrow raised an eyebrow. 'The semen was from someone who had had a vasectomy.'

'Very good,' Amis said with a wry, patronising smile.

'That's very helpful,' French said as they turned to go.

They headed towards the doors, went through them, and then headed down the corridor back towards the lift.

'Doesn't sound like Lucy or Steve are involved,' Garrow said.

French shot him a look. 'We don't know that, do we?' He sounded annoyed. 'Lynne having sex and then being murdered might not be connected.'

Garrow furrowed his brow. 'But there's only thirty minutes between the events, sarge.'

'Let's stick to the evidence, eh?' French said as he pressed the button to call the lift. 'I think that for whatever reason, you've already ruled Lucy Morgan out as a suspect in her mother's murder. And that's unprofessional, Jim.'

'I don't think that's fair,' Garrow replied, but he suspected that French might have a point. It was just his pride and ego that wouldn't allow him to admit it.

The lift arrived, they got in, and there was a frosty silence.

French's phone rang and he answered it.

'DS French?' he said as he listened to whoever was talking at the other end. 'Okay, thanks for letting me know.' Then he looked at Garrow. 'Lucy Morgan has called the station to say that she's started to remember a few more things from Friday night and she needs to talk to us.'

## Chapter 38

'There was someone else there,' Lucy explained as she sat hunched a little in her armchair.

Garrow and French had arrived at Lucy's home five minutes earlier and been let inside by the Family Liaison Officer – FLO – Constable Jenny Wilkes.

Garrow frowned as he pulled out his notebook and pen. 'Can you tell us exactly what you can remember about Friday?'

Lucy blinked as she composed herself. 'I do vaguely remember being at my mum's house.'

'Okay,' French said encouragingly. 'Do you remember arriving?'

'No.' Lucy shook her head immediately. 'Everything is cloudy as if it was a dream.' Then she looked at Garrow with a pained expression. 'I'm sorry. I wish I could remember everything.'

'It's all right. Take your time.' Garrow gave her a kind smile. 'Anything you can remember, however small, is going to be incredibly useful in finding out who did this to your mum.'

Lucy nodded thoughtfully.

Garrow looked into the depths of her soft, brown eyes. Her eyebrows were dark and full, like a child's, lending an aura of innocence to her features. Her cheeks were slightly rounded and symmetrical on either side of her elegant nose. There were gentle creases around her eyes.

Then Lucy frowned as if something had suddenly occurred to her. She looked at them. 'There was someone else there. In the house.'

'Do you know who?' French asked.

Lucy's eyes moved around the room as she searched her damaged memory. 'Mum was fighting with someone in the kitchen. She had a knife in her hand. They were struggling.'

'Do you mean that your mum had a knife?' Garrow asked to clarify.

French frowned. 'Can you see the person who was fighting with your mum?'

Lucy didn't say anything for a moment. Then she furrowed a brow. 'It was a man.'

Garrow looked at her. If she had remembered this correctly, it was a very significant step in finding out who had murdered Lynne. 'Can you describe him?'

Lucy shook her head. 'Sorry,' she whispered, now overcome with the memories of that night. Her eyes filled with tears as she took a breath to compose herself.

Garrow leaned forward. 'It's okay,' he said reassuringly. 'Are you sure that you saw a man fighting with your mum?'

Lucy nodded but looked a little hesitant. 'That's what I can remember. I don't know if that helps?'

'It's very helpful,' Garrow reassured her.

As she turned, Garrow spotted two red scratch marks at the back of her neck.

They were clearly visible as she was wearing her hair in a ponytail.

French looked over at Garrow – he'd clearly spotted them too.

'You've got two scratch marks at the back of your neck, Lucy,' French observed. 'Any idea how you got them?'

Lucy put her hand to the back of her neck. 'These? No, sorry. They were there when I woke up in hospital.'

# Chapter 39

R uth and Nick were now inside the Carden Residential Care Home. Stationed on the main door but out of sight were four armed response officers – AROs – in full combat equipment. Within the police, AROs were referred to as '*shots*', and they were clad in black helmets, perspex goggles, balaclavas, Kevlar bulletproof vests and Heckler & Koch G36C assault rifles. The G36C carried a 100 round C-Mag drum magazine and fired at the deadly rate of 750 rounds per minute. The AROs also carried 9mm handguns attached to holsters on their waists which could be used in more risky situations, especially when hostages were involved. There were another two AROs positioned at the back of the care home and another two waiting on standby in a nearby armed response vehicle.

Ruth noticed that the care home was strangely quiet and still. And despite it being relatively warm outside, the reception area was chilly. The main sweeping staircase turned inward and wound its way up to the space of the upper landing, which could be accessed by only one door.

The space was a large windowless oblong. Daylight streamed in through the open doors at the far end of the reception area. On a nearby solid oak table there was a large vase with thin curving sides and a thick green bulbous neck and flared rim decorated with pink roses. Beyond it there was a recessed alcove in the wall though nothing stood there. After this, there was an archway.

Four uniformed officers marched along the main corridor, through the double doors and towards where Ruth and Nick were standing. While three of them headed for the entrance, the other, a great bear of a man with a goatee beard approached.

'DI Hunter?' he said.

She recognised his voice from their phone call.

'Sergeant Williams,' Ruth replied.

'That's all the residents out of here, ma'am,' Williams explained, and then gestured towards the staircase. 'We've done two sweeps through all the rooms.'

'That's great,' Ruth said and then pulled a face. 'That can't have been easy.'

Williams nodded. 'Yeah, some of the residents were a bit confused and upset. But I explained to the staff that if someone was coming here with a firearm, we needed everyone to be elsewhere for their safety.'

'Where are they all?' Nick enquired.

'The local town hall,' Williams explained. 'The staff there are laying on tea and cakes until we know it's safe for them to come back here.'

'That's very kind,' Nick said.

'Llandudno's that kind of place, sir,' Williams replied in a tone that implied his pride in the town.

'And you located Gethin Stewart okay?' Ruth asked.

'Yes, ma'am,' Williams replied.

Nick looked at him. 'We're going to need to talk to him at some point.'

Williams pulled a face. 'I don't think there's very much point in that, sir.'

Nick frowned. 'How do you mean?'

'Gethin Stewart has severe dementia,' Williams explained. 'I tried to explain what was going on but he just stared into space.' Williams looked at them. 'He also has stage 4 lung cancer. The staff told me that Gethin is receiving palliative care but they don't expect him to live for more than another month. But he's somewhere safe and out of the way.'

'What about the marksmen?' Ruth asked.

Williams gestured outside. 'They're up on the tower of the church. I'll take you up there now, shall I?'

Ruth nodded. 'That would be great.'

## Chapter 40

F rench and Garrow were now back in IR1 at Llancastell nick trying to piece together the evidence they had so far.

Garrow looked up at the scene board. The fact that Lucy had two nasty looking scratches on the back of her neck and Lynne had skin under her nails was a concern. They would have to wait to see what the DNA evidence showed from the skin samples and if they matched Lucy's DNA.

Putting down his mobile phone, French looked over at Garrow. 'That was the boss. They think that Ben Stewart is heading for Llandudno.'

'I can't imagine how scared Georgie must be,' Garrow said.

'And Stewart's 9-year-old son,' French added. 'He's going to be scarred for life.'

'I didn't have a lot to do with DI Stewart last week,' Garrow said thoughtfully, 'but there is no way that I'd have him down as being capable of all this.'

French shrugged. 'Hey, if this job teaches you anything

it's that people can project one version of themselves, when underneath there's a whole other version they're hiding from the world.'

Garrow looked back up at the scene board. 'You think Lucy Morgan is one of those people, sarge?'

'Quite possibly,' French replied. 'Don't you?'

'No.'

'Jim, have you ever thought that maybe Lucy is faking her amnesia?' French suggested.

'No, I haven't,' Garrow said confidently. 'My instinct is that she is telling us the truth. And we haven't found a motive for her killing her mother.'

'Not yet, we haven't,' French countered, 'but I think it's naïve of you to rule her out as a suspect.'

Garrow could feel himself bristle at French's words. 'I'm not being naïve, sarge.'

'Aren't you?' French asked with a raised eyebrow. Then he pointed to his heart. 'You're letting this get in the way of this,' he said, then pointing to his head. 'And that's dangerous.'

There were a few seconds of awkward silence. Garrow knew that French had a point.

French looked at his phone and then over at Garrow. 'CCTV of Mold Road from Friday night has come in.'

'Good,' Garrow replied, glad that they could change the subject as they went over to French's computer. He opened his emails and then clicked on an MPEG file. The file opened to show the CCTV from a high vantage point – possibly a streetlight. It covered some of the Racecourse Ground, the Mold Road but only a tiny fraction of the pavement outside Lynne Morgan's house.

'We could do with more of this pavement here,' Garrow said, pointing. 'If someone had walked along and into Lynne's house, it doesn't look like the CCTV camera would have caught them.'

'Right, let's see what we've got anyway, eh?' French said, sounding disappointed as he started to trawl through the footage. The timecode and date were stamped on the bottom right hand corner of the screen.

Garrow peered intently at the screen. There was part of him that wondered if Lucy would appear on the footage at any point. He found himself hoping that she didn't.

As the timecode showed 21.35, a car stopped on the road directly outside Lynne's house. The car pulled up onto the pavement and then put on its hazard lights.

'Who the hell is that?' French asked.

A man got out of the passenger door and walked out of shot but it was clear that he was heading in the direction of Lynne's home.

French paused the image and they both looked at his face which they now clearly recognised.

Steve Morgan.

## Chapter 41

Ben, Georgie and Arlo were getting closer to Llandudno but because they were using the back roads, it was taking longer. Hovering up in the sky above the fields to their left was an enormous bird. It was a Peregrine Falcon. As Georgie squinted up, she could see its distinctive blue-grey wings, white body and black head. Even from where she was sitting, its wing span was huge. She seemed to remember someone telling her that their wing span could reach four feet and that it could dive at speeds of over 250 mph. As it bobbed and drifted on the rising air currents, it struck Georgie that it was a perfect killing machine.

Seeing a sign for Llandudno, Ben squinted at the dashboard. 'We need more petrol,' he muttered under his breath.

'I need a wee, Dad,' Arlo called from the back.

'Jesus,' Ben snapped.

'Sorry,' Arlo said, sounding scared.

Ben took a moment and then turned with a smile. 'It's

all right, mate. No problem.' He gestured. 'There's a layby just up there.'

Georgie watched Ben closely. There seemed to be a determination to maintain a close, nurturing relationship with Arlo. Underneath all that damage, pain, anger and fear, Ben was trying to do the right thing by his son.

They pulled over on the layby and Ben stopped the car.

'There you go, mate,' Ben said. 'Just pee behind those bushes over there.'

Arlo nodded, opened the door and wandered away. Since the shooting in the car park, Arlo had been very quiet. And even the way he walked seemed to indicate the shock that seeing his father shoot a man had had on him.

Georgie turned and looked directly at Ben.

He frowned back at her. 'What?' he asked defensively.

'You really want a close relationship with Arlo, don't you?' she asked.

'Of course,' Ben said in a tone that implied this was a ridiculous question. 'He's the only decent thing I've ever done with my life.'

Georgie sighed. 'But you're damaging him, can't you see that?'

'No, I'm not!' Ben snapped angrily.

'You've taken him out of school and away from his mother,' Georgie continued, even though challenging Ben seemed risky. 'You're dragging him around North Wales on some revenge killing spree with a police hostage in the car. And you shot an innocent man in the leg in front of him. How can you not see that you're damaging him?'

She saw Ben bristle with anger. Maybe if she could get him to see some kind of sense, he might let Arlo go.

'You don't know what you're talking about,' Ben sneered.

'I get it. Your childhood damaged you beyond repair.

And no one should have had to witness or experience what you did,' Georgie said with an empathetic tone. 'But now you're going to do the same to Arlo.'

'No. It's not the same.' Ben shook his head. 'You have no idea what it was like or what I went through.'

'No, I don't,' Georgie admitted. 'But don't put Arlo through any more. You need to protect him. You need to let him go so he can go home and be safe.'

'I am protecting him,' Ben said sharply. 'He's better off here with me than with that bitch and the scumbag she married.'

'Do you truly believe that?' Georgie asked.

Ben put his hand up angrily. 'Who the hell do you think you are, talking to me about me and my son? How fucking dare you.'

Ben jumped out of the car in fury and went around to the boot. He opened it, grabbed some things from a plastic bag, and then came around to the passenger door.

Georgie's heart was now pounding. Ben seemed to have completely lost his temper and for a moment, she thought he was going to attack her.

As the door opened, Georgie flinched and put her hands up to protect herself in case he did assault her.

Instead, Ben took out a plastic tie, put it over her wrists and then pulled it tight so that the plastic cut into her skin.

'You don't need to do that,' Georgie protested.

'Shut up!' Ben yelled as he tore a long strip of gaffer tape from a roll and then placed it forcefully over Georgie's mouth. 'This will shut you up.'

'What are you doing, Dad?' a voice asked timidly.

Ben turned and then looked down at Arlo who was now standing next to him. 'It's all right, mate,' he reassured him. 'I'm going to tell you something but it has to remain a top secret, okay?'

Arlo looked scared and confused. 'I don't understand what's going on,' he said tearfully.

Ben pointed at Georgie. 'It turns out that my friend, Georgie, has been working for the drug dealers behind my back.'

Arlo frowned but didn't say anything.

'So, I'm going to need your help to take her to a police station as soon as we can so she can be questioned,' Ben explained.

'Is she going to prison then?' Arlo asked, looking upset.

'Probably,' Ben said, and then ushered Arlo into the car. 'Jump up here, mate.'

Georgie was now breathing air in through her nostrils but it was making her feel very claustrophobic. She turned a little so she could see them in the back of the car.

Arlo gave her a suspicious look. It seemed that he had believed his father's fanciful story.

Ben then looked at Arlo. 'Do you think you can help me do that, mate?'

Arlo nodded unconvincingly.

Ben then pulled out the Glock 17 from his waistband, unclipped the magazine and then handed the empty gun to Arlo.

'I might need you to use this,' Ben said. 'So, I need to teach you how to handle it, okay?'

Arlo nodded as he took the gun but it was heavy. His hand wobbled.

'Use two hands, mate,' Ben said, guiding Arlo's other hand so that he was now holding the black, ridged grip of the handgun. 'That's it,' he said encouragingly.

There was something so dark and unnatural about an innocent 9-year-old boy holding the gun.

'Like this?' Arlo asked, seeking the approval of his father.

'Brilliant, mate. That's spot on,' Ben said, sounding delighted. 'Now put your finger on the trigger here.'

Georgie watched uneasily as Arlo put the index finger of his right hand onto the trigger of the gun. She knew it wasn't loaded but the whole thing was making her feel very uneasy.

'See if you can pull it, mate,' Ben said. 'Nice and slowly.'

Arlo pulled a face as he tried to pull the trigger.

Then CLICK.

'There you go,' Ben said triumphantly. 'Just aim here, and pull the trigger slowly.'

He took the gun from Arlo, who was looking very pleased with himself. Ben then took the fully loaded magazine and snapped it back into the gun and handed it back. 'Try that.'

Arlo held the gun again with both hands.

'How's that?' Ben asked.

'Good,' Arlo said excitedly.

'Right, mate. I want you to point it at her, okay?'

'Why?' Arlo asked.

'Because I'm going to pee too,' Ben said. 'And if she tries to escape or do anything bad, what are you going to do?'

Arlo frowned but then pointed the gun at Georgie's face.

*Jesus.*

'Shoot her?' Arlo suggested.

'Exactly. Shoot her.'

Ben wandered away to have a pee.

Georgie looked directly at Arlo who was holding the gun with two hands.

*One slight mistake and he's going to blow my bloody head off!* she thought as her stomach tightened with anxiety.

# Chapter 42

Garrow hesitated before knocking on the door to Lynne Morgan's home. Forensics had now finished so Steve had been allowed to move back in. Garrow waited a few moments, then knocked again.

French, who was standing on the doorstep next to him, gave a frustrated sigh. 'Given what we've just seen on the CCTV, he's probably not going to answer it.'

Garrow nodded but the front door slowly opened and Steve poked his head out. His eyes widened in shock.

Steve tried to slam the door shut but Garrow wedged his foot in the way before he could succeed.

'Bloody hell,' French growled.

With a grunt, Garrow pushed the door open wide enough to step inside and began running down the hallway towards an open door to a utility room and another door that led out into the back garden.

Garrow and French ran through and out into the garden.

'Oi, stay there!' French shouted.

Steve was already racing across the back garden, intent

on making it over a six-foot fence that separated the house from next door.

'Stop! Police!' Garrow yelled.

Steve leapt up onto the fence without pausing while Garrow and French continued after him.

Garrow scrambled to the top of the fence, then jumped off, feeling every bone in his body jar in protest.

On the other side, he spotted Steve sprinting across another garden. However, he tripped heavily on the patio and went flying to the ground.

A second later, Garrow was on him, pulling his hands behind his back and cuffing him.

'You're under arrest,' Garrow said, trying to get his breath back.

## Chapter 43

Having just filled up the BMW with petrol in a remote petrol station, Ben sat looking preoccupied in the driver's seat. Arlo had put his AirPods back into his ears and was engrossed playing on his phone again. Georgie still couldn't get the image of him holding the gun and pointing it at her out of her mind.

Ten minutes earlier, Ben had removed Georgie's gaffer tape once they pulled in. He didn't want anyone to see her like that. He had threatened to put the tape back over her mouth if she continued to verbally badger him. She agreed. Breathing only through her nose was deeply uncomfortable.

Georgie wriggled her fingers for a moment. The plastic tie was still around her wrists and it was tight, making her skin sore.

A mobile phone buzzed from somewhere.

Georgie recognised it as her phone ringtone and frowned. Ben still had her phone inside his jacket and had kept it charged. She had no idea why he wanted it. She assumed that they were moving around so much that it would be difficult to get a GPS fix on them but it seemed careless, nonetheless.

Ben took the phone, looked at the caller ID and then showed it to her – *DI Ruth Hunter*.

'Does she really think you're going to answer the phone?' Ben scoffed.

Georgie shrugged but didn't answer. She thought that the less she said the better given Ben's volatility.

Looking up, Georgie became aware that a battered, red Ford Ranger pickup truck had parked in front of them. It looked like it had been done deliberately to block them in.

A middle-aged woman in a dirty wax jacket and wellies walked over determinedly. Georgie immediately assumed she was a farmer.

'What the fuck is she doing?' Ben asked in an anxious voice.

'No idea,' Georgie replied quietly, but she was getting the feeling that something was about to kick off.

The woman stopped about ten yards from them, pointed aggressively and yelled, 'I know who you two are. I've seen it on the news. And I've called the police. You're going nowhere 'til they get here.'

Ben shook his head. 'For fuck's sake!'

'Ben,' Georgie said. 'Don't do anything stupid. Please.'

Ben gestured to the woman. 'It's not me who's being stupid, is it?' he sneered.

A white Ford Focus with three teenage boys, all in baseball caps, pulled into the garage and parked beside the petrol pumps behind them. Their rap music was playing loudly.

The woman gestured to one of the teenage boys as he got out, then pointed to the BMW and shouted, 'Excuse me. That's the policeman who is on the run. The ones that are on the telly.'

The teenage boy looked confused as he went over to the petrol pump. 'Yeah?'

The woman jabbed her finger at the BMW. 'They're in that car.'

'What?' the teenage boy said as he moved cautiously around to look inside.

The woman pointed again. 'I've boxed them in and called the police. Just keep your car there so they can't get out, eh?'

The teenager nodded anxiously as he leant into the passenger window to talk to his mates. The thudding music stopped.

There was a growing tension in the air.

'What's going on, Dad?' Arlo asked.

'Don't worry, mate,' Ben reassured him. 'There's something wrong with that lady's car that's all.'

Arlo nodded and went back to looking at his phone.

'Right, fuck this,' Ben snapped.

Opening the car door, Ben got out, pulled the Glock 17 from his waistband and aimed it at the woman. 'Move your truck before I shoot you,' he said calmly.

The woman shook her head and glared at him. 'I can't do that. You've got an innocent woman and child in there.'

Ben stepped forward two paces, aiming the handgun directly at her.

'Move the fucking truck, or I'll blow your head off,' Ben growled.

Georgie felt the tension in her stomach grip hold. She took a breath.

'I can't let you leave,' the woman said very confidently. 'You'll just have to shoot me, won't you?'

Glancing at where the truck was parked and then back at the car behind, Georgie could see they really were boxed in. There was no room to manoeuvre.

Maybe this was it? It would be a matter of minutes before the police were there. Then a darker thought. Was Ben going to try and shoot his way out while holding her and Arlo hostage? It didn't bear thinking about.

Striding back towards the BMW, Ben looked in with utter rage. 'Right, get out of the car,' he yelled.

'Dad?' Arlo said from the back.

'Get out of the car, Arlo, now,' Ben snapped.

Georgie moved her hands over to open the door and got out. She had no idea what Ben was planning to do next.

Ben pointed the gun at the woman. 'We're taking your truck.'

The woman shook her head. 'No you're not.'

Georgie couldn't help but admire the woman's courage.

As Ben marched towards her with his gun pointing directly at her head, the woman took her car keys that were in her hand and tossed them into the long grass of a field that was adjacent to the petrol station.

*Jesus Christ!* Georgie thought. *She's going to get herself killed.*

Arlo, who still clearly believed his father's words about Georgie, was keeping his distance from her.

'For fuck's sake!' Ben said, shaking with anger. He went up to the woman and pushed the gun into her temple. 'You shouldn't have done that.'

*Oh God, he's going to kill her.*

There were an agonising few seconds as Georgie held her breath.

She heard the faint sound of police sirens in the distance.

'Dad? What are you doing?' Arlo asked.

'Doesn't matter,' Ben said, turning on his heels and now marching in the opposite direction.

Suddenly, the teenage boy started the engine of his car. He wasn't about to get shot.

With a screech of tyres, the Ford Focus reversed back at high speed, bumped into the air pump and sped away.

Georgie could hear the sound of sirens getting closer.

'GET BACK IN THE CAR!' Ben thundered.

They got back in as Ben jumped into the BMW, but in a flash a marked police car had swerved into the petrol station and stopped behind them.

Slamming the car into reverse, the BMW hit the police car behind.

It was just enough to allow Ben to pull out of the space they had been boxed into.

Pulling forwards, Georgie saw a uniformed police officer run towards their car.

Their exit was still blocked by the pickup truck.

Crunching the BMW back into reverse, they sped backwards. Ben spun the steering wheel. The back of the car skidded around with a loud squeal, clipping the garage wall but not stopping.

He slammed the brakes on and the car juddered to a halt.

They were now facing forwards.

'Dad, I'm scared,' Arlo said from the back of the car.

'It's okay, mate,' Ben said through gritted teeth.

With a stamp on the pedal, Ben accelerated out of the entrance and onto the main road.

With a glance in the wing mirror, Georgie saw the blue flashing lights of a patrol car that was now directly behind them.

'Shit!' Ben hissed.

He pushed the accelerator and the engine roared. He

gripped the steering wheel as they screeched around the bend.

Georgie glanced over at the dashboard.

90 mph!

She felt the back tyres losing their grip and sliding as they cornered a bend at 100 mph.

She looked again in the wing mirror. The police car was slipping further behind.

Georgie glanced over at the dashboard again.

110 mph.

Ben went hammering up the hill, and over the crest. He pulled out to overtake a long articulated lorry, and went past in a blur.

As they careered around another bend, there was a small country lane off to the right.

Throwing the steering wheel, the BMW skidded as they hammered right and along the lane that was bordered by dry stone walls and hedgerows.

'Fuck me, that was close,' Ben said triumphantly.

## Chapter 44

G arrow leaned over and pressed the red button on the digital recording equipment. There was a long, loud electronic beep.

'Interview conducted with Steve Morgan, Interview Room 2, Llancastell Police Station. Present are Detective Constable Jim Garrow, Duty Solicitor Neil Roberts and myself, Detective Sergeant Daniel French.'

Steve was now dressed in a grey sweatshirt and bottoms. His clothes had been taken for extensive DNA analysis. His mouth had been swabbed for a DNA sample and his nails clipped.

Steve gave Garrow a blank stare and then leaned in to talk to Roberts and whispered something in his ear.

French raised his eyebrow. 'Steve, do you understand that you are still under caution?'

Steve shrugged. 'Yeah.'

'Can you tell us why you ran earlier when we came to talk to you?' French asked.

'I dunno,' Steve mumbled. 'It's a natural reaction when I see coppers I suppose.'

'Even when your own mother has been murdered?' Garrow asked suspiciously. 'For all you knew, we could have been coming to give you an update on our investigation.'

'In fact, it might be argued that the only reason you'd run when we knocked on your door earlier is that you were guilty of something,' French suggested. 'Is there anything you'd like to tell us about that, Steve?'

'I'm not guilty of anything,' Steve growled.

Garrow flicked through the pages of his notebook. 'When we spoke to you yesterday, you told us that you had left the house you shared with your mum early on Friday evening and that you didn't return at any time over the weekend. Is that correct?'

'Yeah,' Steve snorted angrily. 'I don't know what you're hassling me for. Why aren't you out there trying to find out who killed my mum?'

French opened his laptop, pressed a button and waited for the screen to burst into life. 'For the purposes of the tape, I am showing the suspect Item Reference 293F.' French leaned over, hit the spacebar and the CCTV footage of the Mold Road on Friday night outside Lynne's house played. As the car drew up and then pulled onto the pavement, French paused the footage. 'This is CCTV footage of the Mold Road on Friday evening. And this section of the road is directly outside the house you share with your mum, Lynne Morgan, is that correct?'

'If you say so,' Steve grunted, looking elsewhere.

French moved the laptop round slightly. 'Steve, if you can look at the screen for me please. If you look across the road, you can see part of the Mold Road stand of The Racecourse Ground. And this is directly opposite your house, isn't it?'

Steve flicked his eyes over to the laptop reluctantly. 'I suppose so.'

'Thank you,' Garrow said.

'And if you see here, this car has parked up on the road outside your house at exactly 9.35pm,' French said, and then played the footage forward so that the figure they knew to be Steve gets out of the passenger side of the car. 'And then immediately, this person here gets out of the car and heads in the direction of your home.' French frowned and looked over at him. 'Any idea who this person is?'

Steve shrugged and gave him a look as though that was a ridiculous suggestion. 'No. How would I?'

French pointed to the face on the screen. 'That looks a lot like you, Steve.'

'Does it?' Steve asked unconvincingly.

'Come on,' Garrow said in a frustrated voice. 'We've run the plate of that car through the DVLA. It belongs to an Andy Morrell, who we know is a friend of yours. We know that's you getting out of the car Steve. And then we know that fifteen minutes later, it's you getting back in the car before it drives away.'

Steve looked down at the floor but didn't reply.

They waited for a few seconds for the tension to build in the room.

Steve then leant over and had a conversation with Roberts in hushed tones.

'Let's put it this way,' Garrow said. 'You lied to us about returning to your home on the evening that your mum was murdered. Can you see how suspicious that looks?'

Steve shook his head. 'I didn't have anything to do with what happened to her. I promise. I could never do that.'

'Then tell us what happened,' French said.

Steve took a few moments and then said, 'I just popped home to get some things.'

Garrow narrowed his eyes. 'Drugs?'

'No,' Steve said, clearly lying.

'Okay, why did you go into your house for fifteen minutes and then leave?' French asked.

Steve didn't reply for a few moments. Then he said, 'I was just picking up some booze, that's all.'

'Jesus, we've got you on camera, Steve,' French snapped, playing the footage forward to where Steve comes back to the car and then pointing. 'You're not carrying any booze with you. Why are you lying to us?'

'All right, all right,' Steve snapped. 'I went to get drugs, okay?'

French nodded slowly.

'Where was your mum when you went in?' Garrow asked.

'Her bedroom door was shut,' Steve explained. 'I assumed she was in bed watching telly or something.'

'She didn't hear you come in?' French asked.

'No.'

'And you didn't go and say hello?' Garrow enquired.

'No.'

French raised an eyebrow. 'Did your mum know that you were keeping drugs in the home?'

'I don't know,' Steve muttered in an annoyed tone.

Garrow reached over to a folder and pulled out a document. 'For the purposes of the tape, I'm showing the suspect Item Reference 325G.' He then turned the document so that Steve could see it. 'This is part of your medical records which we've had sent over from your doctor's surgery. I see that you've been to rehab in an attempt to come off heroin.'

Steve glared at him. 'So what?'

'Any idea how many times you've been to a detox centre or rehab to come off drugs in recent years, Steve?' French asked calmly.

'I dunno.'

'Seven times,' French explained. 'The last one of these was a private rehab near Chester three months ago which your mother paid for. Is that correct?'

Steve rubbed his nose nervously. 'Yeah.'

Garrow pointed to the image on the screen. 'What did your mum think about you taking drugs again.'

'She didn't know,' Steve replied. He looked ashamed.

'Oh, right, she didn't know,' Garrow said. 'So, when you went back into the house on Friday evening to get your drugs, your mum wasn't in bed was she?'

'Yeah, she was.'

'And she wanted to know why you were going up to your bedroom,' Garrow suggested.

'In fact, she knew exactly what you were up to,' French said. 'You'd been doing this for nearly a decade.'

'Did your mum try and stop you getting the drugs you'd hidden upstairs, Steve?' Garrow asked.

'No,' Steve whispered, but he was starting to look emotional.

French looked over at him. 'She wouldn't let you upstairs. And maybe you got into a row. And you had a fight.'

'No,' Steve murmured as he put his head in his hands.

'In the heat of the moment you grabbed a knife and swung it,' French said. 'And it cut her.'

'That's not what happened,' Steve said, his face now in his hands.

'She was getting in the way of you getting your drugs and you just lost it,' French said. 'Come on, Steve. Just tell us the truth.'

Steve started to sob. 'No, that's not what happened.' Then he started to shake.

Roberts looked over. 'I think my client could do with a break.'

French nodded as he closed the lid of his laptop. 'Okay. We're back in half an hour, please.'

## Chapter 45

As they drove along the coastal road, Georgie could see that Llandudno was now only a couple of miles away. She buzzed down the window. The battering wind brought goosebumps to the skin of her arms. She could hear the faintest sound of waves breaking, like a distant shattering of glass, swept in with the sharp breeze and dissipating into the air.

Looking out at the landscape to their right, she saw that the mist was lifting to reveal low hills rising from the shoreline. To their left, the ground sloped up toward gently rolling hills stretching away above them to the east. The sea stretched out with a smooth, colourless luminosity, so that it was difficult to spot where the sea ended and the sky began. It appeared as if they had walked through a gate between worlds.

Moving her hands, which were still tied together, she buzzed the window up again. She wondered if anyone had heard her conversation with Ben in the underground car park on the mobile phone. She had dialled 999 and 55, so the emergency operator should have been alerted to the fact that she was in too much danger to speak. And she knew that she had mentioned they were going to Llandudno to 'visit' Ben's father. Although she prayed that there would be a police ambush waiting in Llandudno to rescue her and Arlo, part of her was incredibly worried about the danger of that.

There was also part of her that didn't want Ben to die in a hail of bullets. She knew that he was a murderer and a corrupt police officer. In fact, she didn't know the extent of the crimes he had committed while he had been an officer. However, he had also been subjected to the most hideous trauma in his life. Watching his mother being killed in front of him as a boy. And then being sexually abused while in care. The emotional and psychological scars of that would damage someone for life.

As she pondered her feelings, Georgie also wondered if she was developing some kind of 'Stockholm Syndrome.' She had learned about it on a CID course she had attended. It was a psychological condition where an emotional bond developed between a hostage and their captor. The increasingly close contact between them meant that a connection formed. This, combined with the fear and terror of the law enforcement trying to rescue them, meant that the hostages started to see their kidnappers as the victims. If she remembered correctly, the theory had originated during a bank robbery in Stockholm in the 1970s where the hostages had defended their captors and refused to testify against them after they were released.

'We need another car,' Ben said, breaking her train of thought.

His comment made her feel uneasy. Taking another car meant possible interaction with members of the public. And if Ben was using his gun, there was always a possibility that something would go wrong. She had suspected that they were going to have to switch cars after a while. The patrol car that had spotted them at the petrol station would have seen the licence plate and make and model of the BMW. That would make them a sitting target once they drove into Llandudno.

Up ahead, there was a large sign – *Grosvenors Farm Shop 1 mile.*

As they approached the turning, Ben indicated and they pulled off the road. A small track led down to three neat, single-storey wooden buildings. There were various adverts outside for *BBQ packs, steaks, free range eggs* and *organic veg.*

To the right of the shop, there was a car park where about half a dozen or so cars were parked up.

Georgie could feel her heart starting to quicken as they stopped.

'Why are we stopping?' Arlo asked as he took out his AirPods.

Ben looked at him. 'As part of my operation, I need to switch cars. I don't want the bad guys to track us. Does that make sense?'

Arlo nodded but Georgie could see that he was confused.

'Right, out we get,' Ben said.

Georgie held up her hands. 'Are you going to take this off?'

'No,' Ben said as he opened the driver's door.

Georgie opened the passenger door, stepped out and then used her body to close the door.

Suddenly the air was filled with the sound of banging dance music.

As they looked up, a new white convertible Mercedes C300 pulled into the car park, music blaring. A middle-aged man in a baseball cap and Ray Ban sunglasses was driving.

'Can we have that car?'' Arlo asked.

Ben smiled. 'I don't see why not. I'll go and have a chat, shall I?'

Georgie watched as Ben strode over to the man in the car.

She glanced over at Arlo, who was keeping his distance from her. 'Arlo, I'm not what your dad says I am. You do know that? I'm a police officer,' she said under her breath.

'I'm not talking to you,' Arlo said with a frown.

Ben approached the man in the Mercedes. 'Nice car.'

'Thanks,' the man replied with a quizzical look.

'Are you English?' Ben asked.

'Yes.'

'Even better,' Ben said. 'I'm afraid I'm a police officer and I'm going to have to commandeer this car from you.'

'Yeah, nice try, mate,' the man said, opening the car door and looking belligerent.

Ben opened his jacket to reveal the Glock 17 sitting in his waistband.

'Give me the keys right now,' Ben growled.

The man looked terrified, nodded and handed the keys to Ben.

'Start walking over there,' Ben said, 'and don't look back until we're gone.'

The man turned nervously and began to walk across the car park towards the shop.

Ben looked at Arlo. 'Ever been in a convertible before, mate?'

'No,' Arlo admitted.

Ben gestured for Arlo to get into the back. 'Well now's your chance, eh?'

Arlo got into the back with an excited smile.

Georgie opened the passenger door and eased herself into the seat slowly as she was unable to use her hands.

Starting the engine, Ben revved the turbocharged engine. Then he glanced over at Georgie with a curious expression. 'Don't worry. This will all be over soon.'

They pulled away at speed sending a cloud of dust from the track into the air.

## Chapter 46

R uth and Nick were standing outside on a viewing area beside the bell tower at the top of the Church of the Holy Trinity on Trinity Square, Llandudno. It gave them a clear view over the square and the entrance to the Carden Residential Care Home.

To their right were two trained marksmen from SCO19 who had designated this spot as the optimum place to take a shot at Ben if anything went wrong with his arrest.

Ruth ended the call she had made to the Chief Constable of North Wales Police and then looked at Nick and the two SCO19 officers. 'Right. I've spoken to the Chief Constable. Given the fact that Ben Stewart is armed and has already used his firearm, and the fact that a police officer and young boy's lives are in serious danger, the use of lethal force is permitted.'

'Understood, ma'am,' the younger of the SCO19 officers said.

Nick took a call on his mobile phone and moved away.

The older SCO19 officer looked at Ruth and pointed

down into the square. 'A traffic unit has been deployed with a stinger at that point in the road. If the suspect tries to escape, the tyres will burst and the target vehicle will slow rapidly. And if the suspect uses or threatens to use his firearm, we will be able to get away a clean headshot from up here.'

'Thanks,' Ruth said feeling the muscles in her chest tighten with anxiety.

Nick approached holding his notebook and gestured to his phone. 'We've had a report of a white convertible Mercedes C300 being taken at gunpoint at Grosvenors Farm Shop which is four miles east of here. Descriptions match Stewart, Georgie and Arlo.' Nick ripped a page from his notebook. 'Here's the reg.'

'Thanks,' Ruth said, feeling relieved that the information had been relayed so quickly. 'Sounds like we've got that intel just in time.' She clicked her Tetra radio. 'All units, this is three six, over.'

'Three six, this is Alpha One, receiving, over,' said the voice of the helicopter pilot.

'Three six, this is Bravo Seven, over,' said the chief firearms officer who was based inside the care home.

'All units, we have a new target vehicle. Repeat, suspect is in new target vehicle,' Ruth said. 'It's a white convertible Mercedes C300. Registration Lima Foxtrot One Nine, Oscar Lima Yankee, over.'

'Three six, new target vehicle received, over. According to our intel, the ETA of target vehicle is imminent. Standby.'

Ruth took a deep breath as she looked down into the square with a growing sense of dread. She knew that Ben Stewart, Georgie and Arlo would be arriving there any minute now.

## Chapter 47

G arrow and French walked down the stairs as they
headed back to start to interview Steve Morgan
again. Having heard what Steve had to say for himself,
Garrow was now convinced that he was guilty of
murdering his mother Lynne. He had the three vital
elements in any murder enquiry – motive, means and
opportunity.

Steve had returned home to pick up the drugs he had
hidden in his bedroom. When Lynne tried to stop him and
confronted him, Steve had lashed out, slicing her throat,
before fleeing the scene. Garrow was all too aware of the
incredibly volatile relationship between addicts and those
they were close to, especially family members. He also
knew that anyone getting between an addict and their drug
of choice was putting themselves in great danger. Garrow
assumed that Lucy had dropped in at the very time of the
attack. The scratches on her neck might well have been
caused by a fight with her brother. Lucy clearly tried to
help her mother as she lay dying, which is why she was

covered in her blood. Steve then knocked Lucy unconscious before fleeing the scene.

'Steve will have to undergo a full body examination,'
French said, breaking Garrow's train of thought as they
proceeded past the reception area of Llancastell nick and
then on to the interview rooms.

'To see if he has scratch marks?' Garrow asked, as that
is what he assumed French was talking about.

'Lynne had skin under her fingernails,' French said.
'Whoever attacked her has the marks to prove it.'

'You mean Lucy,' Garrow said. He knew what French
was getting at as he was less convinced of Steve's guilt.

'I'm just going on the evidence Jim,' French said
frostily.

## Chapter 48

Ben, Georgie and Arlo approached Llandudno from the east on the Colwyn Road. The salty sea air blew and blustered around Georgie's face. She squinted up at the bright sunshine and wished she had a pair of sunglasses. Then it struck her that this was the least of her problems as they might be heading into a gun battle in about five minutes.

Georgie could see the Great Orme – or *Y Gogarth* in Welsh - looming up in the distance. It was a giant limestone headland that rose up nearly 700ft and whose name derived from the Old Norse word for sea serpent. It had been assumed it was given this name by the Vikings as it resembled an enormous sleeping creature as they arrived on the North Wales shoreline.

Beyond the dry stone wall that bordered the road to their left was a swathe of fields. And beyond them, the Irish Sea. There was nothing to the north of Llandudno until the Isle of Man which was over 2oo miles away.

A few minutes later, they arrived in the town of Llandudno and began to weave their way through the town centre to wherever Ben's father lived. He hadn't said any more about where they were going and she knew he wasn't going to.

They turned into Trinity Square very slowly. Ben was clearly taking no chances as he glanced around nervously.

Georgie couldn't help but look around too. She had done her best to alert her colleagues to the fact that they were going to visit Ben's father in Llandudno. However, she had no idea whether that information had got through.

Pulling the car into a space, Georgie looked out and saw that they were only twenty or thirty yards away from a care home in a large Georgian building. She assumed that's where they were going.

They sat in the car for a few seconds in silence.

'What are we doing here?' Arlo asked.

Georgie saw an elderly woman walking past them. She was using a stick to walk and carrying a bag of shopping in her other hand.

'I'm taking you to see your taid, mate,' Ben explained as he pointed up to the building.

'Okay,' Arlo said.

Ben looked around again, presumably to check the coast was clear and then said, 'Right, let's go shall we?' He opened the driver's door.

As Georgie unclipped her seatbelt, she saw that the old woman had stopped at the three large stone steps that led up to the double doors of the care home which were open. She was having an animated conversation with someone inside. She got to the top of steps and started to shout angrily. A few passers-by looked over to see what the fuss was about.

Ben watched what was going on and sat back in the driver's seat again with a frown. 'What the hell's that all about?' he said under his breath.

The old woman was waving her walking stick at someone inside the building and shouting, 'What are you doing? I need to come in to see her!'

Georgie could see that something wasn't quite right. Unfortunately, so could Ben.

'Just wait there, mate,' Ben said cautiously to Arlo.

Suddenly the old woman lost her footing on the top step and fell backwards down the steps and onto the pavement.

'Jesus,' Georgie gasped quietly. 'She's not moving.'

Ben went as if he was going to get out of the car and then stopped again.

A uniformed police officer in high vis ran out of the care home and went down the steps to help the old woman.

'Fuck!' Ben growled as he closed the car door. 'They know we're coming. Put your seatbelt on, mate.'

Slamming the car into reverse, Ben pulled out into the road and reversed back up the road at high speed.

Ben's eyes narrowed as he spun the steering wheel. 'How the hell did they know we were coming?'

Georgie shrugged, trying to hide her deep disappointment. They had been so close to getting rescued.

Stamping down on the accelerator, Ben swung the car forward out of Trinity Square.

The engine roared as Ben sped down the wrong side of the one-way system, weaving past the cars coming the other way.

Within two minutes, they were hammering along the seafront as they left Llandudno. If there were any police units trying to follow them, Ben had managed to lose them.

## Chapter 49

French and Garrow were now back in CID chasing up other leads and evidence. They had continued their interview with Steve Morgan for about fifteen minutes but hadn't learned anything more. Steve was adamant that he hadn't encountered his mother when he returned home on Friday night and had nothing to do with her murder. However, he had refused to submit to a full medical examination unless they were going to arrest or charge him. French and Garrow wanted to see if Steve had any scratches on his body that would indicate he had fought with Lynne. The fact that he had refused to be examined was definitely suspicious.

'Sarge,' Garrow said, looking over from his desk. 'Forensics have confirmed that the blood on Lucy's hands and clothing definitely matches that of her mother.'

French nodded. 'Which is no big surprise.'

Garrow looked at French. 'You think she did it?'

French took a few seconds to respond. 'If I'm going on the evidence, then yes. If I'm going on instinct, then I think Steve Morgan is our prime suspect.'

Garrow went back to the evidence that was on his desk. Fishing into the cardboard box, he pulled out the monthly calendar that they had taken from Lynne's kitchen. Taking it out of the clear, plastic evidence bag, Garrow began to turn back the pages of each month to see if there was anything significant.

The previous month – March – had various appointments written down, but at first there didn't seem to be anything out of the ordinary - *Dentist, MOT, a gig in Liverpool.* On Friday 19th March, something that looked like *Ditton Hamilton* and *3pm*.

With a quick search, Garrow found that there was a firm of solicitors in Wrexham called Ditton Hamilton. That posed the question about why Lynne Morgan had gone to a solicitors firm in Wrexham a few weeks before her murder. It might be unconnected, but it was a lead worth pursuing for the sake of a phone call.

Picking up the phone, Garrow called the firm's number.

'Hello, Ditton Hamilton Solicitors. How can I help?' asked a friendly but professional sounding woman.

'Hi there,' Garrow replied. 'This is DC Garrow from CID in Llancastell. I'm doing some checking into a meeting that a Lynne Morgan had with someone from your firm at 3pm on Friday 19th March. Could you confirm that the meeting took place and who it was with?'

'If you give me a minute,' the woman said politely, 'I'll just check our system.' There was a beat. 'That's right. Mrs Morgan came in to meet one of our senior partners, Mr Speight.'

'Right,' Garrow said. 'Could you tell me the nature of their meeting please?'

'I'm afraid you would have to speak to Mr Speight directly,' the woman said. 'It wouldn't be information that we could give you over the phone anyway, but if you'd like to come to our offices, I'm sure that Mr Speight would be more than willing to assist you with anything that you might need to know.'

'Okay, thank you for your help,' Garrow said.

## Chapter 50

Georgie, Ben and Arlo were now heading inland but Georgie had no idea where they were going. She wondered if Ben had any kind of plan either, or if he was just driving aimlessly. He had hardly said a word since they left Llandudno but was clearly angry that he hadn't been able to take his revenge on his father.

As they came over the brow of a hill, Georgie could hear something.

A deep mechanical drone.

At first, she assumed it was a tractor ploughing a nearby field but the drone got louder, deeper and more rhythmic. The wind also seemed to pick up inside the car, whipping her hair around her face.

*What the hell is going on?*

Georgie glanced up and saw that a black and yellow police helicopter was hovering about three hundred feet above them.

*Great! They've spotted us,* she thought.

Ben looked up and spotted it too.

'This is the North Wales Police. Pull your vehicle over

to the side of the road,' boomed a voice from the helicopter's sky shout public address system.

Ben snorted. 'No fucking way.'

Arlo leaned forward and shouted against the noise, 'Dad? What's going on?'

Ben didn't answer him. Maybe he had run out of lies that he was willing to tell his son.

Georgie turned and looked at him. 'It's all right. We're going to be all right,' she reassured him.

'This is the North Wales Police. Pull your vehicle over to the side of the road and stop,' the voice boomed again.

Georgie glanced up again and saw the helicopter fly overhead and then circle back. She took a deep breath and yelled, 'What are we going to do now, Ben?'

Ben glared over at her. 'Shut up. I'm trying to think.' He was clearly out of ideas. And that made him more dangerous.

They turned onto the main road south. Stamping on the accelerator, the turbocharged Mercedes engine roared as they hit 80 mph.

Georgie had a nervous knot in her stomach. How were they going to get out of this?

Almost out of nowhere, a very tight right-hand turn into a side road appeared.

Without braking, Ben turned the steering wheel sharply.

The back tyres screeched and he completely lost the back end of the Mercedes. Spinning the steering wheel back, he managed to regain control.

'I thought we were going to crash, Dad,' Arlo shouted from the back.

Ben blew out his cheeks. 'Me too, mate.'

As they raced downhill, Ben peered up into the sky. 'Where are you, you bastards?'

Arlo was looking in the other direction. 'I can't see them. I think you lost them, Dad. Well done.'

Suddenly a black shadow came low across the sky in front of them.

'For fuck's sake,' Ben growled in frustration.

Georgie knew the helicopter would have radioed their location. It wouldn't be long before there were police cars on their tail and probably roadblocks. The thought of some terrible armed standoff, with Arlo in the middle of it, made her feel sick.

The helicopter hovered above them before flying ahead and circling back again.

Georgie glared over at Ben. 'We're never going to get away from them. It's over. Just stop the bloody car will you?' She couldn't help herself. Ben had put Arlo and her through enough already.

Ben glanced back at Arlo. 'Don't worry, mate. I'll get us out of this.'

Spinning the steering wheel violently left, Georgie held her breath as Ben drove towards what looked like a narrow dirt track.

*We're not going to make it!*

Closing her eyes for a second, Georgie waited for the Mercedes to smash into the stone walls.

Instead, the car bounced and jolted along the pot holes on the track.

The track appeared to lead down to a thick area of forest that seemed to stretch for miles.

The helicopter had managed to catch them up again but Georgie could see that they would soon be under the cover of the towering pine trees.

As the track started to weave its way through the forest, the sky disappeared behind the huge canopy of trees above.

Ben slowed a little.

There was a right-hand turn which led downhill for about a mile.

At the bottom, Ben brought the car to a stop and turned off the ignition.

Georgie gazed up at the sky which was virtually invisible through the branches and leaves.

The sound of the helicopter had stopped.

For a moment, they all sat getting their breath back and composing themselves.

Then they opened the car doors and stepped out.

Arlo stood frozen, listening intently.

Nothing.

Ben peered up at the sky. 'I think they've gone, mate.'

## Chapter 51

It was getting dark by the time Garrow and French parked up on a side street in the middle of Wrexham and made their way towards Ditton Hamilton Solicitors. Looming over the skyline was the iconic 16th century tower of St Giles' Parish Church. At nearly 140 feet high, it formed one of the 'Seven Wonder of Wales.'

Garrow and French turned left onto the High Street, passing a clothing shop called *Chevron*. On the opposite side of the road, Garrow spotted the small solicitors office sandwiched between two bars.

'There we go,' Garrow said, pointing.

They crossed the road and entered the old-fashioned looking solicitors office. There were old black and white photos on the wall of the office from back in the 1950s. A young woman sitting behind a reception area gave them a smile. 'Can I help you?'

Garrow and French fished out their warrant cards and showed them to her. 'DC Garrow and DS French, Llancastell CID. I spoke to you on the phone earlier about Mrs Morgan,' Garrow explained.

'Oh yes, that's right,' the woman said as she picked up the receiver of a phone that was on her desk. 'Let me give Mr Speight a ring to see if he's free for you.'

'Thanks,' French said.

The young woman said something on the phone, put it down and then craned her neck to point at a nearby office. 'Yes, Mr Speight is just in there if you want to go through.'

'Thanks,' Garrow said with a kind smile.

A man in his 60s, dressed in a smart three-piece suit and generally well groomed, was sitting at his desk looking at documents.

French knocked on the open door. The man looked up. 'We're looking for Mr Speight?' French explained.

'It's Jake, please,' he said with a half laugh.

French and Garrow showed Speight their warrant cards. 'We're from Llancastell CID. We'd like to ask you a few questions about a meeting you had with Mrs Lynne Morgan back in March.'

'Friday 19th March to be precise,' Garrow clarified.

Speight stood up, closed the door and gestured to two dark leather padded chairs beside his oak desk. 'Do you want to sit down for a minute?'

'Thanks,' French said as they entered the stuffy office and sat down.

Speight gave them a quizzical look. 'Yes, I do vaguely remember meeting with Lynne Morgan, although she's not a regular client of ours. But I knew her late husband Mark from the Rotary Club ... So, how can I help?'

Garrow looked at him. 'Can you tell us the nature of that meeting?'

'I'm afraid not.' Speight pulled a serious face. 'That falls under solicitor-client privilege.'

French leaned forward. 'Unfortunately, Lynne Morgan was murdered on Friday night. And that means you're going to have to waive that privilege as we're running a murder investigation.'

'Oh, that's terrible news,' Speight mumbled in shock under his breath. 'How awful … I …'

They waited for a few seconds for Speight to compose himself.

Garrow looked over at him. 'We are going to need you to tell us why Lynne Morgan came in for a meeting.'

Speight thought for a few seconds.

'I don't need to remind you that under the Freedom of Information Act, you do need to divulge the nature of your meeting if we believe that it pertains to a criminal act such as murder,' French explained.

'Of course, of course,' Speight bumbled, putting up his hand. 'I know that Mrs Morgan came in to talk to us about making changes to her will. But I have to admit that I cannot remember the exact details of those changes.'

Garrow and French shared a look. It sounded like they might have found something significant in their investigation – or at least something that needed further examination. And it certainly wasn't the first time that Garrow had come across a crime connected to a person's will and disputes about its contents.

'How long would it take you to dig out the details of the changes Lynne Morgan wanted to make?' Garrow asked.

Speight furrowed his brow. 'I passed it onto one of the paralegals to do the changes so I would need to get it back from them. But I could have something for you by tomorrow morning?'

French nodded. 'That would be great.'

Speight looked at them. 'Of course, if you needed that information quicker than that, you could ask her daughter.

Although I'm sure she's terribly upset by her mother's death?'

French's eyes widened. 'Her daughter?'

'Yes. Amy I think her name was,' Speight replied. 'I can check.'

'Lucy?' Garrow suggested, starting to feel uneasy.

'Lucy, that's it,' Speight nodded. 'I think she came along as a bit of moral support for her mother.'

## Chapter 52

Georgie, Ben and Arlo had now been walking through the trees for about twenty minutes. Although Georgie wasn't entirely sure where they were, if she was to guess then she thought they were in Boldondeb Woods, which was a nature reserve close to Conwy. She could see the mixture of coniferous trees that loomed over them and wondered what was going to happen next.

As they plodded on in silence, the crunch of the leaves beneath their feet and the occasional snap of a twig seemed to echo around the forest. It was getting dark and the temperature had dropped significantly. She didn't fancy spending the night outside. It might be spring but the nights were still cold and she didn't have a coat.

She looked ahead and saw the footpath they had taken was winding down to a steep dip. At its bottom, thick mist had started to settle which seemed to turn the trees into ominous shadows.

'Dad,' Arlo said. 'Are we lost?'

Ben shook his head. 'No, mate. Trust me. Our secret destination is just up here.'

Georgie let out an audible huff. She couldn't help herself.

As they descended into the mist, the forest seemed to grow denser, and the mist thicker. The trees were twisted and gnarled, their branches reaching out like skeletal fingers.

Suddenly, Ben stopped in his tracks, causing Arlo and Georgie to bump into him.

'What's wrong?' Arlo asked.

Ben crouched, putting his fingers to his lips to indicate that they needed to be quiet.

There was the noise of rustling over to their right.

Squinting through the trees and mist, Georgie could see an old man striding along an adjacent path with his black Labrador. He gave a shrill whistle to get the dog's attention before marching away into the distance.

There was a growing noise which seemed to be coming from above the trees. At first, Georgie thought it was the sound of distant thunder. But as the familiar mechanical roar got closer, and the tree tops started to shake and vibrate, she knew that the police helicopter was back.

'Shit,' Ben muttered under his breath.

'Is that the helicopter?' Arlo asked.

'Yes, mate,' Ben replied.

'Are they looking for us?'

'Yes.'

'Why?'

'It's hard to explain,' Ben said. 'It's to do with my job.'

Suddenly, a huge beam of light burst through the trees. Georgie knew that the National Police Air Service - NPAS - used Nitesun, more commonly known as Nightsun, high-intensity searchlights to illuminate large areas.

Georgie thought it was comforting to know that they were still out there looking for her.

Arlo frowned as they all turned to look at the light which was no more than fifty yards away. 'Is it because you're undercover?'

'Yes, that's right.'

Ben pointed to another footpath that led away from where the searchlight was shining.

'Come on,' he said urgently. 'We need to keep going.'

Striding on, they cut through the undergrowth.

Georgie still had her hands tied as she used them to brush away some low lying branches and leaves. It was hard to keep her balance.

Glancing back, she spotted that the searchlight was going in the opposite direction from where they were walking. Ben looked at her with a smug expression.

*Oh just fuck off,* she thought.

'There's a few things that I need to tell you,' Ben said as they marched on. 'You see Arlo, when you grow up you need to remember to stand up against things that you don't think are right. Even if you're scared. If someone is doing something wrong, you need to do or say something about it. Does that make sense, mate?'

Arlo nodded.

Georgie didn't know exactly what Ben was talking about but she wondered if he was referring to his childhood.

Ten minutes later, they got to the top of a hill where the trees had started to thin out.

Ben stopped and looked back at them. 'Bingo,' he said as he gestured to something in the distance.

Georgie was out of breath by the time she got to where he was standing. She peered out at what he was looking at.

About two hundred yards away, the trees had given way to sweeping fields.

And directly in front of them was a large white farmhouse.

There was some washing on the line outside.

Over to the right, there was a new-looking tractor and some other agricultural equipment. Next to that, a Land Rover Discovery.

Ben shrugged. 'I guess we'd better go and say hello.'

Taking some wire cutters from his jacket, Ben turned to Georgie. 'Come here.'

He cut the plastic tie from around her wrist. It felt like such a relief.

A few seconds later, Ben knocked on the large, black wooden door to the farmhouse. He glanced down at Arlo. 'Whatever I say, mate, just play along, okay?'

'Are we going undercover?' Arlo asked, his eyes widening with excitement.

'That's exactly what we're doing,' Ben nodded.

'What about her?' Arlo said, pointing at Georgie.

'She's going to play along too, aren't you?' Ben said in a sinister tone.

'Yes,' Georgie replied. She didn't want whoever lived in the farmhouse to get dragged into anything that might put them in danger.

A moment later, the door opened and a short woman in her 30s looked at them quizzically.

'Hello?' she said.

'Hi,' Ben said with a self-effacing smile. 'I'm really sorry to bother you like this. It's just that we've been in a bit of an accident down there.' He pointed back down into the forest. 'I think the brakes failed on our car and we went off the road and into a tree. There's no reception for my phone.'

'Oh dear,' the woman said, looking concerned. 'Are you all okay?'

'Yes,' Ben replied. 'I wondered if you had a phone we could use?'

'Come in, come in,' the woman said. 'Sorry, I'm Tegan.'

They came into a huge hallway that had a stone floor, a thin rug, and an old grandfather clock to one side.

'Come and sit down in the kitchen,' Tegan said. 'You poor things. That sounds very scary.'

'Thank you,' Georgie said. 'It was a bit. I'm Georgie. This is Ben and this is Arlo.'

'Are you okay, Arlo?' Tegan asked as she smiled down at him.

'Yes,' Arlo said quietly as he nodded his head.

'Arlo. That was my father's name,' Tegan said brightly. 'It means 'hill' in Welsh. Did you know that?'

Arlo shook his head but didn't say anything.

Tegan led them into a large farmhouse kitchen. Two golden-coloured Labradors lay on the stone floor over by an Aga. They looked up as they came in but didn't seem particularly interested in their arrival.

The ceiling was low with dark wooden beams. A Welsh dresser with various bits of china sat over to the right. At the centre of the room was a long oak table with mismatched chairs on one side and a wooden pew on the other.

A small boy with dark hair was sitting at the far end of the table writing in an exercise book. He looked up.

'Oh, this is my son, Rhys,' Tegan said. 'These poor people had a crash in their car down in the woods.'

'Hi Rhys,' Ben said in a friendly tone. 'I'm Ben, this is Georgie and Arlo.'

'Rhys is just finishing up his homework before tea,' Tegan explained. 'How old are you, Arlo?'

'I'm nine,' Arlo replied.

'Oh, the same age as Rhys then,' Tegan laughed. 'Isn't that funny?' Then she looked over at Ben and Georgie. 'Sit down, please. I'll put the kettle on and make you a cup of tea. I think I've got some Bara Brith somewhere.'

'It's fine, really,' Georgie said, trying to hide her nerves. 'If we can use your phone, then we can get out of your hair. We don't want you to go to any trouble.'

'Nonsense,' Tegan said and pointed to the chairs. 'Please sit down. You're probably all in a bit of shock. Tea and cake will do the trick. I won't take no for an answer.'

'That's very kind of you,' Ben said. 'Shall we sit down, darling?'

Georgie bristled but played along. 'Okay. Tea does sound good actually.'

At that moment, the back door opened and a giant of a man, scruffy blond hair and beard, filthy blue overalls and wellies came in.

The whole atmosphere inside the house changed.

Georgie could see the impact his appearance had on both Tegan and Rhys. They both looked instantly scared.

The man looked at them and then over at Tegan.

'These poor people have been in a car accident down in the forest,' Tegan explained nervously.

'Oh aye,' the man said, puffing out his chest. 'How d'you manage that then?'

'I think the brakes went,' Ben replied. 'We went into a tree.'

'Sounds nasty,' the man said with a humourless expression. 'You were lucky to get out all right.'

'Yes, we were,' Georgie agreed. 'Very lucky.'

'This is my husband, Andy,' Tegan explained with a forced smile.

'We wanted to use your phone as we can't seem to get a signal anywhere,' Ben explained.

Andy shook his head. 'Yeah, you won't get a bloody signal anywhere round here.' He then went over to a wooden chair, sat down and clicked his fingers. Tegan scuttled over and began to pull off his wellies.

*Bloody cheek,* Georgie thought. *Who are you clicking your fingers at?*

Andy looked at his watch. 'You won't get anyone out to tow you now.'

'Won't we?' Ben asked with a frown.

'No chance.' Andy shook his head and then looked outside. 'And it's dark. That'll make it ten times harder to get down there.'

Ben looked at Georgie. What the hell were they going to do now?

Tegan looked at Andy. 'They could stay in the annexe?'

'Oh no,' Georgie said. 'We couldn't intrude like that.'

Andy got up from the chair, looked at Tegan and nodded. 'Aye, I suppose so. We rent it out in the summer. It's not much, but there's two bedrooms, a bathroom and it's clean.'

'We'd insist on paying you, of course,' Ben said.

'I won't take a penny from you.' Andy shook his head sternly. 'And I'll drive down with you tomorrow and tow you over to Jack's garage. He'll be able to look at your brakes and get you on your way.'

'That's incredibly kind of you,' Georgie said, feeling very uncomfortable about staying the night at the farm. She didn't know what Ben had planned but she didn't want anyone innocent to get hurt.

Tegan gave them a nervous smile. 'That's settled then. And we've got more than enough food here for you tonight.' She looked at Arlo. 'Chicken hot pot and mashed potato all right for you, Arlo?'

Arlo nodded politely.

Andy went over to where Rhys was sitting quietly and clicked his fingers at him. 'Rhys, get these people clean towels and take them over to the annexe,' he said sternly.

Rhys pointed anxiously to his exercise book. 'I've just got my English homework to finish off.'

From out of nowhere, Andy smacked his hand across the back of Rhys' head. It made a cracking sound.

Georgie winced. *Jesus, what the …*

'Do as you're told, lad,' Andy snarled.

Rhys nodded as he got up slowly from the table, his head bowed in terror. Georgie could see there were tears in his eyes.

'Don't let me catch you crying neither,' Andy snapped. 'Or you know what'll happen.'

Georgie could see the fury in Ben's eyes as his hand went to the handgun that was hidden in his waistband.

*Oh God, he's going to shoot him.*

Georgie knew she had to do something to lessen the tension. She got to her feet. 'It's all right. We can take the towels when we go over there.'

As she glanced over at Ben, she could see that he had now retrieved the handgun and was holding it under the table.

'Nonsense,' Andy said, shaking his head and pointing to Rhys. 'That's the problem with kids these days. They're too bloody soft.' Then Andy looked at Ben, whose face was full of thunder. 'Not like when we were young, eh? As I always say, it never did me any harm.'

Ben looked at him but didn't reply.

Georgie held her breath. It seemed that any second Ben was going to pull the gun from under the table and shoot him.

Andy glanced at Tegan. 'Right, I'm going to get washed up before tea.'

Georgie looked over at Ben who was visibly shaking.

Andy turned and left.

Ben slowly moved the gun under the table and back under his jacket.

Georgie let out her breath slowly.

Andy didn't know how close he'd just come to getting shot dead in that second. However, she didn't know how Ben was going to react if Andy lashed out again.

## Chapter 53

It was 8pm by the time Garrow and French entered the forensic wing of Llancastell nick and headed for the lab to their right. It was brightly illuminated with several rows of forensic equipment – microscopes, fume hoods, chromatographs and spectrometers – as well as vials and test tubes of brightly coloured liquids.

A lab technician in a full forensic suit, mask, and gloves approached them at the doorway. 'Can I help?' he asked.

'DS French and DC Garrow,' French explained. 'We've just had a call that you'd found something in the DNA sample you took in the Lynne Morgan investigation?'

'Oh, yes, that's correct,' the lab technician nodded as he handed them forensic gloves and masks to put on. 'I'll take you over.'

They followed him over to the chief lab technician, Christopher Holroyd. Garrow had met Holroyd on several occasions. Now in his 60s, Holroyd seemed very intelligent but a little eccentric. But in Garrow's experience that was true of most people who worked in police forensics.

'DS French and DC Garrow,' Holroyd said from

behind his dark blue mask. He was holding a test tube of orange liquid and looking at a computer screen with a brightly coloured graph on it.

'What have you got for us, Chris?' French asked.

'We've got the trace DNA that we managed to take from the skin we found under your victim's nails,' Christopher explained. 'After several attempts, we've now managed to get a DNA profile that we can use. So, I've got some good news and some bad news.'

Garrow exchanged a quizzical look with French.

'Okay,' French said sounding encouraged. 'Let's have the bad news first please.'

Holroyd turned and pointed to a large computer screen that showed the image of the DNA profile. 'So, this is the DNA profile of the sample we obtained from the skin under her nails. It's virtually complete.'

'That's good isn't it?' French asked.

'Not really.'

French couldn't help but look a little confused.

'We ran the DNA through the national database,' Holroyd explained, 'but I'm afraid we didn't get a hit.'

Garrow knew that it was disappointing news. Whoever attacked Lynne had never had their DNA taken before.

'We haven't managed to get a DNA profile from the vaginal swab or the semen from your victim yet, but we should be able to do that in the next few hours,' Holroyd explained. 'So, at the moment we can't confirm that the person whom your victim had sex with is the same person who she scratched when she was being attacked.'

'But you think it's likely?' French asked.

'I suppose so,' Holroyd replied. 'I'd like to wait for the test results but I'd suggest it was highly likely.'

'Okay. You did say that there was some good news,'

French said dryly. So far, Holroyd had only made things more complicated and unclear.

'The DNA we took from the skin sample doesn't match that of Lucy Morgan either,' Holroyd stated.

Garrow felt incredibly relieved but told himself to remain completely professional. 'Which means that whoever Lynne Morgan was fighting with, it wasn't her daughter.'

French looked at him. 'Steve Morgan?' he suggested.

Holroyd shook his head. 'No. It's not Steve Morgan either.'

*What?*

'You're sure about that?' French asked.

'Yes. Let me show you.' Holroyd turned and clicked the keyboard. A DNA profile came up onto the screen. 'This is Lynne Morgan's DNA profile. Even though we haven't processed Steve Morgan's DNA profile from the database yet, I can see that the person whose skin was under your victim's nails wasn't related to her. The DNA isn't a familial match.'

Garrow looked over at French. Even though it wasn't conclusive, it looked highly unlikely that Lucy or Steve were involved in their mother's murder.

It also looked likely that whoever Lynne had had sex with, had then attacked and killed her. And that meant they had no prime suspect and were back to square one.

## Chapter 54

'Here you go,' Lucy said as she put a cup of tea down in front of Garrow.

'Thanks,' he said. He sipped it and immediately recognised the taste of his favourite black tea. 'Lapsang Souchong.'

Lucy looked surprised. 'You know your tea?'

'Not really,' Garrow admitted. 'It's my father's favourite tea.'

'Apparently the flavour comes from the leaves being smoke-dried over a pinewood fire,' Lucy explained.

'You know what,' Garrow said, pulling a face. 'I usually drink Yorkshire tea at home.'

Lucy smiled. 'Yorkshire is good too.'

They looked at each other and smiled.

Garrow had arrived at Lucy's home five minutes earlier. Even though it was unprofessional, he thought she needed to know that she hadn't been responsible for her mother's death. Of course, he should have waited until all the evidence had been collated and they had caught Lynne Morgan's real killer. But Garrow couldn't bear to think of

Lucy sitting at home with that overwhelming guilt. It seemed to him that it was cruel not to tell her what they knew.

Garrow looked around at her kitchen. It was tastefully decorated. There were open wooden shelves where a couple of dark blue Le Creuset cooking pots stood. At the other end, a few containers with fresh herbs – coriander, basil and mint.

'You must like cooking?' Garrow said, gesturing to the herbs.

'I love cooking,' Lucy said, and then frowned. 'In fact, I can even remember a recipe for a vegetable curry that I like to cook. Isn't that strange?'

She looked forlorn.

Silence.

Garrow looked at her. 'I'm not really meant to be here.'

'Do you mean on your own?' she asked.

'Yes. I suppose technically I'm now 'off duty',' Garrow said. 'I came here to tell you something. I shouldn't really but I had to tell you. We did some DNA tests and we can rule you out of being involved in your mother's death.'

Lucy's eyes widened. 'What?' she gasped. 'I don't understand.'

'I'm not sure that I should explain it,' he said.

Lucy gave him a pleading look. 'Please. I need to know everything so I can start to put the pieces together of what happened.'

'Your mother fought and scratched whoever killed her,' Garrow explained. 'And so there was skin under her fingernails.'

Lucy looked horrified.

'We tested that skin, got a DNA sample and it's not yours or your brother's,' Garrow said.

He could see that Lucy was fighting back the tears. 'Thank you,' she whispered, and then shook her head. 'That's such a relief. I've been sitting here torturing myself.'

'That's why I wanted to tell you.'

'Do you know who did … kill her?'

'Sorry, not yet.'

Lucy furrowed her brow. 'But what about all the blood? I don't understand.'

Garrow leaned forward over the table. 'Do you want me to tell you what I think happened?'

'Of course,' she sighed and wiped the tears from her face. 'Sorry …'

'When you arrived on Friday night, you interrupted whoever was attacking your mother,' Garrow said very gently. 'You tried to save her, which is why you had her blood on you. The attacker hit you around the head and then left.'

There was a long silence as Lucy took this in.

'But why was I at Pontcysyllte Aqueduct?' she asked.

Garrow shrugged. 'That's the missing piece of the puzzle.'

Lucy reached over and touched his hand. 'You weren't meant to tell me any of that until you had a suspect in custody, were you?'

Garrow moved his fingers and touched the back of her hand. 'No, not really.'

'So, why did you come here?'

'I couldn't bear to think of you sitting here, thinking that you were responsible when you weren't,' Garrow admitted.

Lucy took his hand, looked at him and squeezed it. 'Thank you, Jim.'

## Chapter 55

As Georgie stirred in her sleep, she dreamed that she was standing outside a small cottage. She rang the bell and a small man with a delicate tanned face and a crop of white hair opened the door. He was dressed in Victorian clothes and told her in a firm official voice that she needed to come inside. She felt increasingly scared as the man led her up the wooden stairs and into the room at the front of the house. The small man murmured something and closed the bedroom door so that they were alone. The silence in the room was overwhelming. Glancing around she saw that he had a pair of jeans neatly folded on a wooden rocking chair.

Suddenly, the man was upon her, his hands roaming around her body and then inside her clothes. Looking again, she saw that the small man was now Ben. Grabbing her around the throat, Ben pushed her onto the four poster bed. Then he pinned her down and lay on top of her. She couldn't breathe.

Opening her eyes with a start, Georgie tried to get her

breath back. Her heart was hammering. Blowing out her cheeks, she sat up on her elbows and looked around the small single room in the farmhouse annexe. She had no idea what the time was and no way of telling.

Ben and Arlo had taken the double bedroom further down the hallway. When they'd gone to bed, Ben had made a great show of locking the front door to signal to her that there was no way of her getting out. However, once they had all gone to bed, she had checked the bedroom window but unfortunately it only opened by about six inches.

Sitting up in bed, Georgie realised that she was incredibly hungry. It made a change from being nauseous in the morning. She had heard that some pregnant women had such terrible morning sickness when they were pregnant that they ended up severely dehydrated and hospitalised. She remembered it was called hyperemesis and that Kate, Princess of Wales, had suffered from it.

The sound of a man's voice talking outside broke her train of thought.

Straining to hear, she recognised that it was Ben talking.

*Sounds like he's on the phone*, she thought.

Moving out of the bedroom very carefully, she was trying to locate where the talking was coming from.

She froze, straining to hear the conversation. It was definitely coming from outside.

Creeping slowly into the toilet at the end of the hallway, she stepped on top of the closed toilet seat and stretched up to a tiny window. Pulling down the lever very delicately, she managed to push the window open by a few inches.

As she stood perfectly still, she realised she could now hear that Ben was talking to someone on a mobile phone.

'Listen, we should be able to get to Bangor sometime this afternoon,' Ben said. 'There's a football pitch on Beach Road. It overlooks the marina. Meet us there.'

*Okay, so we're heading for Bangor*, Georgie thought wearily, wondering when all this would end.

## Chapter 56

It was 7am and Garrow had been in the canteen at Llancastell nick for half an hour. He yawned and then popped a green tea bag into his mug and went to pour hot water on it from the machine.

'Keeping you up are we Jim?' said a voice.

It was French.

'Oh right,' Garrow said with a forced smile. 'Takes me a while to get going in the mornings.'

French pointed to his mug of green tea. 'Yeah, well it will do if you drink that crap.'

Garrow rolled his eyes. He was used to French's comments about anything that Jim ate or drank that was vaguely health conscious. 'I'm guessing you're suggesting a mug of industrial strength coffee to wake me up?'

French laughed as he got himself a black Americano. 'Yeah, it wouldn't be the worst idea.'

'I'll stick to this thanks,' Garrow said. 'It's very good for you.'

They turned towards the counter to pay for their drinks.

'Holly Willoughby or Fearne Cotton?' French asked as they waved their cards over the small screen to pay contactless.

'I assume you're asking me which presenter do I think is the most talented?' Garrow said with a wry smile.

'Obviously,' French replied. 'What else would I be talking about?'

'In that case, Fearne Cotton.'

'I knew it!' French said triumphantly as they headed across the canteen towards the exit.

'What did you know?' Garrow asked, trying not to sound defensive.

'I knew you'd pick Fearne. She's all, you know, hippy dippy, well-being, tattoos, mindfulness and ...' French pointed to Garrow's mug, '... she definitely drinks green tea.'

'I'm guessing your pick is Holly Willoughby then is it?'

'Of course,' French said. 'Very funny, curvy, gorgeous, and seems like she'd be great fun down the pub.'

'Right,' Garrow said with a smile as they got to the double doors. It was true what they said. He and French really were chalk and cheese.

Two young male uniformed officers were coming in.

One of them, dark hair, beard and tall, looked at them.

'DS French?' the constable asked.

'That's right,' French replied.

'I've been trying to track you down, sir.'

'Why's that?'

'Last Friday night we were called out to a report of a prowler over in Wrexham,' he explained. 'It was about 8pm.'

'Okay,' French said, but he was clearly none the wiser.

Garrow's ears pricked up. That was close to the time of Lynne Morgan's murder, so he was intrigued.

'The call came from someone living on Primrose Way,' the constable explained. 'We went down to have a look but we couldn't see anything.'

'Where are you going with this, constable?' French asked, trying to get him to get to the point.

'The thing is, 23 Primrose Way backs onto the Mold Road, so the prowler was at the back of those houses at the same time as Lynne Morgan was murdered. I've only just made the connection sir.'

Garrow looked at French. It sounded like a significant development.

'Thank you, constable,' French said. 'Can you email all the paperwork and details over to me?'

## Chapter 57

Primrose Way was a small residential close behind the Mold Road in Wrexham. As French and Garrow parked up, it started to drizzle slightly. The floodlights and steel girders of The Racecourse Ground were visible in the distance.

Spotting where No 23 was, they then walked down to a large patch of grass at the end of the row of houses. There was a wooden fence that allowed them to look over at several back gardens.

Garrow peered at the back of the houses on Mold Road and recognised Lynne Morgan's home from the steel fence that he had climbed over when they discovered her body.

'No 23 virtually backs onto Lynne Morgan's house,' French observed with a raised eyebrow.

'Yeah,' Garrow agreed, thinking this might be the breakthrough they needed. 'Anyone prowling around the back could have climbed into her back garden.'

Then Garrow caught sight of something out of the

corner of his eye. There was something mounted up on the back of a house that by the process of elimination was No 21. At first, he thought it was a security light. However, as he squinted, he saw that it was a home security camera.

'Think we might be in luck, sarge,' Garrow said, pointing to the camera. 'Shall we go and have a word? I'm pretty sure it's next door to 23 which makes it 21.'

French looked and pulled a face. 'I'm praying that the thing actually works and was switched on Friday night.'

They wandered back the way they'd come, went to the front door marked 21 and knocked.

A few seconds later, a severe looking man in his 70s, with slicked-back hair, moustache and a brown cardigan opened the door and looked at them.

'Yes?' he asked, sounding annoyed.

French flashed his warrant card. 'DS French and DC Garrow, Llancastell CID. Do you mind if we come in for moment?'

'Why?' the man demanded.

'Just a couple of routine questions, sir,' Garrow explained politely. 'We shouldn't take up much of your time.'

'Right, well …' The man gave an audible huff, opened the front door wider and ushered them in as though they were children. 'Yes, I suppose so.'

'Thanks,' French said, shooting Garrow a look as if to say 'We've got a right one here.'

'In here, please,' the man said, sounding like a sergeant major.

They came into a large living room which was dimly lit. The shadows from a dull yellow lamp were cast across the large bookshelves. Dusty old hard-backed books lined the walls, their spines filled with names of famous battles and other types of military history. The musty smell was mixed with the odour of glue and paint.

In the centre of the room stood an impressive oak table, its surface lined with tiny plastic toy Napoleonic soldiers, arranged in perfect formation. Beside them, some small pots of paint and a few brushes were spread out clearly in preparation to paint the toy soldiers.

Everything was still, except for the slight ticking of a clock somewhere in the distance.

'I suppose this is to do with that ghastly business over there,' the man said, pointing in the direction of the houses on the Mold Road.

'That's right,' Garrow said as he pulled out his notebook and pen.

'If you're going to write down notes then my name is Commander Stephen Watkin,' he explained as he sat down in an armchair.

'Thank you, Commander,' Garrow said politely.

French looked at Watkin. 'Can you tell us where you were on Friday evening?'

'I was here, of course,' Watkin scoffed as though it was a stupid question.

'Did you see anything or anyone suspicious between 7pm and 11pm on Friday night?' Garrow enquired.

'No. I know that Trevor next door said he saw someone but I didn't,' Watkin said, shaking his head and pointing to the toy soldiers. 'This takes up most of my spare time at the moment. And I have the curtains closed, so I wouldn't have seen anything anyway.'

French frowned. 'But you do have a security camera on the rear wall of this house, don't you?'

'Too right,' Watkin said adamantly. 'I'm not from Wrexham originally. But I married a girl from Ruabon so we moved up here. I'm afraid she passed last year.'

'I'm sorry to hear that,' Garrow said quietly.

'I had to move into this house,' Watkin explained. 'They already had the security camera fixed on the wall but I find it's a bit of comfort. Especially since that bloody football club across the road has started to do well. That Brian Reynolds fellow. Hollywood actor isn't he?'

'That's right,' French said.

'Well Christ knows what he and that other fellow want with a football club up here. But there's hooligans and all sorts wandering all over the bloody place these days,' he grumbled. 'I don't feel safe anymore.'

'Do you have your camera switched on all the time?' Garrow asked.

Watkin shook his head. 'Only once it gets dark.' Then the penny dropped as Watkin frowned and looked up at them. 'You think there might be something my camera picked up on Friday night, don't you?'

'As you said, your neighbour did report a prowler at the back here on Friday night,' French said. 'We're not sure if it's connected to our investigation.'

Garrow stopped writing. 'Do you still have the footage from Friday night?'

'Yes, yes,' Watkin replied, pushing himself up from the armchair. 'I only delete it at the end of the month.' He went over to a PC monitor and hard drive at the far end of the room and turned them on. He was now clearly intrigued by what his camera might have filmed. 'And despite my appearance, I'm not quite the luddite you might expect me to be,' he said with a self-effacing chortle.

Garrow looked at French as they approached. Watkin was starting to soften a little.

'Right, here we go,' Watkin said as clicked on an MPEG file on his desktop. 'This is Friday evening.' He pointed at the timecode. 'I put the camera on at 7.30pm as it was getting dark.'

Garrow peered at the screen. The camera looked over the back garden and then across the back of at least three of the houses on Mold Road that backed on to Primrose Way. From what he could see, Lynne Morgan's house was the middle of the three.

Garrow leaned forward and placed his index finger by the screen. 'I think that's where Lynne Morgan's house is.'

Watkin nodded. 'Yes, that's right. Poor woman. I only knew her to wave to once in a while over the garden fence.'

French gestured to the screen. 'Would you be able to play this forward so we can see if there's anything on this later on?'

'Yes, here we go,' Watkin said. He seemed to be rather enjoying himself playing amateur detective with two police officers. He clicked his mouse and the security footage began to move forward.

Garrow spotted a figure moving at the top of the left hand side of the screen. 'There!' he said, pointing. 'There's someone there.'

Watkin paused the footage.

As Garrow peered closely at the screen, he could see a dark figure climbing over the fence that separated the house to the left of Lynne Morgan's home.

'There's someone there,' French said. 'Can you play it back a little please?'

'Yes, of course,' Watkin said. 'Looks like we might have got this blighter on camera, eh?'

'We've certainly got something,' French agreed.

Watkin played the footage again. 'Right, here we go.'

Garrow squinted at the screen.

The figure appeared to come out of the back door of the house next door, walk across the garden and then climb over the fence. The figure then jogged towards the back of Lynne Morgan's house and went inside via an open patio door.

Garrow's eyes widened as he looked at French.

'8.35 pm,' Garrow said. 'That's pretty close to when we think Lynne was murdered.'

## Chapter 58

It was 8.15am and Ben, Georgie and Arlo had made their way back over to the farmhouse where Tegan had insisted she make them breakfast before going down to their car.

'Here you go, petal,' Tegan said with a smile as she placed a bowl of porridge down in front of Arlo.

'I've never had porridge before,' Arlo said, grabbing a spoon.

'Haven't you?' Tegan said with a laugh, but as she turned Georgie could see that her eye was slightly swollen. She assumed that Andy had hit her last night.

'I normally have chocolate flakes,' Arlo said.

'I'm not allowed chocolate flakes,' Rhys said from the other end of the table where he was also eating porridge. He was wearing a blue school jumper, white shirt and tie.

'Do you like school, Rhys?' Georgie asked, trying to find some normality in the ongoing nightmare of the past few days.

Rhys nodded enthusiastically. 'Yes.'

'He loves it. He's a bit of a whizz at English, aren't you?' Tegan said proudly as she brought over a pot of tea.

Rhys shrugged self-consciously.

'He writes these lovely poems,' Tegan said.

'Bloody waste of time, if you ask me,' said a deep voice.

Andy came in – he had clearly overheard their conversation.

He went over to Rhys who immediately cowered. Georgie couldn't bear to see him wince like that.

'Come on, lad,' Andy growled clicking his fingers. 'Finish that or you'll be late for school.'

Georgie saw Ben bristle with anger at Andy's behaviour. The irony of Ben's clear disgust at Andy's manner in comparison to the crimes that Ben had committed in the past two weeks wasn't lost on her.

Andy looked over at Ben. 'You all sleep alright?'

Ben nodded but his anger was evident.

'Yes, thanks,' Georgie said with a polite smile. 'Very comfortable.'

Andy ignored her and looked at Ben again. 'I've got a couple of jobs to do around the farm and then I'll take you down to your car and tow you into town.' He glanced at his watch. 'It'll be about an hour.'

'Thanks,' Ben said under his breath.

Suddenly, Andy stormed across the kitchen, grabbed the bowl of porridge that was in front of Rhys and snatched the spoon from his hand. 'What did I tell you about being late for that bus, eh?'

'Sorry,' Rhys whimpered.

Andy put his hand on Rhys' shoulder but Georgie could see that he dug his fingers hard into his skin. 'Get upstairs and get your blazer on before I give you a clip.'

Rhys got up and scuttled away.

The tension in the kitchen rose.

Georgie could see Ben seething and prayed that he didn't take matters into his own hands.

'Right, I'll be back in a bit,' Andy said as he went to the door and then he left.

Tegan looked over with an apologetic look. 'Sorry. He gets a bit like that sometimes.'

Ben pointed to her face. 'Knock you about a bit, does he?' he asked through gritted teeth.

Tegan didn't answer as Rhys came back into the kitchen now wearing a blazer and a schoolbag slung over his shoulder.

'You look very smart,' Georgie said brightly, even though her stomach was twisted in anxious knots.

'We don't have a blazer at my school,' Arlo said.

Suddenly the back door burst open and Andy came in, his face full of thunder.

'I know who you are!' he roared angrily. 'I've just heard it on the radio.' He looked over at Tegan. 'He's that copper that's on the run. He's kidnapped them.'

Georgie noticed Ben's hand move towards the handgun.

'No, you've got that wrong,' Georgie said, pretending to look confused. 'I'm his wife. I don't know what you're talking about.'

Andy was having none of it as he marched over to a gun cabinet on the wall, opened it, and pulled out a double barrelled shotgun which he pointed at Ben.

*Oh God!*

'Tegan,' Andy said. 'Go and call the police. Then we'll see if they are who they say they are.'

'Dad?' Arlo whispered.

'It's all right, mate,' Ben said, standing up from the

table and pulling out the Glock 17. He pointed the gun at Tegan. 'If you try to call the police, I'll shoot you all.'

Tegan gave a frightened whimper.

Andy took an aggressive step forward, gesturing to the shotgun. 'You try anything, I'll blow your head off.'

Georgie could feel her heart hammering against her chest. Her anxiety was making her feel sick. She glanced over at Arlo, who was now as white as a ghost, and tried to give him a reassuring look.

Ben shook his head and pointed the gun at Andy. 'Put the gun down.'

Andy frowned. 'No chance.'

Ben took a step forward. 'You need to give me the gun right now.'

'Take another step and I'll shoot you,' Andy warned him.

Georgie couldn't understand what Ben was doing.

'Dad!' Arlo cried out.

Ben took another step.

Andy pulled the trigger.

CLICK.

Nothing.

Ben shrugged. 'Yeah, I spotted the gun case last night. I came back during the night and took the cartridges out.'

Andy's face fell.

Striding forward, Ben pointed the handgun at Andy's head as he grabbed the shotgun from his hands. In one swift move, Ben swirled the shotgun and smashed the wooden butt into Andy's temple, knocking him to the floor.

Tegan was now standing with her arms protectively around Rhys and whimpering.

'Please, we won't tell anyone you were here,' Tegan murmured.

Ben pointed the gun at them. 'Sit down right now, and no one is going to get hurt.'

Ben then marched over to Andy and kicked him hard in the stomach as he lay on the ground. 'That's for being a bullying wanker!'

'Ben,' Georgie said in a cautionary tone as Andy groaned on the floor.

'I spotted this last night too,' Ben said as he went over to a curled up length of rope that was on a kitchen counter. Picking it up, he then took a kitchen knife and started to cut lengths of it.

'What are you doing, Dad?' Arlo asked anxiously.

'It's going to be fine, mate,' Ben reassured him as he came over to Georgie and handed her the rope. 'Tie them to the chairs.'

Georgie nodded as she stood up and looked at Tegan. If they were tied to the kitchen chairs, then at least they were safe. However, she feared what Ben might have in store for Andy.

Ben gave Andy another almighty kick and Tegan let out a scream. Ben glared at her. 'You should be thanking me.'

Grabbing a length of rope, Ben put the handgun down on the kitchen table and then proceeded to tie Andy's hands behind his back and his feet together.

'It's all right,' Georgie said under her breath as she tied Tegan and Rhys to the chairs at the far end of the table. She glanced over to see what Ben was doing. He still had the rope in his hands.

Having finished tying them up, Georgie went over to Tegan, leant in close and looked at her. 'Where are your car keys? And you need to tell anyone that comes here that we're heading for Bangor, okay?' she whispered. Tegan nodded.

Georgie wanted to get the car keys and get Ben out of the farmhouse before any more damage could be done.

With a quick gesture of her head, Tegan indicated a small row of hooks over by the sink. Georgie immediately spotted a set of car keys hanging up. Darting across the kitchen, she retrieved them.

'I've got the car keys,' Georgie said in a serious tone. 'We should go.'

Ben seemed to be concentrating on tying and fastening the rope. 'Not yet,' Ben said angrily without looking up.

*What the hell is he doing?* she wondered with growing unease.

Then her stomach lurched when she saw exactly what he was making.

A noose.

'Arlo, come here please,' Georgie said.

Arlo shook his head. He stood frozen to the spot as he watched his father.

With a sharp movement, Ben threw the rope over the central wooden beam. He moved over to Andy and looped the noose around his neck.

'Ben, what are you doing?' Georgie asked in horror.

'Oh my God,' Tegan shrieked as she realised that Ben planned to hang her husband from the beam in the kitchen.

'Dad?' Arlo said, sounding terrified.

Pulling the rope with his hand, Ben shot a look over at Tegan. 'No?' he asked with a contained rage. 'You want me to let him go? You want me to let him make yours and Rhys' lives a total misery? Is that what you want?'

Tegan looked away, her eyes full of tears.

'Dad?' Arlo said with concern as he moved from where he was sitting at the table.

Ben pulled the rope so that it tightened around Andy's neck and forced him to sit up.

'Please,' Andy gasped. 'Don't do this.'

'Dad? No!' Arlo pleaded again but Ben refused to look at him.

Georgie held up the car keys. 'Come on, Ben. You can't do this in front of everyone. Let's just go.'

'No!' Ben thundered loudly as he pulled the rope again and Andy let out a horrible rasping noise. 'This is what he deserves.'

'Dad?' Arlo said again.

Ben turned sharply to look at him. 'What is it?'

Arlo had picked up the Glock 17 from the kitchen table. He held it in both his hands but they were shaking. 'I don't want you to do it. I want us to go.'

'Woah,' Ben said, his eyes widening. 'Put the gun down, Arlo.'

'Arlo,' Georgie said very gently. 'Just put down the gun.'

Arlo shook his head. 'It isn't right.'

'Put the gun down, Arlo,' Ben snapped.

Arlo shook his head with tears in his eyes. 'No. You told me when I grow up I have to stand up for the things that I think are right. Even if I'm scared.'

'What?' Ben asked, releasing the rope slightly.

'If someone is doing something wrong,' Arlo cried as his hands shook. 'You need to do something or say something. That's what you told me, Dad.'

Ben looked at him, then took a sudden step forward and held out his hand. 'Just give me the gun, Arlo.'

CRACK!

The gun went off in Arlo's hand.

Everyone flinched.

Ben clutched at his stomach and let the rope drop.

'Dad?' Arlo said, sobbing.

Ben brought his hand from where he had clutched at his stomach. It was covered in blood. Then he gave Arlo a quizzical, almost amused look. 'You shot me, mate.'

Georgie approached and then looked at Arlo. 'Arlo, can you put down the gun for me?'

'I didn't mean to,' Arlo sobbed. 'I'm sorry, Dad.'

'It's fine,' Ben said, limping towards him and taking the gun out of his shaking hands. 'It was an accident, mate. I know you didn't mean to.'

Georgie looked at Ben and then down at the gunshot wound in his stomach. 'You're going to need to get someone to look at that.'

Ben gave her a wry smile. 'Yeah, well that's not going to happen is it?' Then he gestured to the door. 'Come on.'

Georgie went over and took the rope from Andy's neck.

'Leave him,' Ben shouted as he and Arlo made for the back door.

Georgie looked back at Tegan and Rhys as she followed. She didn't know what to say.

As they came out of the back door into the farm's central yard, the sun had appeared from behind the clouds.

They approached the Land Rover Discovery and Georgie clicked the automatic locking system which flashed the indicators. She just wanted them to leave the farm as quickly as possible.

Ben winced in pain and stopped for a moment to get his breath. He still had the gun in his hand. 'You're going to have to drive,' he said quietly.

Georgie nodded as she went around to the driver's door.

Arlo, who looked completely traumatised, got into the back of the car.

'Don't you need to go to hospital, Dad?' Arlo asked quietly.

'No, mate. It looks much worse than it really is. Don't worry,' Ben said as he settled himself into the passenger seat. 'Let's just get going first, eh?'

Georgie started up the engine. As she looked over at Ben, she could see how much blood was now seeping through his shirt. If he didn't get medical attention, he was going to bleed to death.

Putting the Land Rover Discovery into gear, she pressed down on the accelerator and drove away.

## Chapter 59

Garrow and French knocked on the door of the house next to Lynne Morgan's. Garrow was trying to process the fact that someone from this house had jumped over the back fence and entered Lynne's home around the time of her murder. It was incredibly suspicious.

After thirty seconds, Garrow banged on the door again but there was still no reply. He listened. Nothing from inside – no voices, no movement.

French walked over to a ground floor window but the curtains were pulled.

'Anything?' Garrow asked.

'Not a peep,' French replied, shaking his head.

'Maybe they're both out at work,' Garrow suggested before he leant down and opened the letter box to see if he could see or hear anything inside. The pungent smell of coffee and toast hit him as soon as he looked through the narrow gap. It was so strong that Garrow reasoned that they had been made very recently.

There was the sound of a key being turned. Then the front door opened very cautiously and Gavin peered out.

He was wearing a red Wrexham AFC football shirt and dark cargo shorts.

'Hello?' he said with a quizzical expression.

'It's Gavin, isn't it?' Garrow asked.

'Yes, that's right,' Gavin said, still seeming to use the door as a shield against him. Then his eyes moved right. 'Horrible what happened to Lynne next door. Have you caught the bastard what done it?'

'We're following several lines of enquiry at the moment,' Garrow explained politely. 'Is it okay if we come in for a minute?'

Gavin's face dropped. 'Erm, I … I'm just in the middle of a couple of things so …'

'It won't take more than a minute,' Garrow reassured him with a nod. 'Then we'll leave you in peace.'

Gavin gestured inside. 'Place is a bit of a tip at the moment to be honest.'

*He really doesn't want to let us inside.*

French, who had now joined Garrow on the doorstep, gave a wry smile. 'I promise you, we've seen a lot worse.'

Gavin scratched his nose and face nervously. 'If you don't mind, I can answer any questions here.' He wasn't hiding the fact that his anxiety was now going through the roof.

French looked at him. 'In the statement you gave to our officers, you said that you and your wife were in all night last Friday. Is that right?'

Gavin nodded. He still seemed to be clutching the door for dear life. 'Yeah. Is that it?'

Garrow raised an eyebrow. 'Did either you or your wife come out of the back of your house and out into your garden on Friday night?'

'No,' he snorted. But now his eyes were moving erratically as he tried to fathom what they actually knew.

'I mean, you would have noticed if someone had come out of your house, then climbed over your fence at the back and gone into Lynne Morgan's house around the time she was murdered, wouldn't you?' French asked with a heavy dose of sarcasm.

The blood drained from Gavin's face. 'I ... I don't know what you're talking about.'

'Yeah, well we've got CCTV footage that suggests otherwise,' Garrow said, fixing him with a stare. 'So, you're going to have to come down to the station with us to help us with our enquiries.'

Suddenly, Gavin slammed the door in their faces.

'Shit,' French said.

Less than a second later, there was a clattering noise of a gate. It came from the back of the house. Garrow took a few quick steps to the left and glanced down the scruffy passageway down the side of the house.

Gavin was sprinting across his back garden towards the rear fence.

'Bollocks,' French said as they set off in pursuit.

'Not again,' Garrow groaned as they ran down the side of the house and opened the wooden side gate.

As they entered the garden, they saw that Gavin had climbed over the fence and down onto a green wheelie bin. He then jumped off that and sprinted into Primrose Way and turned right.

'Stop! Police!' French bellowed as they continued chasing him.

Garrow was now ten yards ahead of French as they ran right along Primrose Way and then right again into Lilac Way.

*He's heading for the Mold Road!*

As Garrow got to the top of Lilac Way, he saw Gavin

running across the main road and narrowly avoiding a van whose driver beeped the horn angrily.

French was way behind now.

Sprinting through the traffic, Garrow got to the other side of the road.

He looked around but Gavin was nowhere to be seen.

Garrow clicked his Tetra radio and said breathlessly, 'This is three-seven to control.'

'Go ahead, three-seven.'

'I'm in pursuit of a male suspect. Red Wrexham football shirt, black shorts. Suspect is heading east on the Mold Road but I have lost visual contact, over,' Garrow gasped.

'Control received …' The radio crackled, 'Be advised, three-seven. Uniformed response vehicle is en route. ETA five minutes,' the female CAD operator told him.

French arrived gasping for breath. 'Where the hell has he gone?'

Garrow shrugged. 'No idea. He's disappeared.'

'The Turf,' French said pointing to a pub further along the road. The Turf was 150 years old and had been the venue for the formation of Wrexham AFC back in 1864. Now a social hub for supporters on match day, it was also the oldest pub or bar within a sporting venue in the world.

Jogging along the pavement, French and Garrow entered The Turf and looked around. It had low ceilings and was covered in football memorabilia – framed shirts, photos, Welsh flags.

It was relatively empty except for a couple of blokes sitting at the bar nursing their pints and watching the large television up on the wall.

French and Garrow took out their warrant cards and approached a middle-aged man with light brown hair and a friendly smile standing behind the bar.

'We're looking for a bloke with ginger hair in a

Wrexham shirt and black shorts,' French explained. 'Ran in here a couple of minutes ago?'

The barman frowned. 'Sorry mate. No-one's come in in the last half hour.'

Garrow wasn't convinced by the barman's response.

French leaned closer to the bar. 'I have it on good authority, this bloke is a Chester fan. Has been all his life. He's only been wearing a Wrexham shirt since the takeover. Bit of glory hunter, if you know what I mean?'

'Oh right,' the barman shrugged and pointed. 'In that case, he's hiding behind the pool table over there.'

'Thanks,' French said as they turned and went over to the pool table.

'Get up Gavin,' Garrow said calmly.

Suddenly, Gavin appeared and launched himself at them.

Grabbing his flailing arm, Garrow twisted Gavin around and used his leg to throw him to the floor.

Taking his cuffs out, he pulled Gavin's arms behind his back and secured the handcuffs on him.

'You're under arrest on suspicion of the murder of Lynne Morgan,' Garrow growled. 'You do not have to say anything, but it may harm your defence if you do not mention when questioned something which you later rely on in court. Anything you do say may be given in evidence in a court of law.'

## Chapter 60

Georgie, Ben and Arlo were speeding through the back lanes trying to get to a decent road that would get them over to Bangor. She prayed that the police got to the farmhouse quickly so that Tegan could relay the fact that they were heading for Bangor. She had no idea who Ben had arranged to meet there or what his plan was for them. However, she was acutely aware that once they were in Bangor, it was less than a mile across the Menai Strait to Anglesey, as well as having access to the Menai Bridge. Maybe the plan was to leave the mainland.

As they stopped at a junction, Georgie heard the sound of police sirens. She assumed that Tegan or Andy had called 999 and that they were heading for the farmhouse. Or that they had the registration of the Land Rover Discovery and were now out scouring the roads for them. She hoped that Ben didn't hear the sirens but his immediate reaction told her that he had.

Looking around frantically, Ben pointed to the entrance to a field across the road. 'Pull in there quickly,' he snapped.

Georgie hesitated for a moment, hoping that a police car would come around the corner and see them sitting there.

'Don't fuck about!' Ben sneered as he pointed the gun at her.

Pushing down on the accelerator, Georgie drove over and into the field.

Ben pointed. 'Drive behind this hedge.'

Slowing down the car, Georgie stopped where Ben had indicated.

A second later, a marked police car with its blues and twos going went past in a flash.

'Just in time, eh?' Ben said with a wry smile. Then he grimaced and clutched at his stomach.

Looking over, Georgie could see that his clothes were completely soaked in blood.

'Jesus,' Georgie muttered. 'That looks nasty.'

Arlo leaned forward to see what Georgie was referring to and then his face fell.

'I'm so sorry, Dad,' Arlo sobbed.

Ben turned round and grimaced again. 'Hey, it was an accident, mate. You didn't mean for that gun to go off, did you?'

Arlo shook his head and wiped the tears from his face. 'No.'

'There you go then,' Ben said. 'Accidents happen, mate.'

Arlo nodded but his eyes were still teary.

Ben opened the passenger door and got out. The effort of even standing was clearly very painful.

He then opened the back door and put his hand to Arlo's face. 'You don't need to cry. It wasn't your fault.'

Ben moved slowly towards Arlo so that their foreheads nearly touched.

'Listen to me, mate. This is really important,' Ben said in a quiet but serious tone. 'Whatever happens, I want you to know that I love you. And I want you to remember that grabbing that gun was the right thing to do. What I was going to do to that man was wrong, okay? And when the gun went off, it was an accident. Do you understand all that?'

Arlo nodded.

Ben kissed him on the cheek. 'Good lad.'

Getting back into the car, Ben tried to get his breath as he looked over at Georgie. 'Right, we can go now.'

## Chapter 61

By the time Garrow and French arrived to interview Gavin, the duty solicitor, Neil Roberts, had arrived and was looking intently at the case files. Gavin was now dressed in a regulation grey tracksuit, as his clothes had been taken for forensics. He had also been swabbed for his DNA and had photographs taken. He sat with a terrified look on his face as his eyes roamed around the room. Taking a sip of water, Gavin took a deep breath.

French reached across the table to start the recording machine. A long electronic beep sounded as French opened his files and gave Garrow a quick look of acknowledgement.

'Interview conducted with Gavin Staples, Interview Room 3, Llancastell Police Station. Present are Detective Constable James Garrow, Duty Solicitor Neil Roberts, and myself, Detective Sergeant Daniel French.' French then glanced over. 'Gavin, do you understand you are still under caution?

'Yeah,' he mumbled, but he was now looking at the floor.

Garrow opened an A4 notepad and took out his pen which he clicked open. 'Gavin, can you tell us why you ran from us when we came to your house today?'

Gavin didn't say anything but his leg was twitching nervously.

'Gavin?' Garrow said.

'I don't know,' he mumbled.

French opened his laptop and then said, 'For the purposes of the tape, I am going to show the suspect Item Reference 838E.' French turned the laptop to show Gavin. 'Could you look at this CCTV footage for me please, Gavin?'

Gavin raised his head a little and peered over.

French played the footage of the figure going over the fence from Gavin's house and into Lynne Morgan's home.

French pointed. 'This is CCTV footage taken by a camera on Primrose Way. Do you know where Primrose Way is, Gavin?'

Gavin shrugged. 'Yeah.'

'Primrose Way backs onto Mold Road, doesn't it? And this CCTV footage shows a figure here …' French pointed to the screen, '… climbing over the fence, going into Lynne Morgan's garden and then into her house. Is there anything you can tell us about that?'

'It's not me,' Gavin said.

'Well, who is it then?' Garrow asked.

'I don't know,' Gavin said, staring intently at the floor.

'Was there anyone else in your home on Friday night except for you and your wife Tracey?' French asked with a sceptical expression.

'No …'

French narrowed his eyes and gave a withering sigh. 'You expect us to believe that while you and your wife were sitting at home on Friday night, someone else that you weren't aware of came into your home, out into your garden, and then over to Lynne Morgan's home? Come on Gavin.'

Silence.

Garrow pulled over another file. 'For the purposes of the tape, I'm going to show the suspect Item Reference 294F. This is a medical document that shows that Lynne Morgan had penetrative sex just before she was murdered. Can you see that, Gavin?'

Gavin gave a nervous sniff, glanced over and nodded.

'For the purposes of the tape, the suspect has just nodded,' Garrow explained.

French fixed Gavin with a stare. 'Did you have sexual intercourse with Lynne Morgan on Friday evening, Gavin?'

Gavin shook his head with a distraught expression. 'No,' he whispered.

'And you're sure about that?' French asked, his voice getting louder. 'Because we have a vaginal swab and semen from Lynne Morgan and that will give us a DNA profile. Is that going to match the DNA profile that we're going to get from you?'

Gavin put his head in his hands. 'No. It wasn't me.'

'I put it to you, Gavin, that you were having an affair with your neighbour, Lynne Morgan,' French said loudly. 'Once your wife had gone to bed, you went over the fence and had sex with Lynne. Then something happened. You got into a row which got out of hand and you killed her. That's what happened, isn't it, Gavin?'

'No, no, no.' Gavin was now in bits.

They waited for a few seconds so that the tension could mount.

Garrow reached over, pulled out another photo and turned it to show Gavin. 'For the purposes of the tape, I'm showing the suspect Item Reference 238H,' Garrow said. 'As you can see, Gavin, this is a photograph that our medical examiner took of you before this interview. Can you tell us how you got those scratches on your shoulders?'

Gavin shook his head and then looked down at the floor.

French moved his chair forward. 'Did Lynne Morgan scratch you when you were attacking her, Gavin?'

Gavin shook his head slowly.

Garrow looked over at him and said gently, 'Gavin, we know that you didn't intend to kill Lynne when you went to see her on Friday. But something terrible happened. You just need to tell us the truth.'

Gavin put his head in his hands.

'Gavin, we know that you and Lynne had a fight. We know that she scratched you because you have scratch marks on your shoulders,' French said. 'And we have DNA from the skin under Lynne's nails. And that DNA is going to match yours, isn't it, Gavin? And the DNA from the semen and the swab are going to prove that you had sex with her. So, you just need to tell us exactly what happened.'

Gavin was now sobbing.

Roberts looked over at them. 'I'd like to request a break for my client.'

French sighed in frustration and nodded.

## Chapter 62

Ruth and Nick pulled up outside the farmhouse that was situated twenty miles south of the North Wales coast. Three marked police cars were parked outside and the area had been taped off by several uniformed officers.

Ruth could see a man, woman and small boy sitting on chairs at the back of the farmhouse being tended to by paramedics and giving witness statements.

Ruth and Nick approached a burly-looking uniformed officer with a moustache and wearing a high-vis police jacket.

'DI Hunter and DS Evans, Llancastell CID,' she said, flashing her warrant card. 'What do we know so far, constable?'

The constable cleared his throat and glanced down at his notepad. Then he gestured to the family sitting to the rear of the farmhouse. 'We've got Andy, Tegan and Rhys Featherstone. This is their farm. Yesterday evening, Ben Stewart, DC Wild and Arlo Stewart arrived here on foot, claiming that the brakes had failed on their car down in the woods and they'd crashed into a tree. Given the time of day, the Featherstones suggested that they stay overnight in the annexe. Then Andy Featherstone was going to help Stewart to retrieve the car first thing this morning and tow it to a nearby garage.'

'What went wrong?' Nick asked.

'Andy heard a description of them on the radio news,' the constable explained. 'He confronted them with his shotgun and told his wife Tegan to call the police. However, Stewart had taken the cartridges from the shotgun overnight. Stewart was armed with a handgun and he ordered DC Wild to tie the wife and son to some chairs. Stewart fashioned a noose from some rope which he put around Andy's neck. He was in the process of hanging him from a wooden beam across the kitchen ceiling when Arlo took the gun and shot him in the stomach.'

'Christ!' Ruth exclaimed and shook her head.

Nick frowned. 'Do we have any idea why Stewart was going to hang Andy Featherstone?'

'No, sir. No idea,' the constable admitted.

'Do we know how badly Stewart was injured?' Nick asked.

'Tegan Featherstone worked as a nurse before she got married,' the constable replied. 'She said he was losing a lot of blood when they left.'

'How did they get away?' Ruth asked.

'They took the family Land Rover Discovery. I've already circulated the colour, make and registration to all units in the area.'

'That's great work.' Ruth then gestured over to the family. 'And how are they?'

'Very shaken up, ma'am.'

Nick raised an eyebrow. 'Anything else that might help us?'

'Yes,' the constable said forcefully. 'Tegan Featherstone

said that when DC Wild was tying them up she whispered to them that they were heading for Bangor.'

Ruth exchanged a look with Nick.

'I'm going to leave all this in your capable hands,' Ruth said as she and Nick jogged back to the car.

'Right you are, ma'am.'

## Chapter 63

French and Garrow were back in Interview Room 3 after a short break. The duty solicitor, Neil Roberts, was talking quietly to Gavin as they entered.

Roberts looked over at them with a serious expression. 'My client would like to fully cooperate with this investigation. However, in return for his full cooperation, he would like immunity from any criminal charges.'

French frowned for a second. 'I'm afraid that's not something that we could guarantee without talking to the Crown Prosecution Service first. And it would be unusual for us to do that in a case like this,' French explained.

Garrow wondered what Gavin had to tell them. There was no doubt in Garrow's mind that Gavin had been the figure on the CCTV entering Lynne Morgan's home.

Gavin and Roberts talked quietly again for a few seconds.

French leaned forward and said, 'Let me put it this way, Gavin. If you do fully cooperate with this investigation, then myself and DC Garrow will make sure that it is taken into full consideration by both the CPS and a judge, should you go to trial. If you have committed something that is considered a minor offence, then it is possible that charges might be dropped in consideration of your help today.'

Roberts looked at Gavin and nodded to signal that this was as good as it was going to get.

Gavin blew out his cheeks nervously as he looked over. 'I was at Lynne's house on Friday night.'

*Big surprise*, Garrow thought as he clicked his pen in preparation of taking notes. 'And you and Lynne were having an affair?'

Gavin nodded and looked embarrassed. 'Yes.'

'And that was you climbing over the fence at the back and going into Lynne's home at 8.35pm?' French asked to clarify.

'Yes.'

'How long had you and Lynne been having an affair?' Garrow asked.

'Nearly a year,' Gavin admitted quietly.

French raised a quizzical eyebrow. 'And your wife never suspected anything?'

'No,' Gavin replied. 'My wife has ME, so she spends a lot of time in bed asleep … I'm not proud of this, but I had nothing to do with … what happened to Lynne.'

Garrow stopped writing and looked over. 'You went over to Lynne's home where you had sexual intercourse with her?'

'Yes,' Gavin said awkwardly under his breath.

'In her bedroom?' French asked.

'Yes.'

'And when you left, Lynne Morgan was alive?' Garrow asked as he scribbled notes on the pad.

Gavin hesitated and then shook his head.

*What?*

Garrow and French exchanged a furtive look.

French narrowed his eyes. 'Lynne Morgan was dead when you left her home?'

Gavin nodded very slowly and looked upset.

French looked confused and sat back in his seat for a few seconds. 'I think you're going to have to explain exactly what happened while you were in Lynne Morgan's home on Friday night, Gavin.'

'Yeah,' Gavin whispered as he pursed his lips. 'Me and Lynne … We were in her bedroom, you know. When we have sex, she … scratches me. You know? I've always got marks on my back and shoulders.'

'Go on,' French said.

'Then afterwards, we heard the front door open and close. Lynne thought it might be her son, Steve.'

'And was it Steve?' Garrow asked.

'I don't know,' Gavin admitted. 'It must have been.'

'And then what happened?' French enquired.

'Lynne had some problems with Steve. He's a drug addict. She'd just paid for him to go to rehab,' Gavin explained. 'Lynne was scared that Steve had drugs hidden in the house somewhere and that he'd come back from being out to get them … So, Lynne dashed out of the bedroom to see if it was Steve. I heard her go downstairs. Then I heard this big row in the kitchen. In fact, it sounded like a fight. There was shouting. And then nothing. I heard someone go out of the door and …' Gavin wiped a tear from his face. 'Sorry …'

'What did you do when you heard all the shouting?' French asked.

'Nothing. I mean, I wasn't supposed to be there, was I?' Gavin said. 'Steve knows me and Trace. I couldn't just go down there …'

'What happened when you eventually went downstairs?' French asked.

Gavin took a visible deep breath to try and steady himself. 'So, I waited in the bedroom for ages. I thought that Lynne had had a barny with Steve, that he'd stormed out and then she'd come back upstairs again ... but she never ... And then after about twenty minutes, I put my clothes on and went downstairs. And that's when I ...' Gavin began to shake and his eyes filled with tears. 'She was just lying there with all this blood.'

'What did you do?' Garrow asked.

'I didn't know what to do.' Gavin looked over and wiped his eyes. 'I didn't know what to do. I could see she was ... gone. And I panicked. I was there on my own. I just panicked.'

'And you left and went back home?' French asked to clarify.

'Look, I know I did a terrible thing leaving her like that. I'm never going to forgive myself for doing that. But I never hurt her. I would never hurt her.'

French and Garrow took a few seconds to digest all that Gavin had told them.

Garrow pointed to his notes. 'You said that you heard a row downstairs. Could you hear how many people were rowing?'

'I think it was just Lynne and Steve?' Gavin replied.

'You heard Steve's voice?' French asked.

'No,' Gavin admitted.

'But you heard a man's voice?'

Gavin shrugged. 'To be honest, I just heard voices. I couldn't tell you if it was a man's voice.'

'Did you hear Lynne say anything or did you hear anything that they were arguing about?' Garrow said.

'No, sorry,' Gavin answered. 'It was just mumbled, you know?'

'What time did all this happen?' Garrow enquired.

Gavin pulled a face. 'I don't really know. I kind of lost track of time while I was there.'

'We know that you entered the house at 8.35pm,' French stated. 'How long do you think it was before you heard the front door open?'

Gavin thought for a few seconds. 'As I said, I kind of lost time.'

French looked visibly frustrated. 'Was it fifteen minutes, two hours?'

'Maybe an hour or a bit less,' Gavin replied.

They knew from the CCTV on Mold Road that Steve Morgan had entered the house at 9.25pm which was 50 minutes after Gavin had arrived.

'Is it possible that the front door opened about 50 minutes after you arrived?' French asked.

'Yeah, that sounds about right,' Gavin said.

Garrow looked at French. It looked like Steve Morgan was back in the frame again.

## Chapter 64

Georgie was driving west towards Bangor. Glancing left, she saw that Ben's wound was getting worse. Arlo had spent a good twenty minutes crying in the back of the car until Ben could calm him down. Arlo was now sitting quietly in the back with his AirPods in his ears watching something on his phone.

'We've got to get that patched up,' Georgie said, sounding concerned. It was hard for her to rationalise that Ben bleeding to death would be a good thing and allow her and Arlo to be rescued.

Looking up, she saw a large petrol station on their right. It had a *Greggs, Costa* and a small supermarket. She indicated and then turned off the road.

'What are you doing?' Ben asked.

Georgie parked the car and then looked at him. 'Seriously. If we don't get some kind of dressing and antiseptic on that, you'll be dead before we get to anywhere.'

Ben looked down at the bloody mess and nodded. He still had the Glock 17 clasped in his hand. 'Well, I can't go in there, can I?' Then he looked at her. 'And neither can you.'

They both in unison looked back at Arlo.

'Mate,' Ben said, turning to look at Arlo who had now taken out his AirPods. 'I'm gonna need you to do me a favour. If you get out and come here.'

Arlo nodded, took off his seatbelt, got out of the car and came to the passenger door that Ben had just opened.

Fishing inside his wallet, Ben took out two £20 notes and handed them to Arlo. 'Here you go. I'm gonna need you to go into that shop and buy a few things. Is that okay?'

Arlo nodded.

'Good lad,' Ben said, and then gritted his teeth due to the pain of his wound.

Arlo blinked tearfully. 'I'm so sorry, Dad,' he whispered.

Ben put out his left arm and gave Arlo a partial hug. 'We talked about this. It was an accident, mate. I know you didn't mean to do it. Okay?'

Arlo wiped his face and nodded.

'We're going to need some bandages, cotton wool, disinfectant and some kind of tape. Sellotape, gaffer tape,' Ben explained. 'Do you want me to write that down?'

Arlo shook his head. 'No.'

For a few seconds, Ben and Georgie watched Arlo jog to the shop with the money clasped in his hand.

Ben gave an ironic laugh and shook his head.

'What?' Georgie asked.

'I know exactly how he feels,' Ben said, then turned to look at Georgie. 'I lied when I told you that my dad beat my mum to death. That's not what happened that night. My dad was beating my mum so I grabbed the shotgun. I aimed it at my dad and told him to leave her alone and get out of the house. I'd never stood up to him before and I was shaking like a leaf. But he came for me, tried to grab the gun and it went off in my hand. It hit her in the chest and killed her stone dead.'

'Oh my God,' Georgie whispered. 'That's so terrible.'

Silence.

Ben gave her a wry smile. 'So, what are the chances of it all happening again, eh? God's got a sick sense of humour, hasn't he?'

Georgie gave a slight nod. She didn't know quite what to say. 'I don't understand. If you've been through all that, why are you putting Arlo in the same situation?'

'I can't let him live in that house with his mum and that man,' Ben growled angrily.

Georgie shook her head in disbelief. 'What, and all this is better is it?'

'He's with me. And I'm his father,' Ben snapped. 'And if I'm honest, he's better off dead than not being with me.'

'You can't really believe that,' Georgie asked in a bewildered tone.

'I do. I know how Arlo feels. Me and him are the same,' Ben said. 'If I die, then he has to come with me. I can't let him stay here to fend for himself without me. I couldn't do that to him.'

Georgie just couldn't fathom Ben's narcissistic and twisted view of the world.

'What about me?' she asked.

Silence.

Ben looked at her and then shrugged. 'I'm in love with you, Georgie. I always have been, ever since we first met. And I know you feel the same. That's why you're here with me and Arlo.'

Georgie narrowed her eyes. 'I'm here because you

kidnapped me at gunpoint, Ben,' she said in utter bewilderment.

'No,' Ben said confidently. 'You could have escaped by now if you'd wanted to. But you haven't. You want to be here with us.'

Georgie glared at him and realised that he was completely delusional. 'I don't, Ben. I assure you I don't.'

Ben looked directly at her. 'I'm taking us to Anglesey. No one knows us there. And we can build a new life there as a family. And with your baby.'

*Okay, he has seriously lost his mind.*

'But you're going to get caught,' Georgie said. 'How's that going to work?'

Ben shrugged again. 'If I go, then I'm taking Arlo and you with me.' Then he pointed the Glock 17 at his temple. 'And all this pain up here will just stop.'

At that moment, a low thundering noise grew in the air above them.

Georgie glanced up.

The police helicopter had spotted them and was now hovering in the sky over their heads.

'Shit!' Ben growled.

Arlo came running back from the shop with a bag full of stuff. He jumped into the back of the car.

'Everything okay, mate?' Ben asked.

'Yeah,' Arlo replied.

Georgie moved her head again as she looked skywards at the black and yellow EC145 police helicopter.

Ben motioned with his bloody hand which gripped the Glock 17. 'Drive.'

# Chapter 65

G arrow and French were stood in front of the scene board. They were 90% certain now that Steve Morgan had killed his mother when he returned home on Friday night, probably to retrieve his drugs.

'Okay,' Garrow said, taking out a board marker and writing on the scene board. 'How does this work in terms of timing?'

'We know that Gavin Staples left his home, jumped over the fence and entered Lynne Morgan's house at 8.35pm,' French said.

Garrow began to scribble this down on the timeline that he was creating.

'Lynne and Gavin have sex in her bedroom,' French continued. 'Gavin heard the front door open and we're assuming that was Steve Morgan returning home to get his drugs from his bedroom.'

Garrow nodded and wrote that on the timeline. 'And Lynne leaves the bedroom to confront Steve. They have a huge argument downstairs in the kitchen.'

'We're assuming that this argument gets out of hand. She's recently paid for his rehab,' French said.

'Maybe she had written Steve out of her will,' French stated, thinking out loud. 'Maybe she tells him this in her anger. Steve loses it, grabs a kitchen knife and attacks her with it.'

'At this moment, Lucy arrives and lets herself into her mother's house as planned,' Garrow said as he wrote on the board again. 'She sees her brother slit her mother's throat and goes to try and help her, getting covered in her blood. Steve hits her across the back of the head, heads out of the house, gets back into the car and drives away.'

There was silence for a few seconds as they studied the timeline.

'We just need something that links Steve to the actual crime scene,' French said in a frustrated tone.

Garrow points back at the timeline. 'After about twenty minutes, Gavin Staples wonders what the hell is going on and where Lynne has got to. He comes downstairs, sees her dead body and flees the scene.'

French's mobile phone buzzed and he answered it.

Garrow went back to looking at the timeline which now made sense in terms of the sequence of events.

French ended the call and gave Garrow a meaningful look. 'We've got him.'

Garrow frowned. 'How do you mean?'

'Forensics found a tiny spot of something on a drawer in Steve Morgan's bedroom,' French said. 'DNA test shows it's his mother's blood.'

'Which gives us our link to the crime scene,' Garrow said with a sense of relief that they now had their killer.

'Let's go and bring him in.'

## Chapter 66

Ruth and Nick were now hammering along the back roads towards Bangor. Ruth was still trying to work out why Ben had decided to abduct Georgie and then Arlo and go on the run. It had to be something to do with the human trafficking investigation they had been working on. And if Ben had decided to go on the run, she could only assume that he had been somehow involved in some kind of corruption that Georgie had uncovered.

'Three six from Alpha One, are you receiving, over?' crackled the Tetra radio, breaking Ruth's train of thought.

Alpha One was the call sign of the helicopter pilot that she had ordered into the air about fifteen minutes earlier to scour the roads south of Bangor for the Land Rover.

'Alpha One, this is three six, receiving,' Ruth said into the radio. 'Go ahead, over.'

'We have visual contact on new target vehicle leaving a petrol station in Llandygai,' the helicopter pilot stated. 'That's about six miles south of Bangor and the Menai Bridge. Vehicle is now on the move, heading north at speed on the A5, over.'

'Received, Alpha One,' Ruth said. 'Continue visual contact and standby.'

Nick glanced over from the driver's seat. 'You think he's going for the bridge?'

'Maybe,' Ruth said, wondering if Ben thought he had a better chance of escaping once he was on Anglesey. 'He might even think he can get the ferry to Dublin up in Holyhead.'

'We need to make sure he doesn't get over the bridge then,' Nick warned her.

Ruth clicked her radio. 'All units, this is three six. Be advised that our new target vehicle is now heading north on the A5 from Llandygai. Proceed with caution as suspect is armed and considered very dangerous.'

'Maybe try the phone again,' Nick suggested, referring to Georgie's mobile which was still ringing. He assumed that Ben had it in his possession.

'Yeah,' Ruth said, taking out her phone which was patched into the car's speakers. She hit the redial button for Georgie's phone and it started to ring.

'Hello?' said a man's voice.

It was Ben.

Ruth and Nick looked at each other for a moment.

'Ben?' Ruth said calmly.

Silence.

'DI Hunter, why do you keep ringing this phone?' Ben asked.

'I want to know how you are all doing?' Ruth replied.

'How we're all doing?' he said with an ironic snort. 'Jesus. Not so great, if I'm honest.'

'I know you've been injured,' Ruth said. 'You're going to need some kind of medical help with that.'

'Yeah, that's what Georgie keeps telling me,' Ben said in an almost friendly tone.

'How is she?' Ruth enquired.

'Georgie? Yeah, she's just fine.'

'All this stress can't be good for her in her condition,' Ruth said.

'Don't underestimate her, DI Hunter.'

'How's Arlo doing?'

'He's with me so he's doing all right.'

'Really?' Ruth asked sceptically.

There was a long silence. Ruth worried that Ben was going to hang up on her.

'I'm sure you're aware that we know your exact location,' Ruth said. 'So, tell me how we find a resolution. We don't want anyone to get hurt.'

'Don't worry, we're all going to be fine,' Ben replied in a weary voice. 'Georgie and Arlo are going to come with me, whatever happens.'

Ruth's stomach tensed. She didn't like the sound of Ben's reply. What was he talking about?

'Listen, whatever has happened to make you go on the run like this, I'm sure we can sort it out,' Ruth said gently, trying to use all the skills she'd been taught on a hostage negotiation course. 'If you can pull over now, I'm not far behind you. Me and you can sit somewhere, have a chat and a cup of tea. You can tell me your side of things. How does that sound?'

Another long silence.

'Yeah, I've got no interest in doing that,' Ben said, and ended the call.

## Chapter 67

G arrow leaned over and pressed the red button on the digital recording equipment. There was a long, loud electronic beep.

'Interview conducted with Steve Morgan, Interview Room 2, Llancastell Police Station. Present are Detective Constable Jim Garrow, Duty Solicitor Neil Roberts and myself, Detective Sergeant Daniel French.'

Steve was dressed again in a grey sweatshirt and bottoms. He stared solemnly at the wall – he looked broken.

French glanced over at him.

'We are re-interviewing you today, Steve, because there have been significant developments in the investigation into your mother's murder,' French explained. 'And there's a few things we'd like to clarify with you while you're under caution.'

Steve didn't even react. It was as though he hadn't heard what French had said.

French leaned forward, took a document from a folder and turned it to show Steve. 'For the purposes of the tape,

I'm showing the suspect Item Reference 347G. This is a transcript of an interview you gave to us under caution yesterday, isn't it, Steve?'

Steve looked over blankly and shrugged.

'In this interview, you admitted that you returned to the home that you shared with your mother Lynne Morgan at 9.35pm to collect drugs, is that correct?' French asked.

Steve leaned over, asked Roberts a question under his breath, and then said, 'Yes.'

Garrow looked over. 'You told us that when you went in, you went straight up to your bedroom to retrieve those drugs and then you left. Is that correct?'

Steve nodded.

'For the purposes of the tape, the suspect has nodded in response to this question,' Garrow said.

French frowned. 'The strange thing is, Steve, the CCTV shows that you were inside the house for 15 minutes. I don't think it could have taken any more than a couple of minutes to go up the stairs, get your drugs and leave. Can you tell us what took you so long?'

Steve shrugged. 'I had a piss.'

French forced a smile. 'You had a twelve minute piss?'

'You told us that you didn't see your mother when you went inside,' Garrow said, looking at the transcript. 'In fact you stated, *'Her bedroom door was shut. I assumed she was in bed watching telly or something.'*

Steve looked confused. 'Yeah. That's what happened.'

French raised an eyebrow. 'You see we have a witness inside the house who heard the front door opening. He then heard your mother going downstairs and having a violent row with someone. When our witness came downstairs about thirty minutes later, your mother was dead. That was you rowing with her, wasn't it, Steve?'

'No,' Steve insisted. 'Who the hell else was in the house?'

It was time to introduce the new evidence which would contradict everything that Steve had told them and back him into a corner.

'So, you're sticking to your story then?' French asked. 'You came in. Took a long piss. Grabbed your drugs and left. And you didn't see your mother?'

'It's not a story,' Steve replied indignantly. 'That's what happened. Why don't you believe me?'

Garrow leaned over, pulled a photograph from the folder and showed it to Steve. 'For the purposes of the tape, I'm showing the suspect Item Reference 923B.' Garrow pointed to the image. 'This is a chest of drawers in your bedroom, isn't it, Steve?'

Steve looked utterly baffled as he looked at the photo. 'Yeah …'

'And that's where you kept your drugs, isn't it?' French asked.

'Yeah,' Steve replied cautiously.

Garrow pointed to the tiny speck of blood that was on the top of the chest of drawers. 'Can you see that mark there, Steve?'

'Yeah,' he said, but he was starting to get agitated.

'Would it surprise you to know that that mark is a speck of your mother's blood?' Garrow said.

There was a long, tense silence as the blood visibly drained from Steve's face.

'Steve, could you explain how a spot of your mother's blood managed to find its way onto the top of your chest of drawers?' French asked. 'The chest of drawers that you just admitted going to retrieve your drugs from?'

Steve's breathing had become quick and shallow. His

eyes roamed wildly as he shook his head. 'No, that's not … I don't understand.'

'Come on, Steve,' French said in an almost friendly tone. 'I get it. You go home to get your drugs. Your mum's there trying to stop you. She's just written you out of her will. You just lose your temper and grab a knife. Your sister Lucy arrives to find that you've slashed your mother. While Lucy attempts to save your mother, you hit her around the head. You run upstairs to get the drugs you came for but a tiny speck of blood falls from your hand onto the chest of drawers. That's what happened, isn't it?'

Steve put his head in his hands and sobbed. 'No …'

Silence.

French looked over. 'Steve Morgan, I am charging you with the murder of Lynne Morgan, contrary to common law. Do you have anything to say?'

Steve shook his head and continued to sob into his hands.

## Chapter 68

Georgie, Ben and Arlo were speeding up the A5. The police helicopter moved away and up towards the clouds, before circling back. Glancing at the rear-view mirror, Georgie saw they had a new problem. There was a BMW 530 marked police car behind them with its blues and twos going.

Ben looked at her, spotted her reaction, and glanced quickly at the wing mirror.

'Shit!' he snapped as he looked over. 'Speed up.'

Georgie pushed the accelerator slightly but they were already doing 90 mph.

Ben's eyes were full of anxious fury. 'Faster.'

'I'm trying,' she protested.

The back of Ben's hand shot up and across, slapping hard against her face. It was sharp and painful.

Georgie pressed the accelerator down with such force that the car bolted; the tyres spun under the sudden burst of speed. She gripped the wheel, trying to control the car. Her heart was hammering against her chest.

Ben raised the Glock 17, leaned across and pushed the barrel against her cheek.

'Understand me clearly, you need to go faster,' he said with menace.

'We're going a hundred,' Georgie said as they overtook a coach which went past in a blur.

'I've made myself very clear, haven't I?' Ben said. 'I'm as happy for us all to die today as I am that we all get away. So, if you don't go faster, I'm going to shoot you. Do you understand?'

'I understand.' Her reply was a whisper. She breathed through her parted lips, her terror complete.

Ben removed the barrel of the gun from her cheek as she pushed the accelerator so that it was hard against the floor of the car.

Her hands clasped the steering wheel so tight that her knuckles were white.

One false move, one tiny mistake, and they would all be dead.

## Chapter 69

R uth and Nick were now hammering along the A5 towards Bangor. According to her calculations, they were about five miles behind the Land Rover that Ben was driving. For the last few minutes, Ruth had been liaising with units in Bangor, trying to arrange for a road block and a stinger to force a hard stop of the vehicle. She had also organised for two armed response units to be on standby. There was no way she was going to let Ben drive through Bangor, across the Menai Bridge and onto Anglesey. Given his state of mind, she couldn't be sure that he wouldn't drive the car off the bridge and kill them all.

'Three six from Alpha One, are you receiving, over?' crackled the Tetra radio.

'Alpha One, this is three six, receiving,' Ruth said into the radio. 'Go ahead, over.'

'We still have visual contact on target vehicle,' the helicopter pilot stated. 'They are now two miles south of Bangor, still heading north on the A5 at very high speed. There are two marked traffic units currently in pursuit, over.'

'Received, Alpha One,' Ruth said. 'Continue visual contact and standby.'

She looked up as Nick pulled onto the other side of the road to overtake a tractor before pulling back. They now had their blue lights, that were located in the radiator grill, flashing and the siren on.

Nick looked over at her. 'I'm praying that Ben has lost enough blood that he's going to be semi-conscious by the time we stop them.'

Ruth pulled a face. 'He sounded pretty lucid to me on the phone.'

'Charlie Tango two to three six, are you receiving?' said a voice on her Tetra radio. It was Inspector Christopher Maxwell from the Bangor Police, whom she had been liaising with.

'Charlie Tango two, three six receiving, go ahead,' Ruth said into her radio.

'We have a road block in place on the A5 one mile south of Bangor town city centre, where the A5 meets the High Street,' Maxwell said. 'Stinger is in place for a hard stop on target vehicle. ARUs are in place and officers are aware that the suspect is armed and very dangerous, over.'

'Alpha One has visual contact with target vehicle. ETA at your location less than one minute, over,' Ruth said, as her stomach tightened at the thought of what was about to happen on the outskirts of Bangor. 'Standby.'

Ruth blew out her cheeks and looked over at Nick.

## Chapter 70

Georgie could feel the muscles straining in her arms with the stress of holding the steering wheel at such high speed. A few cottages whizzed past so fast that it was impossible to make out any of their detail. A sign that read – *Arafwch Nawr – Reduce Speed Now* – flashed past. The irony wasn't lost on her.

Glancing at the rear-view mirror, she saw that both police BMWs were directly behind her. The looming shape of the helicopter was above. There was no way they were going to escape. And now she feared that if they were forcibly stopped by something like a stinger, Ben would shoot her, Arlo, and then himself in a murder suicide that only made sense to him.

A stinger was a long string of metal spikes that would be pulled across the road to burst the tyres of a car and force it to stop.

Turning quickly around, Georgie checked that Arlo was wearing his seatbelt. With a surreptitious feel, she checked that her own seatbelt was firmly in place. Then she glanced over. Ben was wearing his seatbelt too.

However, she now had a plan. It was a long shot but it's all she could think of to stop Ben.

As they cornered a long bend, Georgie could hear the tyres squealing under the car.

To her shock, the road up ahead was blocked off by several police cars with their blue lights flashing.

*Jesus!* She took a nervous gulp.

There were dozens of police officers in high-vis jackets. Traffic cones and police tape had been used to block off pavements and a nearby road. And then she saw several armed response officers crouched behind a police car with their Heckler & Koch G36 assault rifles with telescopic sights pointed down the road.

'Shit!' Ben growled.

Georgie pushed the brakes to slow the car. Her mind was racing with what to do next.

'What are you doing?' Ben yelled angrily. 'Keep driving!'

'I'm not driving through that,' Georgie said in horror.

Ben pushed the Glock 17 hard into her temple. 'Do it. Keep driving!'

Georgie eased off the brakes as she realised that it was now or never.

She had to act now.

*Come on, Georgie, you can do this!*

With a violent turn of the steering wheel, Georgie spun the car hard right across a large patch of grass that was bordered by a dry stone wall.

'What are you doing?' Ben screamed as they were thrown across the car.

As they hurtled and bounced across the grass, Georgie saw Ben point the gun at her head.

*He's going to shoot me!*

With a flick of her left hand, she hit his forearm up as hard as she could.

CRACK!

The bullet smashed through the car roof.

Hitting Ben with her shoulder as they bounced over the grass, she leant down and hit the red button to release his seatbelt.

She looked up and held her breath.

The dry stone wall was about twenty yards away.

Ben glanced at her, realising what she'd done and why.

He tried to grapple with his seatbelt.

The car was out of control, skidding left and right.

A second later, they smashed into the dry stone wall.

*CRASH!*

There was the thunderous sound of metal and glass collapsing.

The airbags deployed with a loud hiss.

Georgie closed her eyes.

She felt her whole body being thrown forward and then back. Her head cracked against the passenger door.

The car came to a rest and for a few seconds there was an eerie silence.

She sat upright in the seat trying to get her breath and clear her head.

Then she glanced anxiously over at the passenger seat.

It was empty.

The windscreen was smashed and bloody.

Outside, Ben's body lay twisted further down the wall. His face was matted in blood and glass.

It looked like he was dead.

Georgie's head swam and for a moment she had double vision.

In the corner of her eye, she spotted police officers racing across the road towards them.

*Thank God, we're safe.*

Then everything went black.

## Chapter 71

A s Ruth and Nick hurtled around a bend in the road, their Tetra radio crackled.

'Charlie Tango two to three six,' Maxwell said in an urgent voice. 'Target vehicle has crashed. Repeat, target vehicle has crashed, over.'

Looking up, Ruth could see the police road block up ahead with its cars, flashing lights and swarms of police officers.

'Charlie Tango two, this is three six, we are at target location,' Ruth said as they sped towards the roadblock. 'What the hell is going on?'

Ruth soon spotted paramedics racing towards something.

Then, to her alarm, she saw that the Land Rover Discovery had ploughed into a wall and was seriously damaged.

'Shit,' she gasped as Nick turned the car towards the crash site.

'Please God let them be all right,' she said under her breath.

'I wonder what happened?' Nick said as he slammed on the brakes and they leapt from the car.

Sprinting across the road, they reached the patch of grass.

Georgie was laying in the grass unconscious as paramedics attended to her.

'Is she all right?' Ruth shouted as she ran over.

The paramedic looked up at her. 'She's breathing, she has a pulse and there are no obvious injuries. But she's taken a nasty bang to her head.'

'She's pregnant,' Ruth said fretfully.

'We'll get her checked out as soon as we get her to the hospital, ma'am.'

'Where's Arlo Stewart?' Nick asked, looking around.

Maxwell marched over. 'We can't seem to get the boy out of the car. His seatbelt got jammed in the crash.'

'How is he?' Ruth asked.

'He's fine. Very shaken up but he's conscious,' Maxwell explained. 'We might have to cut him out.'

'Have you got Ben Stewart under arrest?' Ruth asked, looking around to see where he was.

Maxwell shook his head and pointed to something further along the grassy patch by the wall.

It was a body under an orange blanket.

'Paramedics think he died on impact,' Maxwell said.

There was the sound of some cutting equipment coming from the car as rescuers tried to get Arlo out.

'Ma'am!' the paramedic, who was tending to Georgie, called over.

Ruth's heart was in her mouth for a second.

'What is it?' Ruth asked as she approached them full of terror.

Then to her relief, she saw that Georgie, who now had a clear plastic oxygen mask over her face, was conscious.

Ruth crouched down beside her and put her hand gently to her head. 'Don't worry. You're going to be all right.'

Georgie nodded and then looked at her. 'Arlo?'

Ruth nodded. 'Yeah, he's fine.'

'Ben?' she croaked.

Ruth shook her head. 'No. He's gone.'

She could see the relief in Georgie's face at the news.

Nick came over and looked at her.

Georgie smiled up at him. 'Hello stranger.'

Nick smiled back at her. 'Hey, causing trouble again I see,' he joked.

'Yeah. Now probably isn't the time to have a catch up though,' she said with a wry smile.

They laughed.

Ruth's attention was drawn to the noise of clapping as a fireman carried Arlo out of the wreckage of the car.

'Thank God,' she said, looking at Nick.

The paramedics moved Georgie onto a stretcher and carried her towards the back of the ambulance. She gave them a little wave.

Ruth gestured to where Ben's body was lying and they walked slowly towards it.

'We need to make sure that someone retrieves the handgun that Ben had,' Ruth said. 'I don't want some local finding it in the bushes up there and running around Bangor with it.'

'No,' Nick agreed, and then gave her a look. 'Maybe grab fish and chips on the way home?'

'Sounds good to me.' Ruth smiled and put her hand on his shoulder. 'It really is good to have you back, you know.'

Suddenly, the orange blanket that was covering Ben moved.

At first, Ruth thought it was the wind.

Then, to her horror, she realised that somehow Ben was sitting up.

*What the hell is …*

As the blanket dropped away, she saw Ben looking directly at her.

He pulled the Glock 17 out of his jacket and fired.

CRACK!

'NO!' Nick screamed as he dived to push Ruth out of the way.

It was no use.

She could feel the hot, searing pain of the bullet as it hammered into the top of her abdomen.

Crashing to the ground, she lay on her back, looking up at the blue sky.

There were two more gunshots from an ARO's automatic weapon.

'Boss,' Nick shouted as he rushed to her.

'I've been shot,' Ruth said in disbelief. Putting her hand down to her stomach, she could feel the warmth of her own blood on her hand.

Then the sky darkened.

## Chapter 72

Garrow had arranged to meet Lucy in Acton Park. It had been ten minutes since he had broken the news of her brother's guilt. She had been devastated when he had told her.

Garrow looked across the park as the late afternoon sun cast long beams of pale gold over the grass. Some boys were playing cricket nearby. There was the faint smell of cedar wood and the sound of a distant lawnmower as it moved back and forth in perfect rhythm. A hedge was dotted with raspberry spiraea which shook gently in the warm evening breeze.

'I just can't believe it,' Lucy whispered eventually whilst staring into space.

'I'm so sorry,' Garrow said.

Lucy put her hand on his shoulder. 'I don't know what I would have done without you. You've been with me every step of the way.'

Garrow gave her a caring smile. 'You've been through so much.'

'Yes, but I know that you've taken some short cuts

along the way,' Lucy said, as she moved a tress of hair from her face.

Garrow shrugged. 'I just knew instinctively that you didn't have anything to do with what happened to your mum.'

'I have this thing in my head that I just wish I could go back in time.' Lucy let out a sigh and looked overwhelmed. 'If I could just change what happened on Friday evening.' She then looked at him. 'My brother isn't a terrible person, you do know that?'

Garrow gave a slight nod. 'I guess that your mum got in the way of him getting his drugs and he just had a moment of utter madness. It's so terribly sad.'

'It's a horrible illness, addiction,' she said.

'Yeah, I know. We see the results of it on a regular basis,' Garrow said. 'And I suppose the fact that your mum had written him out of her will would have hurt him too.'

Lucy looked confused. 'What are you talking about?'

'We know that you went to the solicitors with your mother to change her will,' Garrow explained. 'Given your brother's history of drug taking, we thought that she was writing him out of the will. To be honest, we haven't had that confirmed.'

'No, quite the opposite actually,' Lucy said. 'Mum wanted to leave Steve everything. She said she knew that I'd always be all right. But Steve needed as much help as he could get.'

'Didn't that bother you?' Garrow asked.

'It's only money, isn't it?' she said softly.

'I suppose so.'

One of the boys hit the cricket ball with a thwack and it sailed towards them. It bounced on the grass and came to rest by Lucy's foot.

Another boy came running over and gave them a smile.

Lucy picked up the ball and threw it back – with her left hand.

'I didn't know you were left handed,' Garrow said with a curious frown.

'Yep. Always have been,' Lucy said. 'Does it matter?'

Garrow shook his head. 'No, I don't suppose it does.'

## Chapter 73

Sitting in the waiting room of the intensive care unit, Nick took a deep breath. Ruth had been airlifted from the crash site in Bangor where she'd been shot straight to the University Hospital in Llancastell.

Looking up at the television that was mounted on the wall, Nick saw that it was showing the BBC News. A helicopter was flying over where the Land Rover Discovery had crashed as a red banner rolled underneath – *Police officer shot after a high speed chase in Bangor, North Wales.*

Nick saw something in the corner of his eye. It was Georgie. She was attached to a drip and wearing a hospital gown. There was a deep gash across the top of one eye.

'Hey,' Nick said getting up. 'Are you okay? What are you doing here?'

'I sneaked out,' Georgie admitted. Her voice sounded weak.

'Shouldn't you be resting?' he asked with a concerned expression.

Georgie gestured to her tummy. 'They did a scan and the baby is fine.'

'Thank God,' Nick said, putting a hand on her shoulder.

'Once I knew the baby was fine,' Georgie said, 'I needed to see how Ruth was. Is there any news?'

Nick pointed down the corridor. 'She's in surgery at the moment. They're trying to take out the bullet and deal with her internal bleeding.'

A moment later, a figure approached.

It was Sarah. She came over and embraced them both.

'Sarah,' Nick said and then looked at her. 'She's still in surgery.'

A tall surgeon with silver hair, 50s, approached. He was wearing light blue scrubs.

'Are you Ruth's next of kin?' he asked.

'I'm her partner,' Sarah explained.

'Okay,' the surgeon said. 'The good news is that we have managed to remove the bullet from Ruth's spleen. The bad news is that there is a significant amount of internal damage and haemorrhaging.'

'But she's going to be all right?' Sarah asked anxiously.

'We'll know more in the next few hours,' the surgeon said.

'Can we see her?' Nick asked.

'She's just coming up from the theatre,' the surgeon explained. 'You can go and see her in about twenty minutes or so.'

'Thank you,' Sarah said.

## Chapter 74

Garrow was walking Lucy back to her home. She reached out to hold his hand and he took it. The evening sky above them was blue and cloudless. An aeroplane dissected it with a diagonal line of vapour.

As they got to her front door, Lucy looked at him. 'Do you want to come in?'

Garrow frowned. 'I'm not sure,' he admitted as he looked over at his car that was parked nearby.

'Nothing needs to happen between us,' Lucy sighed. 'It's just that after everything that's happened, I don't want to be on my own tonight.'

Garrow thought for a second and then nodded. 'Yes, of course.'

She smiled, leant in and kissed him softly on the cheek.

*Okay, that was nice*, he thought as he felt his pulse quicken.

She opened the front door and they went inside.

'I'm going to need something stronger than tea,' Lucy said. 'I've got some wine in the fridge?'

'Sounds good,' Garrow said.

Lucy gestured to the living room. 'Go and sit down while I get us a drink.'

Garrow went in and looked around.

A poster advertising an Andy Warhol exhibition at the Tate Liverpool in 2021 caught his eye. He remembered seeing some of Warhol's major works there – Elvis, Marilyn Monroe, the famous Coke bottle.

His phone buzzed. It was French. He didn't make social calls so it had to be work related.

'Sarge?' Garrow said, answering the call and wondering why he'd called.

'Where are you?' French asked. The tone of his voice made Garrow feel uneasy.

'I'm just out for a walk to clear my head, that's all,' Garrow lied. 'What's wrong?'

'Jim, I've got some bad news,' French said solemnly. 'The boss has been shot. She's in the university hospital now.'

'Oh God,' Garrow said in shock. 'How bad is it?'

'I'm not sure. They're operating on her now,' French explained. 'If I'm honest, I don't think it's good.'

'Jesus. What about Georgie?'

Lucy came in with two glasses of red wine. She handed one to Garrow, and spotting that he was on the phone, she went over to a record player.

'She's fine. And so is the kid. Just a few bumps and scratches,' French said.

'What happened?' Garrow asked.

'Stewart's pulse didn't register with the paramedics at the crash site,' French explained. 'They thought he was dead. When he regained consciousness, he shot the boss with a gun he had hidden on him.'

'That's terrible.'

'An ARO shot Stewart dead but the damage had been done.'

'Right,' Garrow said. 'Maybe I should get to the hospital.'

Having clearly heard what he had said, Lucy gave Garrow a concerned look from where she was standing over by the record player thumbing through a stack of albums.

'And there's something else,' French said.

'What's that?' Garrow asked, picking up on French's solemn tone.

Lucy put the arm of the record player down and the song *White Dress* by *Lana Del Rey* started to play.

'An angler found the kitchen knife that killed Lynne Morgan,' French said, 'along with a hammer. They'd been partially buried on the river bank but the water washed the sand away.'

'Where was this?' Garrow asked.

Silence.

Garrow watched Lucy as she sipped her red wine, seemingly lost in thought and the haunting sound of the song.

'It was right beside Pontcysyllte Aqueduct,' French said.

*What?*

Garrow's stomach tensed as he realised the implication of what French had told him.

*Oh God.*

'Now we know what Lucy Morgan was doing down there. She went there to get rid of the murder weapon,' French said. 'I'm guessing that her amnesia was a complete fake.'

For a second, Garrow couldn't get his breath. He felt sick to the pit of his stomach.

'Right,' he whispered as he saw Lucy standing over by the record player, mouthing the lyrics of the song.

'Sorry Jim. I know you liked her. Looks like she pulled the wool over both of our eyes.'

'Yes ...' Garrow said, trying to steady his breathing.

Lucy made eye contact with him as if to say *Is everything all right?*

Garrow looked away.

'I'll give you a ring as soon as I hear anything about the boss,' French said, and then ended the call.

Feeling a little unsteady on his feet, Garrow tried to take in what French had just told him. It didn't feel real.

'What's wrong?' Lucy asked, going over to him and putting a reassuring hand on his shoulder.

Garrow flinched, moved back, and stared at her for a moment.

'Jim?' she said with a frown.

There was silence as Garrow gathered his thoughts.

*How the hell did I get this so wrong?*

'Jim?'

'We've found the murder weapon in your mum's murder,' Garrow said very quietly.

'Okay. You seem to be shocked by that,' Lucy said with a frown as she sipped her wine.

'I am. We found the knife,' Garrow explained, and then he slowly looked directly at her. 'It was buried on the river bank at the Pontcysyllte Aqueduct.'

Lucy didn't say anything but just blinked.

'I don't understand,' Garrow whispered in disbelief. 'You killed her?'

Lucy didn't react.

'Say something, Lucy!' Garrow snapped.

She looked at him with an icy stare. 'What do you want me to say? That I killed my mother because she only ever had time for my poor junkie brother, Steve? And she cut me out of her will so that he could snort and smoke away our inheritance?' Lucy shrugged. 'Okay, then that's what I did.'

Garrow shook his head in utter shock. 'The amnesia?'

Lucy raised an eyebrow. 'What do you think?'

'You put her blood in your brother's bedroom to frame him?'

'Of course I did,' Lucy sighed, as though this was a stupid question.

There was a long silence.

'I'm going to have to take you in,' Garrow said eventually. 'You do know that?'

Lucy shrugged and said coldly, 'I think you're going to find it hard to get a conviction against me. Especially when I reveal that we've been sleeping together.'

'What are you talking about?' Garrow asked angrily as he pulled the cuffs from his belt.

'My word against yours,' Lucy said.

Garrow grabbed her hands roughly, put the cuffs on her and ushered her towards the door. 'Lucy Morgan, I'm arresting you for the murder of Lynne Morgan.'

## Chapter 75

Nick, Georgie and Sarah were sitting in silence in the
waiting area of the ICU. Sarah stood up and paced
up and down. She sighed under her breath, 'This is
unbearable.'

Nick rubbed his beard anxiously. Even though he
didn't want to think about it, he knew the terrible destruc-
tion a bullet could do once it entered the human body. It
could ricochet off bones, causing immense damage.

A nurse approached and gave them a kind smile. 'If
you'd like to come and see Ruth now?'

They all nodded, got up and followed the nurse down
the corridor. She opened the door to a small single room.

Nick took a breath as he saw Ruth lying on the bed
with drips, an ECG and a ventilator attached to her.

'Oh my God,' Sarah whispered with tears in her eyes
as she moved over and put her hand on Ruth's.

'I keep thinking this is my fault,' Georgie said quietly.

Nick shook his head. 'You can't blame yourself.'

'If I hadn't gone to Ben's flat, I wouldn't have worked

out that he was corrupt,' she said with a pained expression on her face. 'And then none of this would have happened.'

Nick put his hand on her arm. 'No. Ben Stewart was a scumbag. You can't blame yourself for what he did.'

Georgie's eyes filled with tears as she moved over and buried her head in Nick's chest.

'Hey,' he said comfortingly as he put his arm around her.

Suddenly, there was a loud, continuous electronic beep.

Nick looked around and caught Sarah's startled expression.

'What the hell is that?' Sarah cried in panic.

Nick looked anxiously at the ECG machine where the noise seemed to be coming from.

The door to the room flew open and the surgeon and the nurse rushed in.

'I'm going to need everyone out of here,' the surgeon said loudly as he went over to the ECG machine.

'What's going on?' Sarah asked in terror.

The nurse tried to usher them out. 'Please, she's in good hands.'

The surgeon looked over at the nurse. 'Right, I need the crash team in here now!'

Enjoy this book?
Get the next book in the series
'The Colwyn Bay Killings'
on pre-order on Amazon
Publication date October 2023

My Book
https://www.amazon.com/dp/B0CCGT5NCL

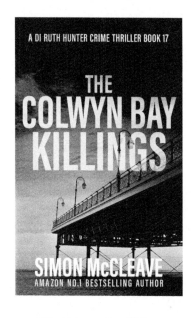

*The Colwyn Bay Killings*
A Ruth Hunter Crime Thriller #Book 17

Your FREE book is waiting for you now

Get your FREE copy of the prequel to
the DI Ruth Hunter Series NOW
http://www.simonmccleave.com/vip-email-club
and join my VIP Email Club

# DC RUTH HUNTER SERIES

London, 1997. A series of baffling murders. A web of political corruption. DC Ruth Hunter thinks she has the brutal killer in her sights, but there's one problem. He's a Serbian War criminal who died five years earlier and lies buried in Bosnia.

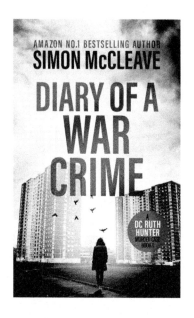

My Book
My Book

## AUTHOR'S NOTE

Although this book is very much a work of fiction, it is located in Snowdonia, a spectacular area of North Wales. It is steeped in history and folklore that spans over two thousand years. It is worth mentioning that Llancastell is a fictional town on the eastern edges of Snowdonia. I have made liberal use of artistic licence, names and places have been changed to enhance the pace and substance of the story.

## Acknowledgments

I will always be indebted to the people who have made this novel possible.

My mum, Pam, and my stronger half, Nicola, whose initial reaction, ideas and notes on my work I trust implicitly. And Dad, for his overwhelming enthusiasm. Carole Kendal for her meticulous proofreading. My designer Stuart Bache for yet another incredible cover design. My superb agent, Millie Hoskins at United Agents, and Dave Gaughran and Nick Erick for invaluable support and advice. And Keira Bowie for her ongoing patience and help.

Printed in Great Britain
by Amazon